Praise for To...

'A lively story and a riveting... society' *The Times*

'Unforgettable' *Sunday Times*

'Storytelling of the highest quality . . . Introduces a detective it is impossible not to believe in. Callaghan is a new voice to be welcomed' *Daily Mail*

'This is a thrilling, intense debut from a powerfully descriptive writer' *Daily Express*

'Establishes Callaghan as a major new voice in crime fiction with his cut-to-the-bone storytelling and descriptive brilliance' *Kirkus*

'Not since *Child 44* have I read something that's left such a memorable impression' Sebastian Fitzek

'Inspector Akyl Borubaev has world-weariness, sorrow, cynical charm, toughness and brains to spare . . . you'll be breathless and begging for more' Peter Spiegelman, author of *Thick As Thieves*

Born in the north of England, Tom Callaghan was educated at the University of York and Vassar College, New York. An inveterate traveller, he divides his time between London, Prague, Dubai and Bishkek.

Also by Tom Callaghan

A Killing Winter

A SPRING BETRAYAL

TOM CALLAGHAN

Quercus

First published in Great Britain in 2016 by Quercus
This edition published in 2017 by

Quercus Editions Ltd
Carmelite House
50 Victoria Embankment
London EC4Y 0DZ

An Hachette UK company

A CIP catalogue record for this book is available
from the British Library

PB ISBN 9781784292430
EBOOK ISBN 9781784290603

This book is a work of fiction. Names, characters,
businesses, organizations, places and events are
either the product of the author's imagination
or used fictitiously. Any resemblance to
actual persons, living or dead, events or
locales is entirely coincidental.

10 9 8 7 6 5 4 3 2 1

Typeset by Jouve (UK), Milton Keynes

Printed and bound in Great Britain by Clays Ltd, St Ives plc

For Akyl, Aizat and Kairat

No change. No exit. A minor flaw.
You die – but start up once more.
It all repeats, just as before.

Alexandr Blok

Chapter 1

We uncovered the last of the dead children in the red hour before dusk, as the sun stained the snowcaps of the Tien Shan mountains the colour of dried blood and the spring air turned sharp and cold.

Seven small bundles, tightly swaddled in plastic bags, all buried in a hurry, just a few inches under the soil. They lay huddled together as if for warmth or comfort, at the foot of an apple tree, one of three bunched in the north corner of a potato field next to the canal. Not a clever disposal: the bags were swollen with the gases of decay, elbowing their way through the sour earth like a crop of misshapen mushrooms.

It was the rancid smell loitering in the dawn air that caught the attention of the farmer who found the first corpse. To begin with, he thought it was a dead hare, wondered why anyone would bother to bury it. A closer look revealed a clump of thick black hair and one small hand, fingers curled into an ineffectual fist. Then he noticed a couple more waxen bundles, decided to go against all his *myrki* peasant instincts and contact the authorities.

He called the *menti*, the local cops, who contacted Murder Squad, asked for an inspector. Since there's only one Murder Squad officer in Karakol, that meant me.

I'd been in Karakol for three months, serving out an unofficial internal exile in the far east of Kyrgyzstan, payback

1

for the chaos I'd caused the previous winter, investigating the brutal killings and mutilations of several young women. A lot of blood and trouble had been splashed around in my attempts to head off a potential coup by the politicians deposed in the last revolution. The local head of the Circle of Brothers mafia ended up face down in a snowdrift, and I helped the Minister of State Security 'disappear' the man who'd ordered his daughter's murder and mutilation.

The man who also happened to be the chief of Sverdlovsky police station, and my boss.

The public were sold some nonsense about a tragic car accident that claimed the life of one of Kyrgyzstan's top policemen; there was talk of posthumous medals, even a state funeral. Being Kyrgyz, everyone greeted the news with the indifference for which we're famous. Truth is, unless it affects our lives or our pockets, we're not too interested in who sits at the big desks, collecting the bribes for favours done. There's always someone who'll do that, whoever's in power. We're too busy wondering how to put *plov* on our plates and vodka in our glasses.

The guys at the top decided it was best if I was out of Bishkek, the Kyrgyz capital, for a while, and Karakol was the ideal spot, being as far away as you can get in my country without a visa. And there are worse places than Karakol; at least I hadn't been posted to the Torugart Pass, the desolate mountain crossing between Kyrgyzstan and China.

There's not a lot in Karakol for an ambitious cop; arresting a few locals overwhelmed by vodka after the Sunday morning animal bazaar is the highlight of most weeks. But my ambition had pretty much died the day I buried Chinara, my wife.

2

Until the call came in.

I was an hour's rough drive north of Karakol, outside Orlinoye, one of the small villages that cling to the landscape like burrs on a sheep's wool. Faint evening mist spilt over the edges of the irrigation canal, a half-transparent shroud over the damp grass and the relics of seven lives ended before they'd really begun.

I'd called Kenesh Usupov, Bishkek's chief forensic pathologist, when I heard there were 'multiple objects of interest'. It's a ten-hour drive from Bishkek, but by late spring the roads are clear of snow and any rockfalls. With the police flashers on all the way, he'd have no problem making the journey.

Even so, I was surprised when I saw an ambulance making its way up the rutted track towards the nearby farmhouse, stopping in the yard beside the police car that had brought me here earlier. Usupov got out of the back, clutching the black leather briefcase he takes whenever he's called out on a case. It contains the basics for a scene of crime investigation; basics because that's all we have in this country.

As Usupov walked through the field towards us, the last of the sunlight flashed and glinted off his glasses, making his usual impassive expression even harder to read. His sense of humour is best described as dry and rarely used, and spending an evening together over a few drinks wouldn't be my ideal night out, but he's good at what he does, methodical, and honest and incorruptible, for what that's worth. Like me, he thinks the dead deserve better than a supporting role as chess pieces for the living, that we owe them the dignity we never bestowed upon them when they were alive.

I smiled when I saw the two plastic shopping bags Usupov

had tied over his shoes, to protect them against the elements. And then my smile faded into a scowl as I looked down at the other plastic bags by my feet.

'Inspector.' Usupov nodded as he joined me. He didn't offer to shake my hand: the burns I carried from my last case were pretty much healed now, but the scarring still looked bad, as if I'd been bitten by one of our mountain wolves. He looked at the two junior police officers, watching from a few feet away, and raised an eyebrow.

'They were here before me,' I explained. 'They've heard what a great crime scene expert you are, and they wanted to trample all around, give you more of a challenge.'

Usupov only grunted in response; my own sense of humour is a little too frivolous for him. He squatted down on his heels, plastic bags rustling like the leaves on the boughs above us.

'How did you get here so quickly?'

'An ex-US helicopter,' he said, 'from Manas Airport. Then ambulance from Karakol. I thought it made sense when I was told there were several bodies to transport.'

I didn't tell him a large suitcase would have been enough, did my best not to show I was surprised about how he got there. Although America has had an airbase in our country for several years, a vital part of keeping the army in Afghanistan supplied, they'd operated a strict hands-off policy in our internal affairs. They'd left lots of equipment behind when they finally pulled out of Kyrgyzstan, including helicopters, but we had very few pilots who could fly them. Which made me wonder what was so special about a report of finding some bodies the other side of Kyrgyzstan, and who had the pull to respond so quickly.

Now it was my turn to raise an eyebrow, but Usupov simply lowered one eyelid in an almost imperceptible wink, turned his attention back to the bodies. He reached into his briefcase, put on a pair of latex gloves, and with fingertips that barely skimmed the surface of the soil, began to brush away loose earth from the nearest corpse. His delicate, precise touch was more like that of a lover than an explorer of the secrets of the dead.

'Did you find the girl?' he asked.

'Girl?' I said, wondering what he meant, what clue he'd spotted that had eluded me.

'Snow White,' he said, never taking his eyes off the ground. 'You've found her seven dwarves, so she must be around here somewhere.'

A grim sense of humour may not be essential if you're a forensic pathologist, but it's not a handicap either, if you don't want death to overwhelm you.

'This is where they were found? In the same position, I mean?'

I nodded.

'We uncovered them one at a time,' and I pointed out the order in which the bodies came out of the ground. 'All buried at the same time, do you think?'

Usupov got to his feet, and I heard his knee joints crack. Like me, he was getting too old to expose other people's cruelties and betrayals.

'Hard for me to say here, better to get them back home and on the slab, but I don't think so. See for yourself.'

He pointed at the smallest package, prodded it with a gloved finger. A viscous squelch made my stomach turn.

'They all seem to be at different stages of decay. But that

could be due to having previously been buried in different locations, in soils with different levels of acidity. Tightly wrapped until the bags split, so we won't get a straightforward timeline from insect and predator activity. But if they weren't transported here all at once, I'd guess they've been buried here one by one, over time.'

That wasn't what I wanted to hear. Seven bodies suggested intent, determination, maybe some ritualistic choice behind the location. It also pointed the finger at a local, and village people are infamously close-mouthed. '*Mne do lampochki*,' they say. 'I don't care.'

'Murdered?' I asked, knowing what his answer would be.

'Can't say. Cot deaths? Stillborn? Who knows, the way infant mortality is around here? But certainly disposed of in suspicious circumstances.'

Usupov turned to the nearest *ment*, beckoned him over. A burly man, with the brown face and hands of a local farm boy, he didn't seem keen to approach until Usupov frowned.

'I want plastic sheeting and tent poles to cover the site, a guard here overnight, and the use of a room in your station, understand?'

The *ment* looked puzzled, as if Usupov had asked for a magic carpet and a dozen Kazakh dancing girls.

'You're leaving them here overnight?'

Usupov sighed; like me, he'd spent a career explaining himself.

'They've been here for quite some time, officer, another night won't hurt if we cover them carefully, and we can examine the scene when there's enough light to do the job properly. Uproot them fully now and we might destroy vital evidence. And it's almost dark.'

The last of the light reflected on the snow was dissolving into darkness, as wind whipped the branches above our heads. It wasn't a spot where I'd like to spend a long moonless night, alone but for the company of seven dead children.

We left one unhappy *ment* to his overnight vigil and trudged back down to the farm courtyard. I was staying at the Amir Hotel in the centre of Karakol, and I'd booked Usupov in there as well. It wasn't the Hyatt, but there was hot water most of the time. Right now, washing off the stink of the dead was the least of my concerns.

I needed to find out who was powerful enough to send a helicopter, what they knew, and why they weren't telling me.

Chapter 2

We excavated the site at dawn, to deter the curious. Usupov trowelled away the damp earth, a few grams at a time, while I stood behind him, taking photographs, using a collapsible ruler to indicate scale. I tried to ignore the smell, a sour confusion of rotting leaves and decaying meat, until I finally stumbled to the canal and vomited into its sluggish brown water, wondering once more what drove me to places like these, to such endings.

The sky was cloudless, the air fresh and clear with the promise of an untroubled future. A couple of red kites circled above us, riding the thermals, scouring the ground for prey. I could hear Usupov behind me, the scratch and scrape of his trowel unsettling and relentless, the echo of a grave being dug.

You never get used to the nearness of death. It taps you on your shoulder when you're least expecting it, breathes a sickening whisper in your ear. 'Could have been you,' it whispers. 'And one day it will be.' You taste the familiar fear in your stomach as you examine the gaping knife wounds, the intestines draped like ropes across the unmade bed, the spatter from gunshots dripping from cheap wallpaper in dismal rooms. Nothing could make you more certain that we're all just bags of guts and bones, whistling in the night to comfort ourselves as the wind mutters threats and the curtains flap like shrouds.

'Inspector, we can take the bodies down now.'

There was no way we could get the ambulance up here, so we had to move the bundles by hand. Unearthed, they looked forlorn, reminders that cruelty is easily forgotten and time erases almost everything.

I picked up the largest bag, trying not to picture the body inside. Chinara was buried just a few miles away, and I pictured her wrapped in the simple shroud in which we Kyrgyz bury our dead, earth and stones gradually settling through her as roots weaved around her bones and mice colonised her skull.

I told the *ment* to take one of the bodies, but he simply folded his arms and stood motionless. I repeated the order, and he simply said, '*Pashol na khui.*' If I'd been in his place, perhaps I'd have told me to fuck off as well.

It took the two of us the best part of an hour to load the ambulance, and by the end I was convinced the reek of rot and slime would never leave me. I wanted to go back to the Amir, hand over my clothes to be burnt, then shower until I'd stripped myself down to raw flesh. It's easy enough to clean your body, harder to scrub images of dead children from your mind.

Usupov had turned the meeting room in the local police station into a makeshift morgue, long tables covered in plastic sheeting against one wall, and – a rarity in any Kyrgyz government building – working light bulbs in every socket, to give him the light he needed. I reflected there was something wrong when a pathologist had more clout than a Murder Squad inspector, then realised why. The local officers were afraid of the death that had entered their lives. A wife-beating, a fight over the last drops in the bottle or a row over a stolen sheep, that was in the nature of things. But dead children, gathered together and hidden where no one could mourn them, revealed an evil outside their experience. I would have liked to say the same.

'I want you to take notes and photographs, Inspector,' Usupov said, his sense of protocol undiminished by being away from his regular slab. 'I'll record my observations, naturally, but it may take some time to get them transcribed. And I'm sure you'll want to press on with your investigation.'

We both knew this case would be mine and mine alone: no one back at Sverdlovsky station in Bishkek would be keen to drag this one along behind them. Dead children, no obvious suspects, all the makings of a career-breaker, one of those failures that outweigh any past triumphs. The chief had many friends before his fall, and they'd all be happy to see me stumble and break my neck over this case. I've learned over the years that every good deed earns you enemies.

The seven bags lay in a row, with the least decayed near the door.

'Why not in the order we dug them up?' I asked. 'Or by size?'

Usupov polished his glasses, snapped on a fresh pair of latex gloves and moved towards the table.

'The freshest ones will contain the most information; what I learn from them might shed some light on the others, where the evidence is less clear.'

He paused, gave me his death's-head smile, thin lips forming a vivid scar, turned and set to work.

Usupov was nothing if not thorough. For almost seven hours we waded through an assortment of bones, skin and teeth, all the shapeless and unseen mechanics of life. By the time we reached the smallest and most decomposed body, all we could do was extract the bones from a mucus-grey soup, and hope that we hadn't lost too many clues. The stench in the room was eye-watering, in spite of the open windows and the face masks we were wearing. We were no longer in a police station, but in a slaughterhouse in hell.

Finally, Usupov assembled the last of seven small skeletons, daubed here and there with cartilage, muscle, tissue, but relatively intact. He gave a half-smile, whether of satisfaction at a job well done or relief it was over, I couldn't tell.

I walked to the window and thrust my head out, desperate for clean air. I was dazed by the carnage, by the knowledge I had no idea where to start this investigation. I turned back to Usupov, held up my cigarettes, nodded towards the door. I've always thought it disrespectful to smoke in front of the dead, though it seems unlikely they care. And anyway, what more harm could anyone do to them?

As I went out into the corridor, I read the health warning on the cigarette pack. None of the children had ever smoked, and they were the ones lying dead, about to be shovelled into a communal hole. Suddenly, I was laughing at the cosmic injustice of it all. A *ment*, one I didn't recognise, scandalised by my reaction, swivelled his head round the corner, withdrew it at once when I stared back at him. Someone else determined to make sure they weren't involved.

Nice to have had the option.

I finished my cigarette, thought longingly about the bottle of good stuff I would have had waiting for me in my hotel room in the days when I drank, suddenly discovered I was hungry, starving, in fact. Hunger is one way of pushing death back into its box and slamming down the lid. Feeding, fighting, fucking; they're all shouts of defiance against our final unwanted visitor.

Usupov called me back into his makeshift morgue.

'In their condition, it's hard to tell the gender at such an early age, as you know, and the skulls are soft, with the fontanelle still unfused.'

I looked down at the skeletons, lined up as if for a school photo. I thought of the children Chinara and I had promised ourselves, of the child we aborted, and my eyes blurred.

'The bleach you use could peel paint off a door,' I said, and made a point of coughing. Usupov stared at me, a rare look of sympathy on his face.

'You take it all too personally, Inspector.'

'Someone has to, Kenesh,' I said. 'And if not me, then who?'

We were silent for a moment, and then Usupov turned back into his emotion-free pathologist persona, and I reverted to being Murder Squad.

'No clothes, no papers, nothing. So tell me how I'll find out who they were.'

Usupov said nothing, but held up several small evidence bags. In each one there was a thin strip of plastic, with some kind of writing on it. They were stained and hard to read, but I didn't have any problem recognising what they were. After all, I'd worn one myself for two years.

'Identity bands. From an orphanage,' I said, and heard my voice splinter and crack.

Chapter 3

I was twelve, the first time I stood in this room. It was just a few months after we declared independence while the Soviet Union collapsed in on itself, a brutal time for everyone in Kyrgyzstan. My father had gone to Moscow two years earlier to look for work, so my mother and I left Bishkek, to live with my grandfather and his second wife in his small farm north of Karakol.

The two women loathed each other with the endless simmering resentment that comes from bad food, cheap clothes and recognising something of themselves in each other's failures. Long silences would settle over the three-room farmhouse the way rainclouds brooded over the mountain peaks to the north, then burst like thunder into a tirade of faults and grievances. Finally, my grandfather declared himself sick of the skirmishes, and my mother packed our cheap plastic suitcase with the split handle and set off to find work in Siberia. I didn't see or hear from her for almost three years.

However, my mother's departure didn't calm her rival; instead she transferred the battle to me. And after the potato harvest, when I'd outlived my usefulness, she bundled me into the back of my grandfather's ancient Moskvitch. Through the scratched rear window, I watched my grandfather shut the gate behind us, unable to meet my bewildered stare. That was the first time I realised just how quickly men will surrender almost anything for a quiet life.

During the twelve-mile drive into Karakol, I wondered if my mother had sent for me, and whether I would recognise her, or she me. Even then, I didn't have much trust in memories.

I spent just over two years in the orphanage, during which I ran away three times. Very few of the children were there because their parents had died. We were known as 'social orphans'; in the chaos of independence, our families had split up, gone off to Russia to look for a job, or simply disappeared. So what little remained of the state authorities got the task of caring for us. And because we couldn't complain, didn't have anywhere else to go and were only children, they took as little care as they needed.

'*Pashol na khui.*'

It wasn't the first time I'd been sworn at; it wasn't even as if none of my superiors had ever said it to me. But I'd never had a one-armed man hug me, then tell me to fuck off.

I glanced around the orphanage director's office. There had been some changes: the scuffmarks of children's shoulders against the wall had darkened, and a different president scowled down from an ornate gilt frame. And there was a different man behind the desk from the last time I'd stood in front of it, waiting to be punished.

However, Gurminj Shokhumorov wasn't your typical official. For a start, he was Tajik, a rarity in our government's ethnic mix, and if you saw him in the street, you'd think he was a farmer, maybe a builder, who'd lost his right arm to an accident or a car crash.

It was shrapnel from an RPG fired by a mujahidin warrior in the Panjshir Valley north of Kabul that smashed Gurminj's shoulder and arm into fragments, and ended his career in the Red Army. To Gurminj, it was a massive joke that the Panjshir is where the majority of Tajiks in Afghanistan live. As he always used to say, back in the days when we'd opened the second bottle of vodka and crushed the cap underfoot, 'If you're going to lose an arm, you want it to be a relative that fucks you up.'

It had been over a year since we'd last met; he was one of the mourners who stood by me as we buried my wife, and he had been with me the following day, when the women came down to the grave and scattered bread and milk on the hard earth.

'Do you honestly think I've got the time to track down some ancient identity bands?' he asked, lifting up the evidence bags Usupov had dropped off the day before.

'You know the right places to go, the right people to ask. Right now, I'm as welcome in Bishkek as a dose of clap half an hour after the town's only pharmacy has closed down. No one will risk their neck to give me the whisper.'

'And if it's me that does the asking, it shouldn't set off any alarm bells; is that what you mean?'

'That too,' I admitted. 'But someone has to do it. Those children didn't get a chance at life; they deserve better than being left to rot by some stinking canal.'

'You know how many people I have to kneel in front of, just to keep this place warm, and stew and bread on the table?' Gurminj asked, throwing his one arm wide. 'I'll tell you, a fuck of a lot.' He smiled, his teeth dazzling white in a thick black beard.

I nodded. My memories of the orphanage weren't great, but I knew Gurminj was a good man. He'd told me once, in the days when I was still drinking, that there was no such thing as a child that couldn't be helped, sometimes even saved. I was drunk in the way I used to get then, with enough anger and despair bubbling under to turn the world into a fleapit hotel with blood on the carpet and screams soaked into the wallpaper. But I wasn't drunk enough to tell him that I'd seen some of the children he cared for grow up to be robbed or raped or murdered. Or to do those things themselves.

He already knew.

Gurminj pushed the evidence bags back towards me, distaste evident on his face.

'Not the nicest present I've ever had.'

'Try being given one when you're twelve,' I said.

He stared back at me, perhaps unsure if I was insulting him.

'I missed my *mama*, my grandfather, even the sour-faced bitch he married. I wasn't a country boy, I didn't know anyone, and they all laughed at my city accent. So I told them they were all *myrki*, stupid peasants. I lost the first few fights, but then I learnt it was easier to just get along with what they said. Or to punch first when I had to.'

'No one ever said living in an orphanage is easy,' Gurminj said, 'but sometimes it has to be better than what went before. You remember the silent ones?'

I nodded. The children who didn't speak, the ones who never caught your eye or smiled or joined in playtime games. The ones who did their best in the showers to hide the scars and burn marks on their arms and backs. And then there were the ones whose scars were all on the inside, who'd given up trying to understand why the world was treating them with such cruelty.

I picked up the envelopes with the identity bands, all that we had to give names, faces to the bodies.

'Seven more silent ones,' I said, memories vivid behind my eyes.

'There's one thing you need to know, Inspector,' Gurminj said, pointing at the bags.

'You've traced the children already?' I asked.

'In a manner of speaking,' he said, produced a sheet of paper from a pile on his desk. 'As you know, I've got contacts in other orphanages. Mainly, we keep each other posted on the latest *nomenklatura* bullshit from Bishkek. But you know, Akyl, there's a market for the children we look after.'

I could sense the anger coming off Gurminj; no one cared more for the orphans under his care, no one was more aware of the need for vigilance against the predators that circle the pack.

'I don't really approve of foreign adoptions,' he said. 'I know all the arguments about finding a better life in America, in Europe. And God knows, anyone that can love a child that isn't their own is a good person. But why should Kyrgyzstan become a baby farm for rich foreigners? What if you lose that sense of who you are, what it means to be Kyrgyz?'

I nodded, although I've often wondered if being Kyrgyz simply means being chained to an endless supply of misfortune.

'We watch out for the traffickers, the illegal adoptions. We've all heard about children being harvested for their organs, or for medicine. Does it happen? Maybe a myth, but who knows? There's no end to the ways in which scum exploit the helpless, so they can have a fancy car, expensive vodka, a bleach-blonde Russian whore with silicone tits. So I keep in touch with some of the security people in Kazakhstan, Uzbekistan, and we watch.'

Gurminj gave a mirthless smile that bared his teeth, held up the paper in his hand. God help anyone who abused a child under his care.

'The identity bands are genuine, no doubt about that. And the different colours show that they come from different orphanages as well as this one, as far away as Naryn and Osh. But that's where the problem begins.'

He paused, and I stared across the desk at him, wondering at his silence.

'The numbers and the orphanages all tally. For once, Central Records didn't balls it all up. But the children who wore them? Your problem is, they're all still alive. And they all left their orphanages at least ten years ago.'

Chapter 4

For a moment, I couldn't make sense of what Gurminj told me. The bands had to be genuine, untampered with. When you were deposited at an orphanage, you were given a band to wear on your right wrist, the number already written on it, the number that tracked your progress or lack of it through the system. Then a lighter was held under the two ends of the plastic to melt them together. There was no way you could remove it without cutting it in half. And when the band got too tight, the old one was destroyed and a new one sealed in its place.

Tamper-proof: what the system captures, it doesn't easily relinquish. The only thing more permanent would have been a tattoo, and even the government wouldn't go that far.

'I don't understand,' I said; this was the first solid fact I'd uncovered so far.

I looked more closely at the bands: I should have realised that they were far too big for such small children. As if he'd read my thoughts, Gurminj nodded.

'It was the first thing Usupov told me, that the bands were too big for the bodies.'

'So why didn't he tell me? I could have started a check on identifying the bands.'

Gurminj shrugged, and pushed his hand towards the ceiling in a gesture of resignation.

'You said he flew up here? In a helicopter? So the case

must be important to someone with plenty of pull, wouldn't you say? Someone who wants the bodies identified. Or maybe wants them staying unknown.'

I'd always thought of Usupov as one of the good guys. We'd worked well in the past, and I owed him. But there's always a first time for everything. The first kiss, the first fuck, the first betrayal, the first death.

Gurminj opened his desk drawer and took out a bottle and two glasses. Not easy with one hand, but he'd had a lot of practice.

'You still don't . . . ?' he said, looking down at the glass he'd pushed towards me.

'Not today,' I answered, the familiar words a lie against the sudden craving I felt. The raw scent of the vodka, the oily look as it swirled around the glass and caught the light, the burn on my tongue and throat, the shudder as the alcohol hit.

'You won't mind if I do?' he asked, poured himself a shot, threw it back.

'Your liver,' I said. 'God help whoever gets it as a transplant.'

'When this shit happened,' he said, pointing at his empty shirtsleeve, 'I used to feel my missing hand wanting to throw a punch all the time. At anyone who got in my way, who felt sorry for me, who assured me that it didn't make a difference but she'd met someone.'

He poured another brimful, let it sit.

'I could imagine the cuts on my knuckles from someone's teeth, feel the blow travel up my arm. The morphine didn't take the pain away, it only pushed it aside, made it seem unimportant, like hearing a TV in the next room. But when it wore off, it was back to having life as my sparring partner.'

This time he sipped, the glass hidden in his one hand.

'So I quit the morphine, hit the vodka, hard at first, then tapered it down to a couple of glasses every two or three days. A kind of equilibrium.'

He tossed the rest of his drink back, pulled a face, smiled.

'Hardly doctor's orders, but it gets me through the week.'

I knew the feeling.

'How about you, *tovarishch*? How do you keep things balanced?'

The concern he felt showed in his face.

I picked up the evidence bags, stuffed them in my pocket, stood up, put my left hand out, a clumsy unfamiliar way to shake hands.

'Balance? It's overrated, Gurminj, hadn't you heard?'

Chapter 5

I walked with Gurminj through half-lit corridors badly in need of a coat of paint, remembering my own time here, how sorrow had been overtaken by a kind of resignation, a belief this was how it was going to be for years to come. I wondered how many of the boys and girls under Gurminj's care felt the same way.

Gurminj stopped by the main door, put his hand on the shoulder of a young boy, maybe eight years old, with a strange, lopsided hairstyle as if he'd cut it himself, using blunt scissors and without the aid of a mirror.

'Inspector, meet Master Otabek, our newest resident,' Gurminj said. 'He joined our happy little gang just a couple of weeks ago.'

I crouched down to look into the boy's face, and smiled.

'I used to live here myself, Otabek,' I said, 'and I made lots of friends. I'm sure you'll like it here, and Director Shokhumorov will take very good care of you.'

The boy said nothing, but simply stared back at me, the way I'd stared when I was told I wasn't visiting, but staying. I couldn't think of anything to say that wouldn't seem totally false, so I smiled again and stood up.

At the gate, Gurminj shook hands again, then embraced me.

'Quiet boy, that Otabek,' I said. 'Reminded me of myself when I was here.'

'He doesn't say much,' Gurminj said. 'In fact, he doesn't say anything. I think whenever he tried to talk in the past, it was beaten out of him. Belts, fists, the usual loving parents. But we'll help him find his voice, his way back.'

I nodded. Gurminj always did his best, and the effort it took was stencilled in the lines on his face. If only everyone tried as hard to live a decent life, maybe I'd be out of a job.

It took me twenty minutes to walk back to the hotel, past run-down shops and patches of muddy wasteland, stray mongrel dogs barking from a safe distance. Karakol feels like it crouches at the edge of the world, with mountains on three sides holding everywhere else at bay. Winter storms can cut the main road back to Issyk-Kul and Bishkek, but the isolation of the place lasts all year round. The people here are suspicious of strangers, and I got several hard stares from the people I passed. No one likes cops, but in Karakol it's become an art form.

As I walked, I tried to find a possible motive behind the deaths. I was pretty sure Usupov would find a cause of death, at least for the less decomposed bodies. I was also pretty certain it wouldn't be from natural causes. But why kill the children in the first place, then bury their bodies together, where the likelihood of them being uncovered was so much greater?

Usupov was waiting for me in the reception area of the Amir. For once, his usual composure seemed to have slipped. I wondered if seeing so many dead children had slipped a scalpel under his skin, then remembered how he'd autopsied all the protesters shot dead by the government at the start of the last revolution. If there was one thing Usupov was hardened to, it was death.

'Inspector,' he began, stopped to polish his glasses. His hands shook slightly; we might have worked together before, cut a few corners, done each other favours, but I was still Murder Squad. Which means I don't have friends, only suspects.

I jerked a thumb at the chairs furthest from the reception desk, and we sat down. The clock on the wall behind the desk stuttered away the minutes, but otherwise the room was quiet. I stared at him, not saying a word.

Few things intimidate people more than silence. Their guilt hangs in the dead air, or they get a taste of what solitary confinement in a basement cell must be like.

'Gurminj told you about the identity bands?'

I showed him the face with the unreadable Uighur mask I'd inherited from my grandfather. A face sharpened by a thousand basement interrogations.

'I'll be looking into that,' I said. 'Not easy, getting hold of those, from all over the country.'

Usupov nodded. Tracking the original owners was going to be time-consuming, but it had to be done. Gurminj had given me the names, but interrogating them was strictly down to me.

'Any thoughts on why the bodies were buried together?' Usupov asked.

I shrugged.

'Seven different dumping sites would mean seven different holes, seven times the risk of being seen, of someone plough-ing a potato field and unearthing a dead child,' I said. 'So one burial place makes sense.'

'You think?'

'It's what I would do. Maybe he was in a hurry, or there's

some kind of ritual involved, a psycho thing,' I said, wondered why the corner of Usupov's mouth twitched, as if hooked. Fear. It was time to press home.

'So what have you got to tell me, Kenesh?'

He looked away. We'd known each other a long time, and I've learnt from long experience how to tell when people lie. And he knew it.

'I was under orders from the moment you called me. To tell you nothing straight away, to report back direct first with whatever I found out.'

I raised an eyebrow, looked disbelieving. I didn't have many friends back at the station, but this seemed a complicated way of screwing up my career even more than it already was.

'Sverdlovsky station.'

It wasn't a question, but Usupov shook his head.

'Worse.'

I waited. Until he said the name I really didn't want to hear.

'Tynaliev.'

Mikhail Tynaliev. The Minister of State Security, probably the most dangerous man in Kyrgyzstan. The father of the dead and mutilated girl I'd knelt beside on a winter night, a brutal wind coming down off the mountains.

I didn't think anyone knew how I'd set up my old boss to admit to having Yekaterina Tynalieva killed. But in the dismal hours before dawn, I'd sometimes lie awake, wondering just how much he'd been hurt before Tynaliev had him put down. Imagining his fingernails being ripped out, his testicles crushed. Having seen Yekaterina Tynalieva's body, and knowing her father's reputation, I would hazard a bet that death was an escape, but not a quick one.

Usupov wasn't stupid; he would have linked Tynaliev with the disappearance of the chief. But he knew better than to enquire into matters that would bring him nothing but problems. I was Murder Squad; it was my job to get myself into trouble by asking the right questions.

'It was the minister who organised the helicopter up here,' Usupov said. 'He told me he wanted a full report, the matter dealt with quickly.'

'Why would Tynaliev show an interest in a case like this?' I asked. 'It's going to reach the papers, but it's not as if it threatens state security. A psycho, maybe a cult, but that's all. So why?'

Usupov finished polishing his glasses and put them back on, clearly more comfortable behind their shield.

'Why is it so important to him?' I repeated.

Usupov smiled, but it never climbed as high as his eyes.

'That's not the sort of question you ask a man like the minister,' he said. 'But maybe it's not about state security.'

I waited for him to add to that. He shook his head, stood up, began to walk towards the lift doors, turned and looked back at me.

'Maybe you should ask if it's about you.'

Chapter 6

I'd last seen Mikhail Tynaliev when his bodyguards had dragged my old boss out of his office to a painful, solitary death. I didn't expect thanks – he wasn't that sort of man – but I had hoped he would leave me alone. As I watched Usupov disappear into the lift, I guessed it was the minister who had ordered me into this internal exile.

I wasn't going to tell the world about the chief's death, but keeping hold of power means making sure the bag is securely tied when you drown those kittens you don't want. If Tynaliev wanted to make sure my tongue stayed behind my teeth, he could have arranged it. A car accident, a shooting in the line of duty. But that wasn't the minister's style. Better to keep me alive but off balance, in case I came in useful later. Everyone said he was devious. No one ever said he wasn't smart.

I knew that since Tynaliev was involved, there was something political floating in the wind. Maybe a power struggle at the White House; I'd heard rumours of a potential palace coup. That was something Kyrgyzstan didn't need; yet another president in less than twenty-five years, the country weakened and looking to Russia for help. But I couldn't see any connection between dead children and whoever was going to be next in line to siphon off our taxes.

At one time, I would have poured myself a couple of shots of the good stuff, oil to lubricate my thinking, push me in directions I wouldn't consider when sober. But the last time

I had a drink, it was to summon the courage to end my wife's cancer with a cushion over her face. And ever since then, I knew vodka would only taste of bile and rot, a dead woman's tongue thrust into my mouth.

I lay back on the hotel bed, its lumpy mattress digging springs into my shoulders, smoked, wondered if I'd finally reached the edge of my abilities, if all the deaths I'd paid witness to had soured and staled me beyond all redemption. The hesitant afternoon light dwindled to black, headlights criss-crossing the bedroom ceiling like prison searchlights.

The call came an hour before dawn, my mobile summoning me from a dry-mouthed dream I couldn't recall but which had left me apprehensive, as if something dreadful had happened while I dozed.

'Inspector, there's a car downstairs waiting for you. To take you to Orlinoye.'

The voice was distant, mechanical, heartless.

Orlinoye. The village where my wife Chinara grew up, and where she now lay in the small graveyard on a bluff overlooking the valley.

'What's this about?'

'There's been a development. New information regarding the death of your wife. The courts have ordered an exhumation, and you are ordered to attend it.'

I shook my head, still fuddled with sleep, sure I'd misheard.

'Some mistake.'

'No mistake. It's a direct order. Go now.'

An elderly Moskvitch with a taciturn uniformed *ment* at the wheel took me past the potato field where the children's bodies had been found. White crime scene tape still fluttered from the three apple trees, a warning to the curious, flags indicating a surrender of sorts.

We didn't slow down, but turned north, onto the road to Orlinoye, passing through a couple of small hamlets, clusters of worn farm buildings surrounded by bare fields, their backs towards the mountains that mark the border with Kazakhstan. The car's worn suspension was no help against the potholed road: I swayed left and right to avoid the worst of the ruts, feeling the holster of my gun rub against my hip with each turn.

We drove for almost an hour until we reached Orlinoye's one road that splits the village in two. With each kilometre we covered, the fear in my stomach grew more intense, a rat gnawing away at me. I was sure no one had seen me smother Chinara in her hospital bed, using the embroidered cushion that had been a wedding present from her grandmother. In those final hours of her life, I hadn't been able to bear her pain, so with half a bottle of vodka inside me, I'd pushed her beyond any further suffering. I told myself it was a mercy killing, that she would have done the same for me. But that didn't prevent her appearing in my dreams, her eyes hurt and accusing.

I'd taken the cushion home, put it away at the back of the wardrobe. Perhaps it had saliva traces, evidence which could convict me. Or maybe this was a set-up; a grave already opened in the hours before dawn, room enough for one more body when I knelt down and felt a gun barrel cold against my neck.

Finally, we turned right down a muddy track past the village power station, and followed it until we reached the graveyard. My final destination? I almost hoped so.

We Kyrgyz believe in paying due respect to the dead, but

we don't believe in wasting good farming land either. The Orlinoye graveyard isn't fertile land that would otherwise be put to good use; it clings to the sloping edge of a small cliff, a river winding through the valley below. There are some eighty graves here, each marked by a headstone and bordered by slender metal railings, most with the Islamic *hilal* – crescent moon – in each corner. A peaceful place, with birds of prey riding the thermals and a spectacular view towards the mountains.

We parked beside two more police cars, and I got out, the muscles across my shoulders tight with anxiety. Spring grass, still sprinkled with night frost and dew, crackled and whispered beneath my boots.

Three men stood by Chinara's grave, one of them Usupov, the other two uniformed officers I didn't recognise. Two others were stripped to the waist, despite the chill of the dawn air, scooping shovelfuls of dirt to one side, the mound of raw earth already partly excavated, three or four feet down.

The last time I visited Chinara's grave, the mound had been stippled with tiny blue flowers, and a single long thorn with jagged blades. A careless beauty, together with a warning not to get too close.

Watching the desecration of my wife's grave, each blow of the spades approaching her body, a sense of finality replaced the fear in my belly. My fingers brushed the cold metal of the gun on my hip, and I undid the leather clasp, making sure everyone saw me do it. I pulled my jacket clear of my gun and walked towards the grave. A thin wind gusted down from the Tien Shan, a whisper of condolence from the Celestial Mountains.

A good place to die, if this was where it was going to end.

Chapter 7

In the distance, high above us, indifferent to our presence, newly risen sunlight burnt pale gold on the snow peaks of the mountains. In the crystal dawn air, my breath plumed and smouldered before vanishing. My eyes never left the men in front of me, watching for hands to make a sudden gesture, a turning away, a stepping apart.

Finally I stopped five metres away, and stared at Usupov. His face was expressionless, unreadable.

'Inspector—' he began, but I raised a hand to silence him.

'There must be a very good reason why you're doing this, and I want to know it. And if I'm not satisfied . . .'

To finish my sentence, I let my fingertips brush the grips of my gun. I tried to keep anger out of my voice. Anger at the men in front of me, at myself for the failures and compromises that had brought me to this point, and shamefully, resentment at Chinara for dying and leaving me adrift, half submerged, like an abandoned rowboat on Lake Issyk-Kul.

'You understand, this is where I laid my wife to rest, on her side, facing Mecca. Where I said my farewells. Kissed her forehead and looked at her for the last time before I shrouded her face with a white cloth. Then wrapped her body in the frozen earth and snow.'

None of the men spoke. The diggers crouched down in Chinara's open grave, watching, knowing they were trapped.

I wondered if the simplest solution to everything I carried

inside me was to start shooting, and let them extinguish me in a dozen heartbeats, place me next to my life's love.

I'd done my best to come to terms with the thought of Chinara's decay. Cheeks collapsing to rest on teeth, eyes sinking back into their sockets, smooth belly distended by the gases of rot. Soft warm skin shrunk into rasping parchment stretched tight over bones before splitting. And slowly, over decades perhaps, turning back into the earth, with only her grave marker to show she'd ever lived and loved and made my heart bright.

I looked at the simple marble plaque in front of the grave. Chinara's profile, copied from a paper silhouette done by a street artist in Red Square beside the Kremlin walls, during the one visit we'd made there. Followed by her name, her dates, and a line she would often quote by one of her favourite poets: *Love weathers all storms.* When we argued, she could always defuse the occasion, simply by saying it, raising an eyebrow and winning my heart once more with her smile.

But I've never been convinced that love can weather a storm as overwhelming as death.

I bent down and brushed the loose soil from one of the blue flowers that had adorned the grave. Sunlight turned the tiny petals turquoise and a gust of wind snatched it from my fingers. It was time.

I like to think I'm not a violent man. I hope the power a police badge, a gun and a basement interrogation room bestow hasn't changed my views on right and wrong. But I also know the clarity when the dice have been thrown, and the speed of your reactions and your willingness to pull the trigger are all that stand between you and a hole in the ground.

Don't think. Act.

It's a clarity that's helped me put people in their graves. So perhaps it's all too easy to deceive ourselves as to who we really are.

The older of the two uniformed officers stepped forward, his hands held palm forwards, as if to reassure me that he meant no disrespect.

'Inspector, we received a call from a very senior government official, ordering us to undertake this regrettable action.'

I looked at Usupov. His imperceptible nod confirmed my suspicion: Mikhail Tynaliev, Minister of State Security. I turned my attention back to the officer. He had taken a step forward, so that my view of his colleague was partially obscured. I beckoned him to move back, ready to pull out my gun if I had to.

'Go on.'

'He told us you're working on a very important case. One with consequences that go to the highest government levels, if you solve it. The very highest. And vital evidence has been concealed in your wife's grave.'

He paused, shrugged.

'He didn't tell us where he got the information. And we were ordered to ask you here, to show that nothing disrespectful to your wife's remains or to your feelings would take place.'

He reached into his pocket, stopped when I shook my head.

'A cigarette, that's all.'

He looked down at the grave.

'This isn't what I signed on for.'

I shook my head again and he withdrew his hand, before beckoning to the diggers to climb out of the grave. They did so, standing well away from the other three. Maybe they didn't know that a Yarygin holds seventeen 9mm Parabellum bullets, more than enough to go round.

I looked down into the dark mouth of the grave. My wife's shroud was smeared and stained with earth, torn in places, the soil around it raw and freshly turned. The roots of the nearby thorn had coiled themselves around the body, as if defending it against incursions such as this one. The white cloth stirred as if caught by a sudden breeze. But the air was still.

Then, a sudden movement, quick, intense. The grey muzzle and black snout of a rat, alert at our intrusion. A rat that had made a home in my wife's body, her ribcage its roof rafters, her belly its nest. The rat stared back at me, unafraid, baring long yellow teeth in a snarl of defiance. Then I was pumping bullet after bullet into the grave, and as the earth gave way under my feet, I fell, to embrace Chinara for a final time.

Chapter 8

I'd had the nightmare before, but its familiarity did nothing to stop me waking, bathed in sweat, heart pounding and my mouth filled with the taste of bile. I switched on the bedside lamp and drank from a bottle of water. Its chill punched my stomach and I thought I was going to vomit.

I looked around the room, bland, unremarkable, but couldn't shake off the impression that something vile had retreated into the shadows, waiting its moment. I sat there, hands shaking, until my heart slowed and the terror in my mind subsided.

I knew the dream was offering me some sort of clue, dredged out from the day's events by my subconscious. When you live in a country governed by the seasons, and the power of nature, there's a deep-seated belief in the sacred-ness of the world around you. To survive in a land this harsh, you need respect. There's an element of shamanism buried deep in Kyrgyz culture, a knowledge that recognises mystic places, sacred mountains, the superstitions and beliefs that underscore the way we live. We never place the round flat-bread *lepeshka* upside down on a plate or fill a cup to the brim with *chai*, we don't disturb brightly coloured cloths tied to a branch or a rock. To do so is to insult the gifts of nature, or to issue a challenge to forces we don't even comprehend.

Sometimes the job's simply about keeping an open mind, rearranging facts until you start to see patterns. But over the years, I've learnt dreams can hint at something, even if I can't always work out what it is. It's more than simply sifting clues or watching how seemingly random patterns form a new way of seeing things.

Dreams let me step away from myself, allow me to reach an understanding with my surroundings, the smells, the sounds, the mutter of wind stirring the grass on the high *jailoo*. The cynical might call it grasping at straws, or following a hunch, or desperation. I call it listening to the songs of the dead, telling me how they died, why, and who stole their breath.

And sometimes it's about seeing the world through the eyes of the thief.

I spent the next two days making phone calls, using the list that Gurminj had given me, of all the orphans whose identity bands were in front of me as I spoke. None of them seemed connected to each other, and a couple hung up on me once I started to explain the reason for my call. None of them had been in the same orphanage at the same time as anyone else on the list. Four men, three women, living in different parts of the country, with nothing in common apart from their time in the care of the state. A time that didn't seem to have many happy memories for them.

I also contacted their local police stations, to see if there was anything against them. One man accused of selling weed, a couple of car crashes, nothing that tied them to seven small bodies.

Usupov was due to go back to Bishkek the following day, taking the bodies with him, to store in the morgue in the hope that we might find out their identities. My new boss in

Bishkek, the replacement for the chief, a paper-pusher and political appointment called Lavrov, had already called me twice, stressing the need for a quick solution to the crime. I did think about asking him if he had any ideas, but the only investigating he'd ever done was looking for his car keys.

Which meant it was time to find out exactly what Usupov wasn't telling me.

'Kenesh, I need to know what's going on.'

We were in the hotel lobby, empty apart from the two of us and a receptionist engrossed in texting her friends. It made sense to talk here; I know enough about wired interrogation rooms to avoid having a conversation in any police station. I sat back on the lumpy hotel sofa and stared at Usupov, saying nothing. All too often, it's what you don't say that gives you the edge.

Usupov looked around, his usual calm gone, avoiding my eyes, his glasses catching the harsh mid-morning light from the window. His unease infected me, and my fingers touched the cold metal of my Yarygin.

'Akyl, the best thing you can do is tiptoe away, and make sure the door doesn't slam behind you. This is a crime you don't want to solve.'

His unusual use of my name was even more disconcerting than the warning he gave. In all the years I'd known him, the formality with which he'd called me 'Inspector' had defined our relationship. Now, I didn't know where I stood with him. I lit a cigarette to buy myself some time to think, and watched the blue-grey smoke as it hung in the air.

'Kenesh, I'm not a virgin. Tell me.'

Usupov shrugged. I picked a fleck of tobacco off the tip of my tongue and stubbed out my cigarette.

'You know I can't just walk away from this. I do and I'm fucked. Lavrov will have me up on the Torugart Pass, inspecting licence plates on the trucks that cross over from China.'

Usupov said nothing, and I felt anger starting to rise.

'If you know something, and I don't, you're a witness, maybe even a suspect,' I said, 'and no one's going to question me if I put you up in a cell for a few days. Maybe with someone you've testified against.'

It was an empty threat, and we both knew it, but I needed to remind Usupov that this was a murder case, and there weren't going to be any get out of jail cards.

'I don't know much,' Usupov said, staring down at his hands. I noticed that they shook slightly.

'So you do know something,' I said. It wasn't a question.

'Not know, more something I suspect.'

'You tell me what you suspect, I'll find the evidence to back it up,' I said.

'You're coming up against some very powerful men, Akyl.'

I shrugged; I'd expected nothing less. And putting a stone in the shoes of the rich and powerful is more satisfying than confiscating some *alkash*'s bottle, or collecting breakfast money fines for speeding.

'It wouldn't be the first time, Kenesh, you know that. It's my career speciality.'

He shook his head, sucking his teeth at my criminal stupidity.

'They'll brush you aside and forget about you the next minute. Traffic duty in Torugart Pass? You'll be lucky not to be in a shroud lying next to your wife.'

Perhaps that was the meaning of my dream, a warning or

a prophecy. The ticking of the clock behind the reception desk was very loud. Silence hung between us like a spider's web, ready to snare the unwary.

'These powerful fuckers, what is it they want, Kenesh?'

Usupov stared past me, and I could have sworn there were tears in his eyes.

'You can't fight them, Akyl.'

'Let me ask you again, and this time with my Murder Squad cap on. Chief Forensic Pathologist Usupov, what is it they want?'

Usupov paused, sighed, world-weary, sickened.

'Fresh meat, Inspector. Young meat.'

He stirred his lukewarm tea, raised the cup to his mouth, put it down again untasted. His eyes were bleak behind his glasses.

'They want children.'

Chapter 9

'It was around this time, about a year ago,' Kenesh began, his eyes avoiding mine. 'I'd been called out in the middle of the night by the duty officer at Sverdlovsky station. They'd found a body just off Chui Prospekt, it was being shipped to the morgue for me to examine. He wouldn't give me any details, except to say it was important the autopsy be done straight away.

'I wasn't too pleased; we'd been celebrating the spring festival, Nowruz, and I knew I had a busy day ahead. But he told me orders from the top, with a police car outside my front door within ten minutes. So I got dressed, a *ment* drove me across town to the morgue.

'The body had already arrived, laid out on the table, covered, just as usual. But what was different was the man sitting on the next table. He was wearing a suit, smart, expensive, so I didn't think he was a policeman; a lawyer maybe, a government official, whatever. But he didn't have that *nomenklatura* look. He was thickset, maybe forty, with the face of a former boxer, all shadows and scars. He sat there on one of the tables, legs swinging, smoking as if he didn't have a care in the world, in his favourite bar with a cold beer in front of him.

'I told him that I didn't allow smoking in the operating room. He looked at me, then at the end of his cigarette, raised an eyebrow.

'"You're worried about his health?" he said, waving the cigarette in the direction of the body.

'"No, but I'm worried about mine," I said. He just smiled, looked at his cigarette again, and gusted a blue cloud in my direction. His smile never managed to climb as far as his eyes.

'"I think you'll find the cause of death was a heart attack," he said. "Tragic in such a young man."

'I pulled back the sheets, and looked down at the body.'

Usupov paused, then reached over and took a cigarette from my pack that lay on the table. He lit it with the uncertain gesture of a non-smoker, coughed as he swallowed the smoke.

'Bad?' I said.

Usupov nodded, swallowed, trying to recapture his normal air of detachment.

'I've seen a lot of shit that people do to each other, Akyl,' he said, and I watched the burning end of his cigarette tremble, as if caught in a sudden wind. I waited for him to speak. From a man who'd spent so much time in the presence of the dead, his silence told me more than I wanted to know.

'He was about twelve, I guessed, but hard to tell from the bruising on his face and chest. Small, undernourished, thin enough so I could see the broken ribs outlined against his skin. The left cheekbone shattered, so his face had collapsed in on itself. Two teeth on the right side slicing through his cheek. His facial injuries came from a hammer; I could see the circular imprint.'

Usupov paused, snapped his fingers to drag the receptionist away from her phone.

'Vodka, the good stuff,' he said. I shook my head, watched

the girl walk away. We waited in silence until an open bottle and brimming glass sat in front of him. Usupov emptied the glass in one swift movement, shuddered as the alcohol blazed in his mouth and throat.

'Go on,' I said, quietly, not wanting to break Usupov's rhythm.

'Bite marks – from more than one mouth – on the boy's thighs. A compound fracture of the left tibia. And bruising from what looked like heavy boots. Not just kicking but stamping, so I could see the tread on the soles. More than one pair of shoes.'

He poured more vodka, watched it spill over the lip of the glass.

'All the time I was examining the body, the man watched without a reaction. I might have been preparing dinner. Then I turned the body over.'

Usupov emptied the glass in a single shot.

'He'd been raped, Inspector, by more than one man, from the amount of sperm I found. Penetrated with something sharp. There was blood on the back of his legs, more bite marks on his shoulders. Twelve, Inspector, that's how young he was. The same age as my eldest.'

I said nothing. There are times when the dead bear witness to such horror that silence is the only possible alternative to a scream of despair. I pushed the thought of a vodka for myself to one side. The clock continued to tick, like a pulse refusing to give up.

'The man said, "I told you, a heart attack," and he stood up, mashed his cigarette out on the floor. It left a blue-black mark on the tiles, the same shade as the bruises on the boy's face. The man stood in front of me, the tobacco on his breath heavy on my face. He had a killer's cold eyes, black, impossible to read. He held up a crumpled piece of paper, pushed it against my chest.

'"The boy's death certificate. I've saved you the trouble of filling it in. Heart attack. Mitral stenosis. It says so in black and white," he said, "and if it bothers you, well, his isn't the only blank death certificate I have. Understand?"

'I asked if the body was to be released to relatives, and he told me not to bother my head with things that didn't concern me. "Concentrate on slicing up the dead," he said. "And avoid joining them."'

Usupov stared at the wall, not seeing anything, and we sat in silence.

'What makes you suspect there's a connection to the case we have here?' I asked.

'You saw the bodies we autopsied,' Kenesh said. 'There were bite marks on some of them. Blows from a hammer. Similar wounds. Done in a frenzy, maybe rage, maybe sexual, I don't know.'

'So you think there's a serial killer responsible for this?'

'More than one, judging from the boy's body,' Kenesh said. 'He'd been raped many times.'

'Can you check the wounds and see if they correspond?'

'Not with the dead boy. I wasn't allowed to take photographs, and the body was taken away, God knows where. But there's one thing I haven't told you.'

'What's that?' I asked, sensing that Usupov might be able to give me my first solid lead.

'The dead boy wore an identity band. From an orphanage.'

I sat back as his words started twisting new patterns and theories in my head.

'So what happened then?' I prompted.

Usupov looked at me for the first time. The fear and shame in his eyes was almost too much to watch.

'God forgive me, Akyl,' he said. 'The man handed me the false death certificate. And I signed.'

Chapter 10

I decided to call Gurminj Shokhumorov, to see if he had any knowledge of local people with an unhealthy interest in children. Orphanages are often targeted by paedophiles; it's a lot easier to pick out children who don't have loving parents to care and watch over them, and fewer people care when they disappear.

His mobile rang, but went to voicemail, so I decided to head over there. The mountains crouched behind a mask of rain, the air damp and cold. I kept trying Gurminj's phone, and I grew more worried each time I pressed the redial button. A police car was parked at an angle outside the building when I arrived, and I knew something was badly wrong. As I got out of the car and approached the front entrance, a *ment* I didn't recognise held up his hand to stop me.

'Crime scene. You can't enter here,' he said, in the pompous voice all small men use when they're in charge.

'What sort of crime?' I asked, the feeling of doom settling in my stomach.

'Police business,' he replied, put his hand on my chest to prevent me going any further. My jacket swung open, and I made sure he saw the butt of my gun on my hip. He gasped, started to reach for his own gun. I grabbed his wrist, held it tight, pulling him towards me.

'I'm Murder Squad,' I told him, staring past the fear and suspicion in his eyes, 'so police business is my business, *da*?'

I used my other hand to fish my ID out of my pocket, held it in front of his nose. The fear left his face, the suspicion remained.

'I didn't know, Inspector,' he muttered, as I let go of his wrist. 'I was told to keep the scene intact, not let anybody through.'

'OK, bad beginning,' I said. 'We both forget this. We start again, Officer . . . ?'

'Kurmanov,' he said, taking a step back, holding out his hand. We shook, awkward, unwilling to admit how close we'd come to a problem of our own making.

'I'm here to see the orphanage director, Gurminj Shokhumorov,' I said.

Kurmanov looked puzzled, then wary.

'How did you know, to get here so quickly?' he asked. 'We only found the body half an hour ago.'

The director's office was still lined with the tidemark of children's shoulders, and the president continued to glare down from the wall behind the director's desk. But now a splash of red paint had stippled the patterned wallpaper, and dripped from the glass of the picture frame. Except it wasn't paint.

Gurminj Shokhumorov lay face down upon the papers scattered on his desk. Spilt red ink stained his hair and bare arms, and pooled a few inches away from his head. Except it wasn't ink.

I could smell cordite, blood and brains, the singed hair blackened around the wound, where the bullet had worked hard to drain his skull. The room was silent, holding its breath in shock. Gurminj's desk calendar had all his appointments and meetings circled in red, now overlaid with a deeper scarlet already turning black. The gun, a Makarov, lay on the floor just behind his chair.

A uniformed officer was idly sifting through the papers on Gurminj's desk, looking up as I entered. I held up my ID, playing the big city Murder Squad guy, and his nervous fingers touched the peak of his cap.

'This is a crime scene. Don't touch anything until the forensic pathologist's inspected the body.'

'It's a suicide, sir,' the *ment* said, holding up a paper. 'Even left a note.'

'Which bit of "Don't touch anything" did I not make clear? Contaminating a crime scene could earn you a bunk in Penitentiary Number One, officer.'

The *ment* dropped the paper as if it had suddenly caught fire. I jabbed my thumb at the door.

'And shut it behind you,' I ordered as he headed out of the room. I walked over to the desk, the smell of blood and shit getting stronger. I've always wondered how despair could so overpower a person that death seemed better than any alternative. Even after Chinara had died, I didn't consider killing myself. Maybe I had too much guilt and remorse not to serve the full life sentence due to me. Perhaps every death seems like a betrayal to those of us left behind.

I used a pencil on the desk to turn Gurminj's note, and read it. The words were barely legible, quickly scribbled down.

Akyl, enough. I want it to end here. I can't answer is why. I honestly don't know. You said balance is overrated; believe me, you should weigh everything, because balance is where answers might be found. G

I tucked the paper in my pocket, looked once more around the room. A framed degree certificate from the American University of Central Asia, next to a row of photos, showing Gurminj with his wife, Oksana, eating *pelmeni* in the local restaurants, hiking through Ala Archa National Park, walking holding hands along Chui Prospekt, Oksana's long black hair hurled upward by the wind. I never knew Oksana; she had died in a car accident the year before I met Gurminj. The loss had almost destroyed him, driving him into his work at the orphanage to fill the hole in his world.

I turned as a senior officer from the station entered the room.

'Our pathologist is on his way, then we can move the body,' he said. 'If that's OK with you.'

I nodded, and took a photo down from the wall. Gurminj, head thrown back, roaring with laughter, surrounded by the smiling orphans he'd cared for, encouraged, given a home they'd never known in their uncertain childhood. For Gurminj, I knew balance was everything. Which made me certain about how he had died.

A single tear-shaped fleck of blood smeared the glass. I wiped it away with my thumb, added the photo to the note in my pocket.

'That's good,' I said, and gritted my teeth. 'I want a complete report from the officer who found him. And you might ask yourself how the director put a bullet in the right side of his head, being as he only had a left arm.'

Chapter 11

Even as I let myself into Gurminj's spartan apartment with the keys I'd found in his desk, I could tell the place had already settled into a sense of loss. I touched the side of the half-empty bowl of *chai* on the kitchen table. Cold, to be rinsed out and forgotten. Time, for all its uncertainties, doesn't linger when we die.

It was clear to me that whoever had killed my friend wasn't too bothered about making it look like a convincing suicide. Probably relying on the stupidity or indifference of the local officers. And that was maybe a clue in itself.

I sat down and looked around the room, open as to what I might find. Clues to a murder are usually all too evident; the bloody knife, broken bottle, bruised throat. But sometimes you have to stare, unthinking, simply letting the scene whisper its secrets. You have to hear the full confession before you can start to separate truth from the lies.

The apartment was almost obsessively tidy, the bed neatly made, plates washed and stacked on the sink. Three chairs stood shoulder to shoulder against the far wall, a table with neatly piled paperwork, a battered coffee tin holding pens and pencils.

In the bedroom, the half-empty wardrobe housing a dozen unused clothes hangers was a reminder of Oksana's absence, of the same emptiness in my own home. A well-thumbed copy of Chingiz Aitmatov's *The Day Lasts More Than A*

Hundred Years lay open on the bedside table. Not when it's your last day, I thought, and closed the book. A torn sliver of paper, used as a bookmark, fell from between the pages. I recognised Gurminj's handwriting; a single word: *balance.*

Between life and death? Good and evil? Sweet and sour? No way of knowing. I remembered our final conversation, and the note Gurminj left behind. But nothing in my life was in balance. Everything was slightly off, a badly hung door that sticks when you try to close it, a window that never quite latches. I checked the jackets in the wardrobe, rummaged through the drawer of the bedside table, lifted the thin mattress. Nothing.

Back in the main room, I leafed through the papers on the table. They were all to do with the running of the orphanage, nothing personal. A small shelf on one wall held a selection of books. Some work books, a couple of popular mysteries, and a thin volume whose spine looked familiar. *Selected Poems of Anna Akhmatova.* The same edition Chinara had owned, one of her favourites that she read over and over, even when the wolf of cancer began to devour her.

I read a line at random: *Here is my gift, not grave-mound roses, not incense-sticks.* Who knows what gifts the dead will accept from us, as we hope to do more than appease our guilt at remaining behind? An imam or a priest might be able to tell you, a philosopher could define the problem, but I'm just Murder Squad. There's only one thing I know how to give the dead. Justice.

I walked back into the kitchen, held the bowl of *chai* under the tap, watched the dark tea leaves swirl and pattern the sink. Some people think they can foretell the future that way, and they might be right. As long as you believe the future is dark, messy, easy to simply rinse away.

I turned the cup upside down to dry, ran a finger over the counter top. No dust yet, but only a matter of time, like everything else.

An old-fashioned brass weighing scale was virtually the only piece of equipment in the kitchen, apart from a frying pan and a three-layer *pelmeni* steamer, presumably a souvenir from Oksana's time. The different-sized weights were cold in my hand as I dropped them into the left-hand pan and watched the right-hand one rise. And then I understood the meaning of Gurminj's note. *Balance is where answers might be found.*

I tipped the weights out of the pan and picked up the scale, turned it upside down, found the paper taped to the underside. I peeled away the tape, looked at what was written on the paper. A mobile phone number, with an international code. A number I already knew.

I poured a glass of water, sat down and sipped, wondering why Gurminj would have this number, or use such a roundabout way of letting me know. Whoever murdered my friend would have forced him to write the 'suicide' note, but his final sentence was a last act of defiance, knowing I would understand and follow the clue wherever it led.

I splashed cold water on my face, sat back down. Sunlight spilt through the window, bouncing off the brass balance and throwing a small spot of light against the shadow on the wall.

I read the paper again, knowing the number was already stored in my mobile. My hand trembled slightly as the dialling tone began and was answered.

A voice said, 'Inspector.' A woman's voice, unsurprised, even slightly amused, honey drizzled over ice cream.

Chapter 12

'Saltanat. *Kak dela?*'

I heard the snap of her lighter, the sharp inhale, the long breath out. I could see the cloud of grey-blue smoke rising in the air.

I remembered unreadable black eyes, a thin white scar running through her left eyebrow.

'You know me, Inspector, I'm a survivor. Like you.'

A pause.

'That's what we do, Inspector, survive.'

Shoulder-length black hair, high slanted cheekbones, a mouth generous with silence and evasions.

'I've been wondering when you'd call me.'

I tried to speak, realised my mouth was dry, took a sip of water.

I hadn't expected to hear from Saltanat after she crossed the border back into Uzbekistan. We'd been untrusting partners of a sort in the Tynalieva case, and, just once, lovers. She'd come to Bishkek to kill me, but decided we were more or less on the same side. While trying to solve the murders of young women across Kyrgyzstan and Uzbekistan, we'd been taken captive by the killers, sent by my boss, the chief. I'd been tortured, my hand half-cooked on a grill. Saltanat had been raped, before killing two of our captors, while I dealt with the third. While I confronted the chief, she'd

52

escaped from his safe house by killing a corrupt policeman. I hadn't seen or heard from her since then, but she'd
remained a presence as constant and terrifying as a loaded
shotgun.

'How's your hand?'

'Scarred. But working.'

'I take it you're not calling to ask how I am?'

'You know Gurminj Shokhumorov.'

It wasn't a question.

'Yes.'

Her voice was flat, empty, giving nothing away.

'Gurminj is dead. A single gunshot to the head. Suicide,
supposedly.'

'But?' I could hear the suspicion in her voice.

'Not many one-armed men shoot themselves on the other
side of their head. Single-handed, you might say. Whoever
killed him didn't really care what I thought.'

When Saltanat spoke, the dismissal in her voice was
absolute.

'So why did you call me? For the pleasure of breaking the
news?'

I paused, marshalling my thoughts, wondering at her
hostility.

'I'm working on a murder case. Seven small children, buried together in a field. I don't know if Gurminj knew
something about it, but if he did, he didn't tell me.'

Saltanat laughed.

'You're not the easiest man to trust with secrets, Inspector.
You have your own agenda, and it doesn't always tie in with
the law. Or the safety of other people.'

'I never knowingly put you in danger.'

She paused, the lighter snapped once more, the inhale and exhale.

'You weren't the one who was raped, Inspector.'

I thought back to that evening in my apartment, after we'd escaped, after she'd showered for hours until the water ran cold. We'd watched the sky darken and turn all the different shades of blue into night. Now, as then, I had no words to give her, no comfort. Then, as now, the cruelties people do to each other can't be washed away or justified in words. All we can do is survive as best we can.

'Gurminj hid your number for me to find. A clue, you might call it. So I know he wanted me to contact you. The only thing I don't know yet is why.'

When Saltanat spoke, the hostility in her voice was softened by a kind of sorrow.

'I'm sorry about Gurminj. He was a good man. He was helping me with a case.'

'To do with the dead children?' I asked.

'Perhaps. In a way,' Saltanat replied. 'We should meet.'

Now it was my turn to be silent. We'd never been able to completely trust each other, except with our lives. And I still carried a smudge of guilt about sleeping with her so soon after Chinara's death.

'Where? You want to come here?'

'Karakol? No.'

I saw the logic behind her refusal. It's about as far from Tashkent as you can get in Kyrgyzstan, and there's only one road in and out. All too easy to get trapped, the mountains on one side and the lake on the other.

'Then where?'

'Remember where you last saw me? No, don't say it, but there. Tomorrow. Noon.'

'I remember,' I said, suddenly wondering if my phone was being tapped.

'Be careful, Inspector. And silent.'

Then she hung up, leaving me to wonder just what the hell was going on.

Chapter 13

On the long journey back to Bishkek, I reviewed Gurminj's death. Or rather, his murder; I knew Gurminj wouldn't kill himself, after all he'd survived. The note was in his handwriting, but there was something off about the tone. A gun to his head as he wrote? I remembered our evenings spent demolishing a bottle of vodka, his outrageous snores as he'd slept on the sofa in our little apartment. Chinara had never complained; she adored him, and constantly tried to matchmake him with any of her friends who were currently unattached. Pointless really, since Gurminj was as devoted to the memory of his Oksana as I was to become to my Chinara. He and I had both discovered that the death of the one you love is the final snapping of the chain that binds you to the rest of the world.

Before I left, I'd interviewed the orphanage staff and older children; no one seemed to have heard anything. I asked about the silent boy, Otabek, was told that he hadn't been seen all afternoon, no one knew where he was. Maybe a runaway, I thought; after all, I'd been one myself. Or maybe he was something else, a witness perhaps. Or a murderer.

For the first few kilometres, I half-expected to see him trudging along the side of the road, but there was no sign of him. I didn't think he'd shot Gurminj, but I've learnt never to rule out any possibilities when it comes to murder.

One of the delights of spring in Kyrgyzstan is the way our

rivers come to life, having been silenced throughout our long winters. Snow-melt dances and splashes, refreshing the fields, and the first hint of leaves and new grass begin to appear. What we lack in wealth, we make up for in beauty, with the Tien Shan mountains reflected in the mirror of Lake Issky-Kul. As far as I'm concerned, it's a good trade-off.

I reached the centre of Bishkek, parked next to the Metro Bar, crossed Chui Prospekt and began to walk down Tureshbekov towards Frunze. The air was still cold, with a sour hint of coal smoke, but the trees lining the street were starting to bud, the promise of winter's end and the start of spring. I didn't look behind me to see if I was being followed; that's a certain way to tip off your pursuers you know they're there.

I turned off towards the Dragon's Den restaurant where I'd last seen Saltanat, but stopped when I saw the SOLD sign outside. A sense of regret swept over me, for times past, opportunities lost, melting snow suddenly cascading from a roof. From the look of the restaurant sign, faded and rusting slightly at the edges, the place had been closed for a while. I wondered what had happened to the long wooden bar, the elegant photos of traditional Kyrgyz nomadic life. I hoped they'd found a good home, that people were still sitting at the bar sipping Baltika *pivo* or vodka, admiring the ornate dresses of the pretty girls in the photos. I like to think some things don't fall apart with the passage of time, that what we make can sometimes survive us.

I was shaken from my reverie by the blare of a horn. A black Lexus with tinted windows was parked across the street, outside the inaccurately named Grand Hotel. The driver's window was open, Saltanat Umarova waving to me to hurry up.

I clambered into the passenger seat, making sure the back seat was empty. I might have been in partnership with Saltanat once, but that didn't mean I trusted her. I hadn't closed the door when we took off with a screech of tyres that could have been heard in Talas.

As always, Saltanat wore black, a long leather coat, jeans tucked into shin-high lace-up combat boots. As she changed gear, I noticed that her crimson fingernails matched her lipstick. Her eyes were hidden behind wrap-around mirror sunglasses, the sort that conceal your thoughts, balanced on cheekbones that could etch glass. She'd cut her long black hair since I'd last seen her, cropped back to almost boyish length, emphasising her elegant neck and jawline.

'You couldn't live without me?' I said.

'Fuck off,' she explained, and pressed down on the accelerator.

'I'd love to, but first, where are we going?'

Not bothering to reply, Saltanat threw the Lexus down a series of narrow alleyways, left, right, straight ahead, until I was completely lost.

'I think you've shaken them off,' I said. 'If they were ever there.'

'They were. Count on it.'

I hadn't seen anybody; if we were being watched, it was by professionals.

'You're going to tell me what this is all about.'

'Eventually,' she answered, steering the Lexus at high speed towards a metal garage door, opening the door with a remote control. I winced as we scraped through the gap, braced myself against the dashboard for the inevitable crash. The abrupt halt threw me forward and then back, as Saltanat drove in and slammed on the brakes.

'Out,' she commanded, impatient as I fumbled with the seat belt and then the door. She didn't look to see if I was following when she strode through the side door of the garage. We were in the side garden of a small hotel, surrounded by high walls and with an impressive double-wide steel gate. A traditional felt yurt stood in one corner of the garden. Across from the yurt, a sloping roof sheltered an open-air wooden bar from rain and snow. Something about it looked familiar, and I realised it was the bar that had graced the Dragon's Den.

Saltanat took a bottle of Baltika out of the fridge, uncapping it and taking a good swallow. She pointed at her beer and raised an eyebrow. I shook my head, aimed a finger at a bottle of water. She shrugged, passed it over, no glass.

'Still staying away from the vodka? Not even an occasional *pivo*?'

I shook my head. I'd never told her, or anyone, but I knew that a single *pivo*, or a hundred grams of vodka, would send me hurtling down a slope of guilt that could only end in eating my Yarygin.

Saltanat took another swallow, set the bottle down on the bar. The rings it made on the wooden surface reminded me of handcuffs. She looked over at me, as if assessing what she saw, not much caring for it. I do the same in the mirror every morning. A creased, worn face, cropped black hair silvered with the first hints of grey, black eyes under thick eyebrows. Tatar cheekbones, higher than the average moon-faced Kyrgyz. A flat, impassive stare, slowly changing from wary to merely weary. I'd always believed in keeping on keeping on, but increasingly I wonder why.

'You didn't have a problem getting here?'

I shrugged.

'You mean driving here, or leaving the case I'm on? I'm not flavour of the month in Bishkek, as I'm sure you know.'

'I'd heard,' she said. 'And about the infant murders, and what happened to your old boss. I guess a couple of years' exile in Karakol is the price you pay for being a semi-honest cop.'

I didn't ask how she knew about the murders; as a member of the Uzbek security service she probably knew as much about what was happening in Kyrgyzstan as Mikhail Tynaliev. In my country, you can always find a little bird who'll sweetly sing if you put enough *som* in his bowl.

'You're going to tell me why you wanted me to come all this way?'

'We both want to track down who killed Gurminj, don't we?'

'So you think he was murdered as well?' I asked.

'Sure of it. So are you,' she said.

I nodded, looked at the hotel. All the windows were curtained, and the place had the air of being abandoned. But I knew Saltanat was not the sort to leave anything to chance. I guessed she would have reinforcements only a few seconds away. Or a marksman sighting down a rifle barrel, with me on the receiving end. My forehead itched, as if cross hairs were pressing down on me.

'There hasn't been an official report, so I'm wondering how you know.'

Saltanat simply smiled, enigmatic as ever. I wondered for

a moment if she'd been behind Gurminj's murder, dismissed the idea out of hand. I couldn't fathom any motive she might have had, and Saltanat has never done anything without a good reason.

As if reading my mind, she turned the full intensity of her gaze upon me. I felt my breath catch in my chest.

'When I first met you, Inspector, I wasn't certain whose side you were on, whether I should kill you or not. I didn't know whether or not you were wetting your beak with the help of the bad guys.'

I tried to smile.

'I hope I convinced you. And call me Akyl, no need for ceremony, surely?'

Saltanat raised one impeccably plucked eyebrow.

'Maybe. Later. But first, cards face up?'

It was my turn to raise an eyebrow. Saltanat has ever shown a full hand in her life. But if it gave me a lead to solving the case of the dead children and the murder of my friend, who was I to argue?

She gave a smile that punched me in the heart. Who can name the exact moment when a woman's smile reminds you of your dead wife? A woman who made the act of living worthwhile, whose breath you stole away, and buried on a snow-covered hill?

'You're the investigating officer, right?'

'Officially? The dead children. Unofficially? I'm putting Gurminj's killer on my to-fuck-someone-up-beyond-belief list.'

I told her about the dead infants, the puzzle of the orphanage identity bands, Usupov's belief that I'd been exiled to Karakol on the orders of Mikhail Tynaliev, the sham autopsy that Usupov had been forced to sign off. She nodded as I told her about seeing Gurminj sprawled dead at his desk, the apparent suicide note, her mobile number hidden beneath the balance.

I paused, looked over at Saltanat.

'Your turn,' I said. Saltanat folded her arms and sat back, her face set in the determined look I remembered from our previous encounters. If anything, she looked even more deadly than when she smiled.

'I hope you weren't followed back to Bishkek, Akyl. And that nobody knows you're here.'

She paused, lit a cigarette, uncoiled pale grey smoke into the air.

'We could both be in a world of trouble.'

Chapter 14

I stared at Saltanat, and she looked back, her gaze unwavering. I don't know much about women. I'd met Chinara when we were both at school. There hadn't really been anyone else besides her. She was all I ever wanted. But it was getting hard to remember her, radiant, beautiful, as she had been before the cancer feasted on her. Loss is like that, submerged rocks that from time to time break the surface of the water. It looks safe to dive in, then you break your neck.

'I don't see where you fit into all this,' I said. 'Or me, for that matter.'

Saltanat looked down and began to pick at the label on her beer bottle with her fingernails. I'd only ever once seen her looking vulnerable, after the rape. Now she gave off a sense of uncertainty, unwilling perhaps, or unable, to tell me what she knew.

'I never told my bosses what happened to me,' she said. 'They don't give you medals for failing, for getting into situations you can't control. The only people who know about what happened are you and me. Best that way.'

'Didn't you talk to anyone?'

She looked up, stared at me. A tear in her eye? The air was cold, and it's easy to make mistakes like that.

'My decision not to tell,' she said. 'My right.'

I looked down at her hand. Out of reach, out of range.

'Three months ago, we arrested a guy shipping a

consignment of DVDs out of Tashkent to Frankfurt. We'd had a tip-off, nothing too specific, just saying there was a box that we might be interested in. The guy was nothing special, low-level, but the box was interesting. We put the pressure on him, a bit of a slap now and then, a friendly punch or two, but he wouldn't tell us anything. He was more scared of his bosses than of us, and believe me, that takes some doing.'

I nodded, remembering the basement of Sverdlovsky police station, with its easy-clean tiled floor and wash-down walls, the kind of interrogations that had been carried out there. Down there, you were a very long way from help of any kind.

'We sent him to one of our safe houses, to keep him quiet, maybe make him change his mind about singing to us.'

Saltanat paused and lit another cigarette.

'Two days later, someone got past our security, over a three-metre wall, drove an icepick through his forehead. No clues, nothing. And of course, he hadn't sung a single note.'

'And the shipment of DVDs?'

'We found maybe fifty DVDs, all called *Welcome to Uzbekistan*, with pictures of Tashkent and Samarkand on the covers. The first one we played had five minutes showing the Guri Amir, Tamerlane's mausoleum, then it cut to a scene in a bedroom.'

'Porn?' I asked.

'Yes,' she replied, 'but mild, all soft focus, kisses, wistful stares and romantic music. Nothing I hadn't seen before.'

'Until you hit fast-forward, right?'

Saltanat stared at me, suspicious, then nodded.

'Pretty obvious,' I said. 'A double bluff. Put people off by pretending to be a travelogue, then make them think they're watching some mild stuff. I take it what followed was a lot harder?'

'I'd never seen anything like that before.'

She took another mouthful of her beer, then stubbed out her cigarette. Putting the bottle down, she wrapped her arms across her chest.

'Children, tortured, raped, with men queuing to take their turn. Boys and girls, begging for help.'

Saltanat looked at me, her face white, her eyes wide with disgust.

'Help that didn't come.'

I swallowed the nausea that rose in my throat. I've seen my share of porn films. It's hard not to, when you're a serving police officer. And I know there's big money to be made. But I hadn't encountered anything as extreme as the films Saltanat described.

I reached over, took a cigarette out of her pack, lit it, blew cancer at the air.

'That's terrible,' I said, thinking that it must have felt like death, watching such things, having been raped herself. 'But I'm not sure why you were talking to Gurminj.'

'There was nothing in the DVDs to show where they'd been shot. The children, they were naked, so no clues there, but they were all Asian.'

I nodded. There was nothing I could say. When I think about what so-called humans do, perhaps being born is a criminal offence, with a life sentence to follow.

'At the end, one man, wearing a leather mask, burly, tattoos down both arms, would come forward, while the others held the child down.'

She paused, picking at the beer label. Her voice was low, hoarse.

'And then he'd kill them.'

The label came free from the bottle, and Saltanat smoothed it out on the bar top, gently, the way you might stroke the forehead of a small child lying in bed with a fever.

'So why did you contact Gurminj?'

She paused, looked over at me, as if I were the enemy, not a former lover.

'I knew his reputation, he was quite a legend in his field. Honest, incorruptible. And because the children in the films were all wearing Kyrgyz orphanage identity bands.'

Chapter 15

I stubbed out my cigarette, feeling the tightening in my stomach that leads to anger. Anger at the random cruelties we impose on those weaker than ourselves, anger at a deity who either leaves us drowning in shit or doesn't exist. Anger at my own helplessness, my inability to make amends, for Chinara, for the victims who needed me, for myself.

'Gurminj must have found out something,' I said, 'and it earned him a bullet in the brain. Why didn't he say anything to me?'

I sat back, put my feet up on the stool next to me. I'd always done that when I was living in the orphanage, used to tell the teachers it helped me to concentrate. Truth was, I was just looking for an argument, a clip around the ear, a reason to hate them all the more. Funny, over the years, the lie gradually became the truth. Maybe something to do with the flow of blood to the brain. Or from it.

Saltanat looked away from me. I stared, knowing there was a problem.

'I spoke with Gurminj about getting you involved,' she said. 'We both wondered if there would be a problem.'

'What kind of a problem?' I asked, trying to keep my voice calm and measured.

'Your involvement with Tynaliev. The summary execution of your old boss. We both know he didn't die in a car crash.'

I stared at her, didn't reply.

'There's money, big money, involved in this sort of filth. And if it's connected to senior government people in some way, then they have a hold over you.'

Saltanat didn't look me in the eye. The sort of body language that says I don't know whether you can be trusted.

I felt a surge of anger, because in her position I'd have wondered exactly the same thing.

'I'm a cop in exile. Not because I can be bought off, but because I can't.'

She nodded.

'I understand. But—'

'But you don't know me that well,' I interrupted. 'You slept with me but you don't know if you can trust me.'

Saltanat held up her hand, but I was in full flow, unable to keep the bitterness out of my voice.

'I get threatened by the Circle of Brothers, I kill my wife's uncle when I find out he works for them, I get tortured,' and I held up my scarred hand as evidence, 'then I get shipped out to the arse end of nowhere. But hey, I might still be selling kiddie snuff movies. Thanks, Saltanat, a real vote of confidence.'

I turned my face away from her, not wanting her to see the anger, the sorrow, that crossed my face.

'I should have known,' she said, her voice hardly more than a whisper.

'Known what exactly?' I replied. 'What I'm like in bed? Why I carry on doing this shitty job? What?'

'Akyl, someone has to want to make a difference, or there's no hope for any of us. Like it or not, you're the designated carer.'

So much burden, so much effort, to make the dead sleep soundly.

I thought of the fragments of barely begun lives unearthed next to a stinking canal at the far ends of the earth.

And of Chinara, lying in earth only now beginning to thaw.

Chapter 16

I'd used up the day's ration of self-pity, turned to face Saltanat.

'We both want to find who killed Gurminj,' I said.

'And the babies you uncovered. And the children butchered in those films,' she added. I nodded agreement.

'We put the past behind us?' she asked.

'All of it?' I replied, remembering the warmth of her body next to mine on the one occasion that we'd slept together. She didn't blush, or smile at the memory. Tough to the core.

'Let's clean this mess up first, see where we stand after that. Right now, I want Gurminj's killers far more than I want you.'

But she spoke with a half-smile that said she knew she could control me, as long as we avoided getting killed first.

'There's a squealer I want to talk to,' she went on. 'Hangs out at one of your favourite bars.'

I winced. I don't have fond memories of the Kulturny, Bishkek's seediest, dirtiest bar. Lubashov, a hood I'd put in the ground, had been the bouncer at the Kulturny, and most of the current inmates at Penitentiary One had enjoyed a few shots of the good stuff there in their day. If I had my way, I'd weld the steel door shut, with all the regulars locked inside, and push a bowl of *plov* inside twice a day. To call it a shithole full of shits was to insult shits and shitholes everywhere. But it was the best place to push and shove, put some stick about, see what kicked off.

The sky had grown steadily darker while we'd been talking, storm clouds tumbling and spilling down from the mountains. The first drops of rain began to fall, cautiously at first, then with increasing violence. We ran back to the car, and I felt a curious exhilaration. The sense of helplessness I'd had ever since we unearthed the dead babies was melting away. I didn't know if we'd solve anything, avenge anyone, but we were at the beginning of something fresh.

Saltanat was with me, as a comrade, if nothing more; the rain fell more heavily, and the windshield wipers could not sweep clear the blurred future that lay ahead of us.

After repeating the same series of alleyways and passages in reverse, we emerged onto Chui Prospekt, heading east. Pools of water that had already formed on the road reflected traffic lights, reds, yellows and greens vivid against gun-metal grey. The giant red and yellow flag by Ala-Too Square flapped in desperation, threatening to rip apart and fly away. The air crackled with electricity, tense, dangerous. My Yarygin sat cold and heavy against my hip.

'I should check on my apartment, get some clothes,' I said. 'What time are you meeting your squealer?'

'Not for a couple of hours. We've got time.'

The tyres of the Lexus threw up sprays of water that sparkled in the air. We turned right, onto Ibraimova, towards my apartment block, a *Khrushchyovka* pre-cast concrete relic from the country's days as a far-distant outpost of the Soviet Empire, named after the Soviet Premier who'd ordered their building throughout the USSR. As we drove up towards the top end of Ibraimova, to make a U-turn, I looked over towards my building.

'Don't turn,' I said. 'Keep going straight and go right at the top.'

Saltanat nodded, kept the Lexus over to the right, pulling into the filling station just beyond the Blonder pub, then down a narrow road lined with birch trees.

'Stop, but keep the engine running,' I instructed, looking out of the window back towards my building. We were parked very near to where I'd found Yekaterina Tynalieva's body a few months ago, and the coincidence didn't escape either of us. Nothing left there now to show anything had ever happened. How quickly we die and are forgotten.

'Problem?' Saltanat asked. She opened the glove compartment, and I saw the dull metal sheen of a Makarov.

'Two police cars, tucked away by the trees next to my place.'

'Why would they be waiting for you?'

'A question I'd like answered,' I said, and reached in my pocket for my mobile. I called up the contact list, memorised a number, removed the battery.

'Give me your mobile,' I said. Saltanat reached into her jacket, pulled out an elegant smartphone, and handed it to me.

'Apple? Uzbek security must be raking it in. All those children forced to pick cotton instead of going to school,' I said.

Saltanat glared at me.

'Bought and paid for. By me. OK?'

I raised a hand to appease her, dialled the number, heard the ringing tone, waited until a familiar voice answered.

'Usupov. You know who this is. No need to say my name. Can you talk?'

'Yes. Where are you? You're in Bishkek?'

'No need to know exactly where right now. I just want answers to a couple of questions.'

'If I can.'

Usupov's voice was strained, cautious. I'd always seen him, if not as a friend, then at least as an ally in the cause of doing the right thing. After our last conversation in Karakol, I wasn't so sure where his loyalties lay any more, but there was no one else I could ask.

'Whose mobile are you using? This isn't your regular number. It's a foreign number.'

I laughed. Even in Kyrgyzstan, we know how to track a mobile's location, and any of the service providers would be happy to earn points by helping the police. Or anyone else with enough clout.

'There are two police cars packed with *menti* outside my apartment block. Any idea why?'

There was a long silence before Usupov spoke, in little more than a whisper.

'There was a call last night. Anonymous. A tip-off. Saying you were involved in something pretty bad, that there was some illegal material stashed in your apartment. So Sverdlovsky sent a couple of men round. You weren't there, otherwise they'd have arrested you. And given you a good kicking down every flight of stairs.'

There wasn't anything in my apartment that could have been a problem. But anyone who knows how to pick a couple of locks can leave something incriminating and then call it in.

'What was it they found? Drugs? You know that's not my thing.'

Usupov paused for even longer. When he spoke, there was a note of disgust in his voice.

'We go back a long way, Inspector. I'm giving you the benefit of the doubt. For the moment.'

My stomach tensed, and when I spoke, my voice was hoarse.

'Go on.'

'DVDs. Child porn, I heard on the grapevine. Stuff you couldn't imagine, the sort that visits you in nightmares. Torture, rape. And murder.'

Saltanat watched as I failed to hide the disgust on my face.

'Kenesh, this is a set-up, believe me, I know nothing about this. Maybe it's because I'm investigating all the deaths in Karakol? Maybe linked to the fake death certificate you had to sign?'

There was a long pause before Usupov spoke.

'They know you're not in Karakol. Orders are to stop and arrest you. Maximum force permitted, if necessary.'

I knew what that meant. Maximum force obligatory. Whatever it was someone high up thought I knew, they'd make sure I couldn't spread the word. Relentless rain hammered against the car roof.

'Akyl, if I were you, I'd head for the border. Any border.'

Chapter 17

I explained the situation to Saltanat, saw concern cloud her face.

'I'm being stitched up,' I said. 'Think about the timing. If I was involved in any of this – and I'm not – I'd know about you arresting the porn mule in Tashkent. The last thing I'd do is raise my head above the parapet.'

Saltanat nodded, seeing the logic of what I was saying.

'But why would someone go to all this trouble?' she asked. 'They could simply put a bullet in the back of your head. Or a car accident. A fire in your apartment because of faulty wiring.'

'Kill me, and it doesn't end there,' I explained. 'The case is on file now, so it has to be investigated. And so does Gurminj's death, now I've reported it as suspicious. Some other inspector takes over, and if they were close to uncovering the truth, then they'd have to be dealt with. But if I'm discredited as a notorious pornographer and child murderer it all dies with me. Case solved, the culprit's shot resisting arrest, end of story, everyone's happy.'

'So now what?'

'Right now, we need to put some distance between us and my apartment. They're expecting me to show up. If they'd had any sense, they'd have been waiting inside. Their carelessness gives us a few hours. Let's head over to the Kulturny, see what your whisperer has to say.'

I slumped down lower in my seat, grateful for the tinted windows of the Lexus. Saltanat handed me a baseball cap from the glove compartment, and I completed my temporary disguise with sunglasses.

The scarred and battered steel door of the Kulturny looked as uninviting as ever when Saltanat parked outside. A steroid junkie disguised as a doorman in a cheap leather jacket slouched against the wall. He looked appreciatively at Saltanat as she climbed out of the car.

'No need to go in there, darling, not if you're looking for a man. He's right here in front of you,' he said, patting his crotch just in case Saltanat might have misunderstood him.

Saltanat smiled, walked up to him, pouted, blew a kiss, then kicked him in the balls. As he dropped to his knees, eyes bulging, gasping with shock and pain, she stepped around him and pushed at the steel door. The unlit stairs down to the basement bar looked horribly like a mouth, ready to devour us, and I remembered that there was no other way in. Or out.

I looked down at the doorman, wondering why he looked familiar, then I placed him.

'Your name Lubashov?' I asked.

He looked up at me, wiping a string of vomit from his mouth.

'What's it to you?' he snarled.

I pulled back my jacket to show I wasn't in the mood for any shit.

'Your brother?' I said. 'Who used to work here? Who got a free ride to the cemetery? Any more tough-guy nonsense from you and you'll be joining him.'

I raised my hands to show that I wasn't reaching for my gun, then stuck a finger in his face.

'We're cool, right? It ends here.'

The doorman simply grunted, turned away to be sick again. Unimpressed by my bravado, Saltanat gestured at the doorway.

'After you.'

'No, no. ladies first.'

'And what makes you think I'm a lady?' she replied.

I pointed at the doorman, wiping away the vomit on his jacket and almost succeeding.

'You're not as far as he's concerned, that's for sure,' I said, and stepped inside.

The Kulturny might have acquired a new doorman, but otherwise the place remained depressingly unchanged. The dark stairwell leading down to a barely lit hovel. Half the light bulbs either burnt out or simply missing. Two prostitutes in a corner sucking on cigarettes with far more enthusiasm than they ever did for their clients. Boris, the barman, checking the glasses to make sure they were still dirty, and topping up the bottles labelled Stolichnaya with rotgut s*amogon*. And of course, the overlying reek of piss, *pivo* and *pelmeni* that gave the place its unique charm.

Saltanat looked around with her usual impassive glare, pointed to an overweight and balding man leaning against the bar.

'Your squealer?' I asked.

She nodded, and walked slowly towards him. The distance hadn't given him enchantment, and it got worse as we drew closer. Beads of greasy sweat trickled down his forehead and over his acne-raddled cheeks. It wasn't warm in the

Kulturny – heating costs money and that means less profit – so I guessed he was dripping with fear. He had a thin, mean mouth, like a newly opened scar, and dark eyes that never stopped dancing around in case of trouble. He wore one of those threadbare cheap suits you find in the bazaar, the sort that look shapeless and worn from the moment you put them on, stretched shiny and tight across his shoulders. His bald patch was highlighted by the way his remaining hair was pulled back into a greasy ponytail. I've encountered a lot of lowlife wearing ponytails, and there's an arsehole underneath every one.

I was willing to bet every *som* in my wallet he'd ask for money before he'd talk. I was equally certain Saltanat would beat any information out of him before a single banknote changed hands.

'Kamchybek?' Saltanat asked, her voice surprisingly gentle.

The man nodded, took a long pull at the glass in front of him. A half-empty bottle of Vostok vodka announced it wasn't his first drink. Rocket fuel to dampen down the fear, anaesthetise the nerves. The way his hands shook, I was surprised he managed to drink without adding to the collection of stains on his lapels.

'Who's this?' Kamchybek asked, his voice a surprisingly high falsetto in such a big man.

'He's with me,' Saltanat replied, not answering the question. Finding out I was Murder Squad and on the run wouldn't inspire him with confidence, I knew that. So I kept my mouth shut and my jacket closed to keep the gun from scaring him.

'I said only you,' Kamchybek whined, in a squeak so high I looked around for bats.

'Do I look that stupid?' Saltanat asked.

I thought she looked deadly, a warrior queen dressed in black, but saying so wouldn't be helpful.

'He's here to protect you,' she continued, her eyes never leaving his face.

'Protect me from what?' he asked, his eyes wide and terrified.

'From me beating you into a coma if you've wasted my time, if you lie to me about anything.'

'Hey, I called you, right? Why would I lie?'

'Let's call it misdirection.' Saltanat's mouth smiled, her eyes threatened.

Kamchybek took another blast of rocket fuel, pointed first at the bottle, then at us.

I shook my head. Saltanat merely looked pained.

'I'll be honest with you, OK? I'm not saying I've never done anything wrong, who can? I sell a little *travka* to smoke from time to time, maybe a DVD player or a mobile that's a tiny bit toasty. But I have limits, principles. You understand?'

We both nodded: I knew where this conversation was taking us.

'I keep my ears open, always good to know what's hot, what's not, get a stride ahead of the competition. But I was in here the other night, a little bit of business, and there are two guys, hammered, talking some shit, real shit, you understand?'

Saltanat looked over at me, made a gesture of impatience. I held up my hand to stop her, nodded encouragement to him. Good cop, bad cop routine. I've done a lot of interrogations over the years; it's always more productive to say as little as possible, let the truth fall through the silences in between the lies.

'They were boasting to each other about the sex they liked. Rough stuff. Kids. Said it didn't matter, boy or girl. Long as the kids got hurt.'

Saltanat's eyes narrowed, so I spoke before she could kick off.

'Two drunks talking in a bar. Spinning the usual lies about how often they get laid, and with whom. Nothing new there. Maybe all just fantasy,' I said.

Kamchybek shook his head, and looked across at the two street-meat women.

'That's what I thought at first. This place doesn't attract the best kind of crowd.'

He paused, demolished another vodka.

'Anyway, they finished their bottle, staggered off with a couple of working girls for an alleyway fuck. But one of them, the one with the beard, he left his mobile behind. One of those fancy ones that connect to the internet. Worth a few *som*. So I slipped it into my pocket, finished my shot, headed for home. I didn't want them coming back and asking me if I'd seen a mobile waiting to be stolen. They both looked pretty tasty, not big, but muscular, and I'm in no shape to be running. Never was much of a fighter, either.'

'And?' I prompted.

'Got home. Switched it on, pressed a few buttons. And a film started playing.'

Saltanat and I waited as Kamchybek wiped his forehead with a handkerchief that had been clean around the turn of the century.

'Well, it was . . . well, I'd never seen anything like it. And

I've been around. Even used to be a bit of a ladies' man when I was younger.'

Now it was my turn to be impatient. The longer I stayed in the Kulturny, the more likely it was someone who knew me would put a call into Sverdlovsky station, and then I'd be dancing in the soundproofed basement room where we do the hard talking.

'Let's speed it up, shall we? What made you decide to call my colleague here?' I asked.

'The two men, I got the feeling they were connected, protected. Just the way they didn't seem to give a fuck whether anyone was listening. I'd heard a whisper about that porn mule being arrested in Tashkent, so I put in the call, got your colleague here. Didn't want to risk talking to the wrong person.'

Kamchybek reached into his pocket and pulled out an iPhone. Still not speaking, he pressed a couple of buttons and the mobile lit up. He handed it over to me as a film clip started playing.

The clip was shaky and slightly out of focus to begin with, then became clearer. It opened with a close-up of a wrist, wearing an identity band. The sight of it tugged at my guts, remembering the one I wore in the orphanage. I tilted the mobile so that no one else in the bar could see the screen, and muted the sound. Saltanat moved closer to me so that she could also watch.

What we saw was horror.

The boy must have been about nine, but the look of terror in his eyes was ancient. His mouth was open, a silent scream, which stopped only when a man's hand slapped him hard across the face.

I heard Saltanat gasp beside me, and felt her turn away.

'I've seen this,' she said, disgust overwhelming her voice. 'In fact, I can't stop seeing it.'

I watched on, the rape, the murder. The bar's stink of *pelmini*, sour beer and stale piss smelt stronger, my stomach rising in nausea. The images swam before my eyes, as if I was watching from the bottom of Lake Issyk-Kul, and I wondered if I was going to faint.

Then I was bending forward, dry retching, the taste of bile sharp as razors in my throat.

That was when I felt a sting in my left shoulder, looked up to see Kamchybek's eyes open wide, as a red poppy bloomed on his chest.

Blood. Not his blood. Mine.

Chapter 18

Ignoring the fire in my shoulder, I turned to see Lubashov, the doorman from outside, Makarov in hand, struggling with the magazine, his face twisted with rage and fear.

I reached across my waist to grab my gun with my right hand, but Saltanat already had her Makarov out, left hand gripping her right wrist, the gun pointed arm's length at Lubashov's head. I've always believed that centre mass of the body is the best target to put someone down – it's how I'd killed his brother – but there's no doubt staring into a small black circle of death focuses the mind to a surprising degree.

'Down. Don't think about it, do it. Gun down or I put you down,' Saltanat commanded, taking a step forward. I could see Lubashov calculating the odds on unjamming his gun, taking aim and pulling the trigger. He didn't stand a chance.

It was one of those moments when time freezes, cigarette smoke suspended against the ceiling lights, a moment of grey, where everything becomes electric and vivid. I looked over my shoulder. There was a scorch mark on my jacket as if someone had tapped me with a red-hot poker, and a certain amount of blood, but nothing I'd need a transfusion for. If I hadn't bent down to gag though, it would have been very different. With no need for a blood transfusion.

Like a man doing a mime act in extreme slow motion, wading through particularly sticky glue, Lubashov lowered the gun down on the floor. It looked as if Mother Lubashova wouldn't need to buy a second tombstone. But Saltanat didn't take her eyes off his hands, her gun off his face.

'You've got a good explanation for trying to kill a police officer?' she said.

Lubashov looked about to burst into tears.

'My brother,' he mumbled, said something nonsensical about revenge. Over the years of what I laughingly call my career, I've learnt that the weakness of all these wannabe gangsters is that they mistake violence for an instant solution instead of a last resort. But shooting a Murder Squad detective will bring a wealth of shit down on everyone, even if he's wanted for questioning.

Saltanat moved forward, beckoning Lubashov back with her gun, until she could pass his gun back to me.

'How badly are you hurt?'

I shrugged, nonchalant, immediately wished I hadn't.

'We can pick up some bandages once we leave. It's just a graze; I've had worse shaving cuts.'

More bravado on my part that Saltanat chose to disregard.

'What do you want to do with this one?' she asked, nodding at Lubashov, who now knelt down and laced his fingers behind his neck.

'Not much I can do, is there? Can hardly ask for him to be taken down the station, unless I'm keen to share his cell.'

I looked at him, the usual cheap mix of arrogance and uncertainty clear in his face. Bullet fodder, if not now, in the future. I pondered for a moment, then drew my Yarygin, awkwardly, with my right hand.

'I could save us some trouble and kill him,' I suggested, sighting down the barrel in the general direction of

Lubashov's balls. Or where they would have been if Saltanat hadn't drop-kicked them into his pelvis.

Lubashov's face grew smudged with grey.

'Plenty of room for you next to your brother,' I added, 'and then your dear old *mama* only needs one *marshrutka* bus ticket to visit the pair of you. Convenient, eh?'

I moved closer to Lubashov, never letting my eyes drop until my gun loomed large in his life. Despite what he might have thought, I wasn't going to shoot him. In fact, I've never killed or wounded anyone except in self-defence. Maybe that makes me less of a detective. And it certainly doesn't mean that the innocent dead don't rise up before me at night. They all stare with accusing eyes, wondering why I hadn't protected them from the monsters outside, why they'd had to pay such a price in order for me to catch the bad guys. And if they could talk, they'd all ask me the same question: 'Why me?'

'If you're going to do it, then just fucking do it,' Lubashov said, with an unexpected and rather admirable flash of spirit.

'Not my style,' I said, stroking his cheek with the gun barrel while Saltanat kept him covered with her Makarov. 'I only shoot villains, not half-arsed hopefuls who don't even know how to put a clip in a gun.'

I gave him one of my special smiles, the one that never reaches my eyes.

'I'm a pretty forgiving kind of guy, but, my job being what it is, I can't help wondering if there's another reason you want me dead, other than your brother snoozing in the cemetery. So tell, who put you up to ruining my second-best jacket?'

'Inspector, we really don't have time for this,' Saltanat said, impatience clear in her voice.

I sighed, knowing she was right. I holstered my piece and unloaded the clip from Lubashov's gun. The metal felt cold, oily, like the name plaque on a tombstone, like death itself.

'You need to check the tension on the spring, rotate your bullets, keep everything clean, oiled and wiped. Or one day you'll come up against someone who isn't as considerate as me, and while you're wrestling with a misfire, they won't miss firing at you.'

I looked around at the rest of the bar, at the people frozen in front of me.

'Everyone keep their sticky little hands where I can see they're not going to give me any trouble. Nice and calm, like taking a walk in Panfilov Park.'

I nodded towards Saltanat, gestured towards the stairs.

'Don't forget our parrot; I don't think we've heard all his amusing repertoire yet.'

Saltanat took hold of Kamchybek's arm, and we started off back to the daylight and fresh air.

And that's when the shooting started.

Chapter 19

One of the first rules of policing is to make sure you've cleared every room, not just the one you're in. But I must have been feeling less than first-rate because I didn't check out what laughingly passes as the Kulturny bathroom, a piece of guttering fixed to the wall on a slant, so that urine dribbles down into a pipe leading to the sewers.

A classic mistake. And a deadly one.

The man who burst through the door could barely squeeze through the frame. Two metres, easily, and almost as many wide. Hair down to his shoulders, dark glasses hiding his eyes, mouth stretched wide in a scream that echoed around the room. Almost as large, and just as frightening was the Glock 17 semi-automatic pistol he gripped in one meaty paw. He collided with the wall as he raised the gun, fired off two shots. In that confined space, the noise was deafening, an express train roaring through a tunnel.

I was off balance, unsighted, and that gave Lubashov the opportunity to pull at my leg and bring me down. I managed to keep hold of my Yarygin, slammed the butt against Lubashov's nose. The bone shattered and I was drenched as his blood spurted across my face.

'Maxim!' Lubashov yelled. 'Kill them!'

Maxim fired off another shot which shattered the mirror behind the bar and sent bottles cascading and splintering. That was all the time Saltanat needed to fire her own weapon twice, hitting Maxim in the shoulder and stomach, the shots knocking him back on his feet. Surprise turned to an expression of pain as he watched blood leaking out of his shirt. He looked puzzled, the way people do when they suddenly realise they've lost a filling, or their apartment keys are missing. He put out an arm to steady himself, gain time, decide on his next target. I watched as his life struggled to hang on, a man dangling by his fingertips over a spring-swollen river. And then he staggered backwards, dropping the gun as he fell.

Gunsmoke rose in a lazy spiral towards the ceiling. The room held its breath in shocked silence. Lubashov clutched the ruins of his face, whimpering to himself. I hauled myself up, holstered my gun.

'Akyl, we have to get out of here,' Saltanat murmured. 'Before the law arrives.'

I nodded, looked round to see what Kamchybek was doing.

'We have a problem,' I said, pointing at our not-so-little songbird.

'Fuck,' Saltanat said, looking at the hole in Kamchybek's face. His left cheek, torn away by one of the Glock's bullets, revealed an uneven row of yellowing teeth. His face had the sullen cast of a particularly bitter sneer. One eyelid drooped lower than the other, giving him the look of a lecherous pimp who has just reeled in a live one.

I reached forward, picked up the iPhone, slid it into my pocket.

'Come on,' I said, stepping over Lubashov, pausing only to bring my boot heel down hard on his gun hand, before heading for the stairs. 'Let's hope it's stopped raining.'

*

We pulled up once more outside Saltanat's hotel. I saw the hotel's name embossed on the high metal gates. Umai, after the Kyrgyz goddess of fertility and virginity. Umai is supposed to be the special protector of women and children, so I suppose she's my boss in the long run. I didn't think I could rely on any special favours from her. But I'm always willing to hope.

Saltanat tried the remote, but the gates remained shut. She hit the horn, and the gates finally swung open to let us enter. A burly, shaven-headed man in his fifties stood behind the wooden bar under the canopy, sheltering from the rain. Saltanat climbed out of the car, ran over and kissed him on the cheek. He greeted her warmly, looked at me as I joined them. While not openly hostile, he looked at me as if I'd be the cause of trouble for him, his hotel and his friend.

'Inspector Akyl Borubaev, Bishkek Murder Squad.' Saltanat made the introductions.

'*Privyat*,' I said, held out my hand. He took it, nodded, his face thawing slightly.

'And you are?' I asked.

'Rustam,' he answered, his accent Uzbek. He gestured at the fridges behind the bar, stocked with bottles of *pivo* and vodka. 'Help yourself. I'll organise food,' and with that, he walked towards the hotel's side entrance.

I turned away from Saltanat, looked down at my hands. They didn't shake or tremble; a bit late in the game, perhaps I was getting used to killing.

'Who do you think that guy was?' Saltanat asked. Her hands were as rock-steady as mine.

'Two thoughts,' I said. 'Either just some *gopnik* layabout in a tracksuit getting rid of the day's *pivo* when we walked in. Or . . .'

'Or?' she prompted.

'You were set up by Kamchybek's call. You were meant to go there, and get hit. But they didn't expect I'd be with you. Or that Lubashov would try to avenge his brother. That made it all turn to shit.'

'Which do you think it was?'

'I look like I believe in coincidence?'

'Who would set it up?' she asked.

I shook my head; better to assume everyone was against us.

'And the iPhone? Why bother if they were going to put me down?'

'A good way to find out just how much you knew, how much you might have reported back, before putting one in your ear.'

I didn't want to tell her I thought she wouldn't have been killed, not just then. She would have been dragged somewhere quiet, where the occasional scream goes unnoticed and people pretend a gunshot is a car backfire. The same sort of place where Saltanat had been raped, probably the same kind of people.

I put my hand on hers, just for a moment, then uncapped a bottle of Sibirskaya Korona, pushed it towards her. She hesitated, then drank.

'It helps me relax,' she said. 'You should try it.'

'You think I can't relax unless I'm halfway down the hundred grams?'

'You used to drink.'

'And now I don't.'

'For ever?'

I shrugged, pretended nonchalance I didn't feel.

'For today will do, for now.'

Saltanat considered this for a moment, smiled, nodded. Once upon a time, in my drinking days, before Chinara, this would have been when I kissed the evening's girl, smelt lemon shampoo in her hair, felt the heat of her skin, the softness of her lips.

But those days are dead and buried deep. And I don't think they'll be coming back, at least, not for Mrs Borubaeva's boy. It's the death all around that's corroded me, not the drink.

Saltanat leant back, finished her beer, said, 'Time to eat.'

I thought, Time to kill.

Chapter 20

Saltanat and I sat under the shelter of the sloping bar roof, the rain cascading down around us. We'd eaten the vegetable *pelmeni* and bowls of *lagman* Rustam had brought out to us, wondered if the storm would ever end. Up in the mountains behind us, occasional rolling peals of distant thunder punctuated our conversation as we planned what to do next.

I thought I knew the streets and alleys of Bishkek better than most *tacsi* drivers, but I'd never heard of the Umai Hotel. And judging by the apparent absence of any guests, neither had anyone else.

'How do you know about this place?'

Saltanat lit a cigarette and sucked down the first smoke, then let it merge with the fine grey mist of the rain.

'I was at school with Rustam's daughter. Anastasia. We knew each other, not well, enough to say hello. When she was at university in Tashkent, she was attacked by three men.'

She paused, stared at me.

'I helped catch the men who did it. One of them was killed trying to escape. By me.'

Her look challenged me to disagree with her. I simply raised an eyebrow.

'I'd do it again. Rustam knows that too. So I stay here at his insistence, every time I'm in Bishkek. I can't pay for anything. Embarrassing, really.'

After a final draw on her cigarette, she threw the still-lit stub out onto the grass, listened to its half-hearted hiss before dying.

'I don't think your people – your ex-people – know I use this place, but we'd better keep on the move, just in case.'

I followed her to the car. From the hotel porch, Rustam raised his arm in farewell, jacket collar turned up against the rain. As the Lexus started to move towards the gates, Saltanat turned to me, her face impassive, betraying nothing. Her voice was calm.

'Eighteen months later, Anastasia killed herself.'

And then we were through the gates, tyres sending up a black spray against walls on both sides.

Chinara always said I felt too deeply for the victims in the cases I handled, that my emotional involvement would lead me to make mistakes, to follow one line of investigation excluding all others. At the same time, she knew it was the only way I could operate. My unconditional need for her and my need for justice for the dead were what made me the man I was. But things change, and so did I.

'Love weathers all storms'? Perhaps. But I've learnt that without love, nothing shores our lives up except rage, darkness, death. The story Saltanat had shared gave me one insight; we both endured the same sense of loss on behalf of the dead. Chinara had been my soulmate; Saltanat was my mirror image.

'Our plan?' I asked.

'We go somewhere no one will look for you. You can't hide in Bishkek; too many people know you. And my contact down in Jalalabad can deprogram that phone's security features.'

'It's the only lead we've got,' I agreed. 'But wouldn't it be better if we split up? Why should you get involved with this?'

'Because I want whoever killed Gurminj,' she said.

'And those children.'

'Yes. And those children.'

Which meant heading south-west towards Jalalabad, snowcapped mountains rising up on either side of us, soon to be stained with the setting sun's blood.

Chapter 21

We have a legend in Kyrgyzstan that at the world's beginning, God handed out countries to all the different races. However, the Kyrgyz man was asleep, probably after a long night on the vodka, and when he woke up, all the earth had been given away. 'But where am I going to live?' he asked, I expect in a whining, rather resentful voice. God considered the matter for a moment, said, 'There's one country I've been saving for myself. So beautiful, with flowing rivers and lofty mountains, clear air, rich grass, splendid trees. I suppose you'd better have that.' And that's how we Kyrgyz ended up in Kyrgyzstan.

I couldn't help remembering the story as we negotiated the hairpin bends that wind up into the Tien Shan mountains on their way to the south of Kyrgyzstan, towards our second-biggest city, Osh. The narrow road climbs to three thousand metres above sea level with terrifying drops down into the valleys below. The air is crisp, cold, so your chest aches and your head feels giddy. Splashes of snow still lined the roadside, and every few miles Saltanat would have to steer past debris left from the winter's rockfalls. But I felt alive, in a way I hadn't felt for a long time. Most people think life is about seeking joy, or making and spending money, or fucking and drinking yourself into oblivion. But for me, it's about justice, providing endings. And when I'm at my least cynical, it's about love.

The road is a hard drive, even in the summer months, let alone in spring. But I wouldn't risk a commercial flight to Osh, and no way was I going back to Karakol. Halfway between Bishkek and Osh, Jalalabad was near enough to the Uzbekistan border to make an illegal crossing possible, if I needed to. But first I had some deaths to avenge.

'You were in an orphanage as a child, weren't you?'

It wasn't something I shared with most people, but I shouldn't have been surprised that she knew.

'Uzbek security work overtime on my files?' I asked.

Saltanat laughed.

'I think you exaggerate our skills,' she said. 'No, Gurminj told me, said you were there while your mother was working in Siberia.'

I felt my chest tighten. Saltanat was entering a dark part of my life, stirring up memories I tried to keep buried. I needed a moment to decide what to reveal, what to keep concealed.

'Can you pull over for a moment? Piss stop.'

Saltanat stopped the car, I got out, walked to where the side of the road ended in a drop of hundreds of metres. The slope was bare of everything but scree and the odd patch of sparse grass. I kicked a pebble over the edge, watching it bounce and spin until it was lost from sight.

I pretended to urinate, then walked back to the car. By the time we were moving again, I'd made up my mind what to tell Saltanat.

'I was tucked away in the orphanage for two years. My grandfather's second wife didn't like me living with them, and with my *mama* away, well, you know how that fairy tale goes. The wicked stepmother. And my grandfather didn't need the earache she gave him.'

I paused, surprised at how strong my memories were.

'It wasn't a bad place, I suppose. Somewhere to sleep. Get fed. They even tried to teach us, although God knows we were a mixed bunch. But it was never home, never a place where you felt secure, loved, wanted.'

Saltanat stared ahead as she drove, listening intently to every word.

'I ran away twice. First time after a couple of weeks, missing my grandfather, the smell of *papirosh* tobacco when he hugged me, pinched my cheek, told me what a fine boy I was. I don't know what I was expecting when I got back to the farm. A loving welcome, I suppose, *plov* on the table, a cup of hot *chai* and the rasp of Grandfather's stubble on my cheek as he kissed me. Surprise, it didn't work out that way. His wife had me back in the orphanage the next day, but not until she'd whipped me with a belt while my grandfather looked on, helpless.

'So the second time I ran away, I had a little more of a plan. Hitchhike to Bishkek, find a job in a restaurant, or unloading the lorries that come over the Torugart pass from China. But it's almost four hundred kilometres from Karakol to Bishkek, and I didn't even manage to get to the eastern shore of Lake Issyk-Kul before the traffic police saw me and delivered me back.'

I paused and stared back out of the window.

'And after that?' Saltanat asked, twisting her head slightly to look at me.

'Long story,' I said, hearing the rasp in my throat, as if I'd swallowed a peach stone. 'Boring too.'

'We've got a long drive,' Saltanat said. 'It'll pass the time.'

I paused as the memories came back, unstoppable, rising in my mind the way vomit rises in your gullet.

'What you have to know about the orphanage is that it wasn't a bad place to be. It was clean, warm, and the food was OK. We slept in dormitories, boy in one, girls in another. That's not to say that the older boys didn't try to sneak in with the girls after lights out, but there was always a staff member on duty, so that was pretty much a no-no.

'There was a certain amount of bullying, nothing too serious, the sort of thing I was used to from school, bigger boys trying to prove who was top dog by hitting the little ones. And again, the teachers did their best to stop it happening.'

Saltanat waited for me to carry on, but I simply stared out of the window, at the snow on the mountain caps, smeared by the red stain of the setting sun. Like blood blooming against a white tiled floor.

'Towards the end of my second year at the orphanage, I was pretty much resigned to living there, at least until I was sixteen, in two years' time. Treading water, you might say. Then a new boy arrived, Aleksey Zhenbekov. He was tall, maybe fifteen, with the sort of muscles you get on a farm where the only machinery is in your arms and your back. His face was almost black from the sun, and his temper was just as dark. From the beginning, he was determined to cause trouble, show the world he wouldn't tolerate any disrespect. Especially from the younger ones, the weak ones, the ones who'd never learnt to fight.

'He called it "discussion". With fists as enduring as rocks, slaps like being struck by a shovel. Like all bullies, he could smell fear the way a cadaver dog can lead you to the dead.'

I paused, my mouth suddenly dry. This was a story I'd always thought should be left unspoken, its details covered over with earth and quickly forgotten. Sensing my mood, Saltanat pulled over to the roadside and stopped. We got out and walked in silence to the drop-off. With dusk almost upon us, shadows growing thicker, the air this high up had a bite as savage as the wolves that live in these mountains. I felt we were balanced at the edge of the world, that a sudden wind could sweep us away into darkness.

'There was one boy, Adilet, the same age as me. One of those boys who spoke only when spoken to, who tried to shower on his own, who didn't join in any of our playground games.

'Adilet was a godsend to Zhenbekov, someone with whom he could debate his "discussions". So we'd find Adilet with bruises on his face, arms, legs. If we ever saw him in the showers, he'd have fist-sized dark brown marks that slowly turned purple and yellow. And over the weeks, Adilet spoke less and less, sat on his own in the classroom. At night, we sometimes heard him weeping in his bunk. And what did we do? Nothing.'

I lit a cigarette, stared out into the gathering dark.

'Of course we were scared of Zhenbekov. None of us wanted to replace Adilet as an object of discussion. But we could have ganged up on him, kicked eight kinds of shit out of him. Or just reported him to the staff. But we didn't. We were cowards, simple as that.'

I felt the taste of tobacco in my mouth, the smoke curling out into the evening air as if the fire of my life was slowly dying down.

'What happened?' Saltanat said, and I saw sympathy in her face, a shared understanding that life is an obstacle course.

'It was one of those summer days where the heat gives way

to a sudden shower, clouds coming down from the mountains, warm rain, sweet, gentle on your face. The kind of soft rain the land loves to drink. And suddenly, we were all called out into the yard, to stand there while the rain plastered our hair down into cowlicks and formed puddles in the earth beneath our feet.

'We stood in silence as a police van entered the yard, parked beside the shower block. After half an hour, the rain stopped, and we watched as two policemen struggled out with a body on a stretcher, placed it in the back of their van, drove off.

'We were all herded back into the orphanage, told the police would be questioning us over the next two days. I looked around, realised I didn't see Adilet anywhere. The boy who'd almost perfected the art of invisibility was missing.'

I threw the butt of my cigarette over the edge, and watched the glowing spark tumble and disappear into the dark.

'That evening, I sneaked into the shower block. The staff had made a pretty good attempt to swab up the blood, but I could still see a few droplets and spatters on the tiled floor.'

'Did you ever find out who killed Adilet?' Saltanat asked.

'You've got it wrong,' I said, scowling at the memory. 'It was Zhenbekov who'd lost his final discussion. Adilet had waited with a length of rusty steel pipe, smashed it into Zhenbekov's skull. Three times. Adilet didn't kill him, but Zhenbekov wasn't going to be bullying anyone again. The police picked Adilet up about five kilometres from Karakol. We were told he didn't say a word, either then or at his trial.'

The sun had almost set, and I could see our breath spilling out into the air, backlit by the moonlight.

'Years later, I found out that Adilet's twin sister had been murdered by their stepfather, beaten, kicked to death, for who knows what? Not sweeping the floor to his satisfaction? Spilling a cup of *chai* and scalding his fingers? Struggling when he tried to enter her bed? Adilet did what he did to regain the control he'd lost when his sister died. No matter that you can't always avenge the dead.'

I felt Saltanat reach out for my hand, felt her palm press against mine, sexless, supportive. And then we were silent as we walked back to the car and continued our journey.

Chapter 22

We spent an uncomfortable night in the car, having turned off the main road and down a track leading to one of the narrow rivers that saunter through the valley. In two or three months' time, there would be other cars here, tents perhaps, a base for people who wanted to hike through the mountains. But in early spring, the weather is still too cold, and we had the place to ourselves.

Saltanat had cold meat *samsi* and water for us, even a couple of blankets, and I managed to get two or three hours of uncomfortable half-sleep, filled with images of the gun fight in the Kulturny. The wound in my shoulder felt as if I'd been burnt, but it had stopped bleeding some hours ago. Saltanat had done her best to clean and bandage it from the first aid box under the spare wheel, but she had nothing to give me for the pain. So while she slept beside me, I stared out of the windscreen at the sheet of stars above us, and wondered what to do next.

The dawn crept up over the mountains, a burglar on tiptoe, each movement imperceptible, gradually swelling and filling the sky with the lightest of blues. I looked at Saltanat as she slept, then stared at myself in the mirror. Damaged, bruised, still in mourning, without a future as far as I could tell. So instead I watched the sun begin to colour the snow a deceptive gold . . .

By noon, we were only a few hours from Jalalabad. Earlier, I'd left Saltanat asleep and went to wash in the Naryn river as it danced and kicked its way downstream. The brutality of the snow-cold water on my face punched me into wakefulness, so I unwound the dressing on my shoulder and looked at Maxim's handiwork. The flesh around the wound was red and inflamed, and I knew I'd have to get some antibiotics. I could feel the muscle tug, and resisted the temptation to pick at the raised dark-brown scab. I'd probably need stitches, but asking a doctor not to inform the local *menti* of a gunshot wound would need either a big bribe or a quick getaway.

Once we'd finished the last of the *samsi*, we set off on the last leg of our journey. I'd checked Kamchybek's iPhone, but hadn't been able to get a signal, not really surprising, given the mountains towering around us.

'I'll get my colleague in Jalalabad to see what information he can track down from the mobile,' Saltanat said. 'There'll be numbers on it that could give us a lead, maybe documents and emails.'

'I'm grateful for you getting me out of Bishkek,' I said, aware of course that I sounded ungrateful. 'And believing me about the set-up with the child porn. Wanting to help me track down whoever killed Gurminj. But the longer we stay together, the more you're at risk.'

Saltanat frowned; I was treading on the toes of the Uzbek security forces.

'Close to the border, and it's easier to cross over without drawing attention to ourselves, if we have to,' she said.

'You've got agents there? Safe houses?'

'Akyl, just trust me on this, OK?' she answered.

Which was, of course, no answer at all.

The mountains shrank to mere hills, long flanks of grass and meadows on either side of the road. We were entering the Fergana Valley, some of the most fertile agricultural land in Central Asia, land that's been squabbled over, seized and retaken for thousands of years. One of the many Silk Road routes ran through here, carrying Chinese silks, spices and sweets from India and finely crafted Persian silverwork. These days, the trade also includes heroin and *krokodil*, semi-automatic rifles and trafficked people. Of course, they're not being carried by camel any more. On the other hand, business is a lot more lucrative.

Jalalabad isn't a particularly large city, or a bustling one. As Saltanat parked the Lexus on Lenina Street, the main drag that runs through the centre, it felt like we'd left Kyrgyzstan behind when we'd driven out of Bishkek. Most of the men were wearing Uzbek skullcaps instead of Kyrgyz *kalpaks*, while the women wore headscarves and long narrow trousers under their brightly coloured dresses. Some young women dared to defy tradition and walked bareheaded, but they were few and far between. We were near the main bazaar, and I wondered if that was where Saltanat intended to meet her 'people'.

'Why don't you take a walk, maybe pick up some fruit in the bazaar?' she suggested.

'What about you?' I asked. 'You don't want me to come with you?'

Saltanat simply shook her head.

'I'll see you back here in a couple of hours, OK?'

And with that, she was gone, slipping into the river of people flowing down Lenina.

I decided to leave my gun in the car, wrapped in one of the blankets and safely stowed under the passenger seat. I didn't think I'd need that much firepower, and it was too bulky not to be obvious. Instead, I pocketed the Makarov I'd taken from Maxim, headed into the crowd.

The bazaar was packed, stalls clustered together to form narrow lanes, tables piled high with local produce, vegetables, shapeless hunks of raw meat, scrawny chickens hanging up by their feet or still alive, looking anxious in small wicker baskets. There was fruit everywhere, the first of the summer crop, melons, figs, plums, oranges, and, of course apples. Scientists believe apples originated in Kyrgyzstan, and we're more than happy to claim credit. We don't have a wealth of world-changing achievements to our name, but creating a fruit that's colonised the world has to be one of them.

The sky was a clear pale near-white blue, the inside of a porcelain bowl, and the day was hot for early spring. I ordered a bowl of *lagman*, our spicy lamb and noodle soup, at a food stall run by a plump *babushka*. It came with a glass of *kumiss*, the salty, slightly alcoholic drink we make from fermented mare's milk. I pushed the glass to one side, concentrated on scooping the noodles out of the bowl.

Then a voice behind me said, 'I strongly recommend you leave the gun in your pocket, Inspector Borubaev.'

A strong voice, used to issuing orders, used to being obeyed without question.

Mikhail Tynaliev, Kyrgyzstan's Minister for State Security.

Chapter 23

I placed my hands palm down on the table, slowly, deliberately. This was no time to be making false moves. When I'd first met Tynaliev to break the news of his daughter's death to him, he'd been surrounded by security guards, trained to fire first and then apologise afterwards. Except they usually didn't say sorry.

'I can recommend the *lagman*, Minister,' I said. 'Not too spicy, and the noodles are fresh.' I was trying to keep my voice as calm as possible. Not easy when you're talking to one of the most powerful men in the country, someone who could have you sharing a cell with half the criminals you've sent there, or sleeping in an unmarked hilltop grave.

'I'm not here to arrest you, Inspector,' Tynaliev said. I turned to look at him. Broad shoulders, a thick neck and hands that told you he'd done his fair share of slaps and punches down in the basement interrogation room of some police station or army barracks. Black eyes that never blinked. He looked fearless, immortal.

The last time I'd seen Tynaliev, his men were dragging my old boss out of his office and to death. Tynaliev had ordered me to bring him the men who'd killed his daughter, and I'd known better than to disobey. He'd told me he was in debt to me, which really meant he owned me, whenever he chose to reel in the line and hook.

'With all respect, Minister, why are you standing in the

middle of Jalalabad bazaar, talking to a lowly inspector like me? You don't have more important matters to deal with?'

Tynaliev's smile didn't fill me with confidence.

'Inspector, I know you far too well to consider you a mere *ment*, an empty head in a big green cap and uniform. In my opinion, for what little that's worth, Akyl Borubaev is a pretty apt name.'

I should explain that my first name, Akyl, means 'clever', and 'boru' is the Kyrgyz word for 'wolf'. It's been a running joke with my colleagues for a long time. But to me it's no joke; staying alive means being clever, and if you're Murder Squad, no one hunts better than a wolf. Or knows when it's being hunted.

Tynaliev pulled out the rough wooden stool next to me, sat down. I could smell his expensive cologne, see the immaculate cut of his suit, the brilliant polish on his shoes. Next to him, I looked like a piece of shit.

'I heard about this child porn and your involvement. I was surprised; maybe I'm not such a good judge of character as I think I am, I said to myself. Then I remembered the respect you showed my Yekaterina, the diligence you showed in catching those responsible. So I think you've been set up because you're investigating the Karakol murders, as your girlfriend seems to believe. Or rather, you were.'

He paused, watched as I held up my cigarettes, nodded his permission. The *babushka* behind the counter started to protest, saying she had other hungry customers to serve. Without taking his eyes off me, Tynaliev gestured and one of the burly unsmiling men nearby handed her a bundle of thousand *som* notes, leaving her smiling her gratitude and shooing away her regulars.

The cigarette tasted good in the open air, nicotine buzzing straight into my brain. I wondered if this would be the final one for the condemned man.

'How did you know I was here, Minister?' I asked.

Tynaliev smiled and folded his arms.

'Contrary to what the uninformed might think, my counterpart in Tashkent and I see eye to eye in a great many things. Neither of us wants civil unrest, looting, killing, either side of the border. I remembered about the delightful Miss Umarova, and how closely you'd worked with her. So I called her boss, he called her, she carried out her orders. And here we are.'

It was what I'd suspected ever since the minister sat down, but the thought of Saltanat's setting a trap for me made the *lagman* rise in my throat. I've always known there are no certainties, apart from perpetual change, but that doesn't stop me wanting something, or someone, in whom I could invest some hope. I wondered if I was going to vomit, and if I could manage to spew on the minister's gleaming shoes. Not much of a revenge, but all I could think of at the moment.

The minister put his hand on my shoulder, the way a father does with a young son who's fallen over and scraped his knee.

'Miss Umarova was very specific that she wouldn't do anything that might bring you harm. She even offered to resign.'

Tynaliev paused and raised an eyebrow.

'In fact, she promised to "put a bullet in any fucker who harmed you". So I'd say you've made quite an impression upon her.'

'What is it you want from me, Minister?' I asked, and didn't bother to sound polite.

He sat back and looked at me, his eyes narrowed. I knew I should be afraid of him, worried about the click of his fingers that would see me dragged upright, arms twisted behind my back, off to a waiting car, a cell, a grave.

But somehow, I really couldn't give a fuck.

'Interesting question, Inspector,' Tynaliev answered. 'I would have expected you to ask if I could get you out of the rather unpromising situation you find yourself in.'

Tynaliev certainly had the power to make any evidence go away, strangle any investigation. I'd stood by while he disappeared my old boss, said nothing. But you can't live with fear gnawing away at your soul until the day you decide to stand up and discover you've no soul left.

'I have enemies, Inspector Borubaev, I'm sure you're aware of that. People who'd like to see me fall, and then take my place. Rivals constantly searching for any sign of weakness, ready to put the poison in the right ears.'

I said nothing. It was a story I'd heard before. And it explained why we were meeting in this remote town, rather than in Bishkek, where Tynaliev's every move would be under observation, where someone would recognise and report me.

'I may not be perfect,' Tynaliev continued. 'I have to take strong measures at times, but believe me, Inspector, I'm a thousand times better than anyone who could take my place. No one can accuse me of being corrupt, not putting my country first. And that means my fist in the mouth of anyone who wants me out.'

Tynaliev paused, gestured to the *babushka* to bring him a bottle of Baltika beer. He wiped the neck of the bottle, took a mouthful.

'You don't drink, do you?'

I shook my head. I couldn't imagine that Tynaliev knew why I stayed sober, but he was too clever not to make some assumptions.

'You stopped just after your wife died?' he asked, assuming a look of concern that fitted him about as well as a puppet's mask. 'Strange, I would have thought such a tragedy would make most people drink more.'

I knew he was probing, even if we weren't in a downstairs interrogation room, with me lashed to a chair and my tongue counting the number of loosened teeth.

'Did you drink more after your daughter's murder, Minister?' I asked, trying to take the offensive, not caring if he felt insulted. I saw his bodyguard stiffen, ready for an order.

'I celebrated when you caught her killers,' he replied, his face giving nothing away, 'and I celebrated as they were being punished.'

I lit a cigarette, looked away at the cold beers in a bucket of ice by the *babushka*'s feet. Condensation trickled down the dark glass sides of the bottles, the labels sodden and starting to peel away. My mouth was suddenly dry with craving, and I could taste the cold sweetness of the beer, picture the gentle slide towards oblivion.

'Well, Minister, I didn't have anything to celebrate when my wife died. And I think I'll be waiting a long time before anyone can capture the cancer that killed her.'

'We've both known a terrible loss,' Tynaliev said, and I could hear genuine sorrow in his voice. 'We've both buried a loved one long before their time. We should let that unite us, not divide us.'

I threw the last of my cigarette onto the earth, and mashed it into the ground with my boot heel.

'What do you want from me, Minister?' I repeated, trying to keep my voice calm and my face expressionless.

'These killings, the children, the orphanage director, I want them solved. But solved in a way that means justice is served, but without publicity, without the spotlight of the press casting up all sorts of unnecessary shadows.'

'Nothing that could make you look weak, ineffectual?' I suggested, knowing I was pushing too hard, not really caring. Tynaliev was the leader of a wolf pack, the alpha male. But if he showed any sign of weakness, the younger males would be upon him, getting bolder, nipping his flanks, finally ripping out his throat, leaving his blood scarlet on the snow.

'Precisely. I want justice, Inspector,' Tynaliev said, 'and I don't care what it costs, how you do it. But make sure the shit stays off my boots. No hint I don't have complete control.'

I didn't say anything, I didn't have a choice. But having a protector in Tynaliev could prove useful. It could also prove fatal.

'Working with Ms Umarova; it served you well in the past,' the minister continued, 'but I don't want it to turn into a double-edged sword. Make sure it cuts away from me. Or mine won't be the head that it severs.'

I didn't know what Tynaliev had to hide, or who he was protecting. But warnings didn't cut much ice with me any more, no matter who issues them.

'I can't lift the order for your arrest, Inspector,' Tynaliev said, getting to his feet. 'Not without tipping my hand you're working for me. But I'll make sure other cases have a higher priority. Once the "news" reaches us that you've probably fled the country, I don't think anyone will be looking too hard for you.'

'I still don't understand why you're personally involved, Minister,' I said, keeping my face as expressionless as possible. 'It's not as if you don't have more important matters to tend to.'

Tynaliev nodded.

'You're right, Inspector, normally I'd let the police handle the matter. But there's a problem with this case.'

'Which is?'

Tynaliev stared hard at me, a look saying I was about to take one step too far.

'You're the policeman. Murder Squad. I'll let you figure it out.'

He looked around, satisfied with the outcome of his meeting, drained the last of his Baltika.

'You still have my private number?'

I nodded. If Tynaliev didn't want the police involved, some high-up people might be responsible for the porn, the murders.

'Good. I'm glad we see eye to eye on this. And speaking of seeing . . .'

I look around to see Saltanat walking towards us, sunglasses hiding her eyes, her face giving nothing away.

'I'm sure Ms Umarova will be a more entertaining companion, Inspector. But remember, I want to hear from you. Soon.'

With that, he and his bodyguard walked away, leaving me to face a woman I desired, feared and felt betrayed by.

Chapter 24

Saltanat sat down beside me, pulled a bottle of beer from the ice bucket. The *babushka* uncapped the bottle and Saltanat took a long swallow. She put the bottle down, started to pick at the edge of the label.

I said nothing.

'So you met with the minister then?' she asked.

I didn't reply, merely looked at her, raised an eyebrow. Saltanat reached over and took a cigarette from my pack, lit it, blew the smoke away as if she were doing her best to keep her temper, and wanted me to know it.

'I obey orders, like you. Except when it suits me not to. Again, like you,' she said, took an angry swig at her beer. 'I want to help you. I want to catch whoever put a bullet through Gurminj's head, and neither of us will succeed in that minor task if Tynaliev wants our heads on stakes in Ala-Too Square, will we?'

I knew pragmatism and acceptance were called for. But pride has a strange way of making us turn away from the sensible path, watching us trek over the mountains instead of through the valleys. So I simply shrugged, feigned indifference and watched the *babushka* pour *ashlam foo* into bowls, the eggs settling on cold noodles, fat glistening in the sunlight.

Saltanat sighed, concentrated on her cigarette. Then the *babushka* spoke.

'Don't be a *gopnik*, you,' she said, her accent thick with the slurred vowels of the south, harsh from a lifetime of smoking strong *papirosh* and working in the bazaar. 'A low-class like you should give one of his balls that a woman like this should even speak to you, not scrape you off her shoe.'

She slammed another bottle of beer down in front of Saltanat, gestured at me with a grimy forefinger.

'You get a *devotchka* like her once in your lifetime, you, listen to me.'

I risked a glance at Saltanat, and though I couldn't catch her eye, I could tell by the way her shoulders shook she was amused.

'Listen to me, boy, I know you think I'm just a peasant, a nothing. But I tell you this. I lost a father in the Great Patriotic War, defending Moscow. I lost two sons in infancy. I've buried two husbands. If there's one thing I know, if you can't find room for someone, then there's no room for anything else worth having. Go on, laugh at me.'

'Forgive me, Granny,' I said, reached for one of her hands, wrinkled and clawed with arthritis. 'I am a stupid man, who doesn't know when a wonderful person has stepped into his life. You're kind to teach such a lesson to such a fool. *Spasibo.*'

I turned to Saltanat, removed the sunglasses that hid her eyes. 'I ask your forgiveness for my rudeness, stupidity, bad manners. If it happens again, just pull the trigger before I shoot myself anyway.'

She said nothing, merely nodded, and my heart twisted in my chest as she gave one of her rare smiles, intoxicating, like sunrise sliding across snow. She took my hand and squeezed it, and I felt the burden on my life, the obsession to

avenge the dead, lift for a moment. I knew it would return –
none of us change that easily or so quickly – but at least I
now had someone to keep me company part of the way on
my journey.

I paid the *babushka* for the food and drink, left a generous
tip, turned to Saltanat.

'Now what?' I asked.

'Back to the car,' she said, 'and then find a hotel.'

Chapter 25

We lay fully clothed on the double bed, having checked into the Roza Park Hotel and demanded a suite. I'd produced my police ID, which got a favourable discount as well as the promise that we had the best room in the place. We'd walked up the stairs, holding hands, locked the door behind us, decided it was time to talk.

'I never thought I'd see you again,' I said. 'Not after you killed Sariev and disappeared.'

'No?'

'I thought you'd decided "Mission Accomplished" and gone back to your life.'

'I knew I couldn't stay in Bishkek, not then. I didn't know what had happened to you, and murdering a serving police officer wouldn't have gone down well with your people, would it?'

'I don't think too many people were upset by Sariev taking the long trip. They probably had a "free beer all night" celebration in every bar in Bishkek,' I said.

'Were you angry with me?' she asked, her eyes never leaving my face, searching for signs of hesitation.

I thought about it for a moment.

'Hurt. Confused,' I said. 'Scared you might kill me. Afraid you might leave me. Which you did.'

'But I'm back now,' she said, and kissed the corner of my mouth. Her breath was sweet on my face. I pulled her towards me, but she put her hands on my chest, laughing, fending me off.

'We've work to do,' she said, and walked towards the bathroom. 'I need to shower. I might even save you some hot water.'

I emerged from the bathroom to find Saltanat already asleep, fully clothed, on top of the bed. I lay down beside her and drifted off into that aimless half-sleep that you fall into in the middle of the day.

It was still light when Saltanat shook me out of a confused dream about being trapped in a maze of thorn bushes. My mouth was dry, sour, and I regretted the absence of a toothbrush.

'We have to go back to Bishkek,' she said. 'I'll tell you about it on the way.'

I winced. I love my country as much as the next Murder Squad detective, but that doesn't mean I want to bounce up and down for hundreds of kilometres on twisting mountain roads twice a week.

We took the stairs down to the hotel lobby, handed the key in to reception. Outside, we stopped to savour the sunshine's warmth, the pale blue sky above us.

'The iPhone is state of the art,' Saltanat said. 'The emails and contact numbers are all encrypted, impossible to crack, supposedly.'

'So what did you find?' I asked.

'All incoming calls were from a blocked number,' Saltanat answered. 'And any attempt to reopen any sent or received emails automatically deleted them.'

'So we've come all this way for nothing?' I said.

'Not quite,' she replied. 'He managed to trace the blocked number.'

I raised an eyebrow, not liking the idea of Uzbek security operating on Kyrgyz soil.

'It's a Bishkek number, and we've located an address.'

'And a name?'

'Not yet. That's why we have to go back to the city, stake the place out. Once we know the name, you can start kicking down doors.'

I was about to suggest that perhaps with her contacts, she could find a way of getting me on a plane without my name getting flagged up and a squad car waiting to arrest me.

But then the shooting started. Again.

Chapter 26

For a second, I thought a nearby car was backfiring, a curious popping sound, like an old man coughing. Then glass shattered behind us, and I pushed Saltanat down to the ground, slamming myself down hard at the same time. The scab in my shoulder split open and begin to bleed. Somewhere back in the hotel, a woman screamed.

I rolled left as Saltanat threw herself to the right, snatching at our weapons as we reached the cover of a couple of cars parked nearby. I released the safety on my Yarygin, peered beneath the car in the direction of the shots. I could see feet, but I couldn't be certain if they belonged to the gunman. No point crippling an innocent passer-by, getting myself into even more trouble.

I waited for a couple of moments, finger tense on the trigger. When no further shots came, I raised my head above the bonnet of the car, watched Saltanat do the same.

I didn't see any masked gunmen waiting to pick us off, so I levered myself up off the pavement. The sleeve of my jacket was torn, and the material dark where fresh blood had joined the old stain. I felt the nausea of shock rise in my stomach, dread at the knowledge death can tap you on the shoulder with unexpected precision, accurate and inevitable.

'Nice way to treat tourists,' I said.

'See anyone?' Saltanat asked. I shook my head.

'I only heard the shots,' I answered. 'And a scream from inside the hotel.'

I holstered my gun, walked back to the hotel. A middle-aged man sprawled on the floor by the reception desk, not moving, while a woman frantically rubbed at one flaccid hand thrown across his chest. No point in going in, nothing we could do to help. And the local *menti* were sure to be on their way.

'You need to buy me a new shirt, then I can dump the jacket,' I said as we walked back to the car, not running but not loitering either.

'There are some clothes in the car,' she replied, looking straight ahead, her gun hanging unobtrusively by her side. 'Let me find a pharmacy so I can clean that slight scratch you're complaining about.'

Fifteen minutes later, we were on the far side of Jalalabad, parked outside a pharmacy, from which Saltanat emerged with everything she needed to inflict a little torture on me.

The burn of the hydrogen peroxide hurt far worse than the bullet, as Saltanat used swabs to clean away the crusted black blood. After she had finished dressing the wound and getting to work with needle and thread, I felt as if I'd gone through a five-hour interrogation at the hands of one of the Sverdlovsky station's best, complete with slaps, kicks and punches. But at least now I didn't look as if I'd been rolling around on the floor of a butcher's shop.

I struggled into the oversized shirt Saltanat had produced from the boot.

'And now back to Bishkek, I suppose?'

She nodded and I sat back, wondering when the pain-killers would kick in, if there was any way of getting out of the mess we were in. As we drove down Lenina Street, a middle-aged man with cropped grey hair and a greasy leather jacket stopped to watch our car as we passed. There was something familiar about his face, a memory I tried and failed to tug out of my past and into the daylight. Then we turned a corner and he was gone.

Chapter 27

'You're sure this is the right address?' I asked as we pulled up down the street from an imposing building a couple of blocks away from Chui Prospekt.

The journey back to Bishkek had been just as tiring as the outbound leg, and I needed a shave, a bath and a bed, not necessarily in that order. I smelt like an old goat, but at least I didn't detect any sign of my shoulder turning septic. Saltanat, as always, smelt divine, and looked as if she'd had an uninterrupted eight hours' sleep in a five-star hotel.

The house was on Frunze, in the elite district of town, where money bought you privacy, CCTV cameras and very high concrete walls. Sunlight sparkled off the broken glass that ran along the top of the wall, further reinforced by a wire fence that I was certain would be electrified. Solid steel gates kept the world out, brutal spikes mounted at the top to impale intruders.

There was no sign of bodyguards, sentries, no-necked men with bulges under cheap leather jackets. Only the upper part of the house was visible, shuttered windows glaring down at the street. A massive satellite dish squatted on the roof. Whoever lived here would have enough clout to get Saltanat whisked back over the border and me enjoying ten years no-star bed and board in whichever prison was most remote and unpleasant.

I said as much to Saltanat and she rewarded me with one

of those enigmatic stares that lasted until I had to break eye contact.

'You want to drop this, Akyl?' she said, surprise in her voice. 'Go back to your apartment and wait for your old colleagues to drag you down the basement to discuss your crimes? And then life in prison, at least until your fellow inmates discover you were a policeman?'

I knew she was right. But we had to be more careful than going in guns blazing.

'No, I don't want to drop it,' I said. 'Gurminj was my friend as well as yours. There are the seven dead babies who deserve some justice. And the children in those films.'

I paused, swallowed. The saliva in my mouth tasted thick and oily, as if I'd gone for weeks without cleaning my teeth. Pain pressed into my shoulder, its fingers probing underneath the stitches, like a small creature trying to escape.

'Can you pass me the iPhone?' I asked.

Saltanat reached for her bag and handed it to me.

'What are you planning to do?' she asked.

I gave her the mirthless smile that had become my speciality ever since watching Usupov uncover those scraps of bodies in the field near Karakol.

'There's such a thing as being too subtle, Saltanat. Sometimes you have to piss on the bushes and see what emerges. Like tethering a sheep up in the mountains and then lying in wait until the wolves come down.'

Saltanat raised an eyebrow. Perhaps I was being a bit too philosophical.

'I'm just going to make a quick call,' I said, and hit redial.

I listened to the dialling tone, which matched my heartbeat, rapid and worried.

And then I heard a voice.

'*Da?*'

A man's voice, deep, cautious. Speaking in Russian, but not with a Kyrgyz or Russian accent. English or American, at a guess. The Voice. Raw, like skin scraped on gravel.

'A friend of yours lost his mobile, and I'm sure he'd like it back.'

Silence. I cleared my throat and continued.

'These smartphones, not cheap, are they? So I'm sure there's a reward for its safe return. With all its contacts, photos and videos. Particularly the videos.'

More silence. Then the Voice again.

'What did you have in mind?'

'I was thinking maybe twenty-five thousand?'

'Twenty five thousand *som*?'

'No,' I said. 'Dollars.'

'*Pashol na khui.*'

'Well, I can certainly fuck off if that's what you really want, but then you don't get the smartphone back,' I said, putting a smile into my voice I certainly didn't feel. 'And then who knows whose hands it might fall into? Perhaps I should just hand it in at Sverdlovsky station. The police could probably trace the owner.'

'I'll call you back,' the Voice said, broke the connection.

Saltanat looked over at me, genuine approval in her eyes.

'A small-time crook gets lucky, decides to try a spot of blackmail. Arranges a meet. Bites a bullet,' she said. 'Except he's not a small-time crook. And he doesn't.'

I smiled again, the one that never reaches my eyes.

'Devious minds think alike, Saltanat. We've put the pot on

the stove. Now we let the ingredients simmer. And speaking of which . . .'

'Yes?'

'I'm hungry.'

An hour later, back at the outside bar of the Umai Hotel, I finished off the last of the *pelmeni* dumplings a taciturn Rustam had brought us, sipped my *chai*. Saltanat had refused to eat, had instead worked her way through most of a Baltika beer, staring at me with obvious exasperation.

'Now your belly's full,' she said, 'how about we get back to work?'

I winked, knowing it would irritate her further.

'Wolves aren't stupid, you know. When they see a sheep tethered, they wonder whether it's a trap. So they hide up by the rocks or the trees, scenting the air to see if any hunters are nearby. Only when they're satisfied there's no danger do they race towards the sheep. Then the hunters open fire.'

'Thank you for the natural history lesson,' Saltanat said. 'I understand the metaphor. But that's not an answer.'

'We know where they are, not who they are. They don't know who or where we are. So we have the advantage. But they know what we have, the danger it means for them. So they have to reach out to us.'

I tapped the iPhone.

'They'll ring, don't worry.'

So we sat there as the shadows grew longer, smoked cigarette after cigarette, waiting for the call.

'Ten thousand dollars,' the Voice said, no introduction, no greeting, straight to business.

'No,' I said, and broke the connection, switched off the phone.

'Why did you do that?' Saltanat demanded, anger in her eyes.

'I want to show them we're greedy, that we'll be careless when it comes to the meet and exchange. And it puts them on the back foot, which isn't a bad thing.'

I threw the remains of my cigarette out onto the grass.

'I'll turn it back on in an hour. And I guarantee it will ring a minute later.'

Which was exactly what happened.

'Twenty-five thousand dollars, very well,' the Voice said. I was pretty sure it was an American voice, confident, no sign of hesitation or anger.

'It's very expensive to keep me waiting,' I said, injecting a note of annoyance into my voice. 'The price is now thirty thousand. Dollars.'

Silence on the other end of the line.

'Who are you? Circle of Brothers?'

I smiled. This was a dance only one person could lead. And if the American thought I might be connected to the organised crime gang spread throughout Russia and Central Asia, so much the better for piling on pressure.

'Call me Manas. The local superhero. Top dog. *Bratski krug*.'

'Very clever, Mr Whoever-you-are.' Anger in the Voice now, the first hint of carelessness with an undercurrent of worry.

'I'm turning this mobile off in ten seconds,' I said, 'and I won't be switching it back on if we don't agree now.'

I could sense the man's hesitation, almost smell his desire to hit and stamp and kill me.

'Ten, nine, eight . . .'

'OK, we have a deal, but where do we meet?' he asked.

'Instructions in an hour, call me,' I told him and switched off the phone again.

'What do we do until then?' Saltanat asked.

I nodded at the hotel.

'I'm sure Rustam has a room to spare,' I said and walked around the bar to where the cold beer was kept.

'Another Baltika?'

She shook her head, lit another cigarette, stared at the empty sky.

Chapter 28

Like most Murder Squad detectives, I keep a stash of not strictly legal weapons, 'just in case', as I always tell myself, stuff I don't want to risk keeping at home. Divide and conquer is a pretty good motto when it comes to illegal weapons. I rent a small storage space near the big bazaar on the other side of Bishkek, not in my name. That's where I hide two passports, one Uzbek and one Russian, also not in my name, a couple of Makarovs and ammo to go with them, a switchblade, lock picks, several changes of clothing, including bulletproof vests, and other useful items. I think of it as an additional insurance policy, in case we have another revolution and someone decides I'm not cheering fervently enough.

Saltanat kept watch while I taped the two Makarovs and ammo to the underside of the car, having made sure they were loaded. If we found ourselves caught in crossfire, I wanted cover to hide behind and enough firepower to shoot our way out. We both stripped to the waist and strapped on the vests, before putting our shirts back on.

'Comfortable?' I asked.

'If you enjoy mammograms,' she said, checking her own Makarov and slamming the clip home.

I slipped the fake passports into the glove compartment, padlocked the storage space, then we were off, back down Chui Prospekt, car headlights already on to combat the dusk, the greater darkness that lay ahead.

I could smell leaves, grass and the hint of rain in the air. Spring was striding towards Bishkek, the rivers starting to swell with snowmelt. Shepherds would be thinking about moving their flocks back up to the grasslands of the high *jailoo*, and the city girls would be hunting out their summer dresses packed away months ago. I wondered if I would be alive to see them parade across Ala-Too Square, young, hopeful, an eternal future ahead of them.

'Take a right here, and then a left,' I said, peering out at the familiar streets.

'We're going to the Kulturny?' Saltanat asked, following my instructions.

'This is my city,' I replied. 'I know how it works here. So yes, the Kulturny.'

There was a confidence in my voice I didn't really feel, but I knew we had to keep moving forward. Losing momentum means losing advantage. And unlike wolves, we didn't have anywhere to shelter, anywhere to hide.

Right on time, the call came.

'OK, where?'

'You know the Kulturny?' I said. 'The most stylish bar in Bishkek? The French champagne, fine vintage wines, haute cuisine, sophisticated clientele?'

A grunt was the only response.

'When?'

'Forty-five minutes,' I replied. 'But don't be late or they'll give our table away.'

'How will I know you?' the Voice asked.

'Don't worry about that,' I said. 'I'll know you.'

I ended the call just as Saltanat pulled into an empty space, across from the bar.

The street was pretty much empty; this part of town doesn't see much action, once the daylight starts to go. The yellow puddles from the few streetlights we have become stepping stones in a dark and dangerous lake. I could see Lubashov leaning by the steel door, his balls presumably recovered from meeting Saltanat.

I put on one of the midnight-blue wool ski masks I'd taken out of storage, and handed the other to Saltanat. With only eyes and mouth visible, it would be difficult for anyone to identify us, unless we were dead, in which case it was all academic, and Usupov would do the final honours.

You set up something like this by arranging the meet to give them the bare minimum time to get there, with not enough time for an ambush, making sure you're already in place. You wait until they arrive with a shriek of tyres, hurl themselves out of an armour-plated Hummer like a Spetsnaz team on high alert, cover the street with Kalashnikovs primed to fire.

But nothing happens, no gunshots from the dark, no grenades thrown from the rooftops. So everyone starts to relax and get sloppy, the adrenalin beginning to flush out of their systems.

They all tense again as the car door opens, always the front passenger door, and the big guy, the number one, the *bratski krug*, gets out and takes the few steps to the meet door and safety.

That's when everyone is waiting for the hit. Which is why you don't do it then. You wait. Wait some more. A bit more after that. And then you hit them.

We were invisible, thanks to the car's tinted windows and our dark clothing. I reached up and switched off the courtesy light; no point in giving someone a clean shot.

I heard Saltanat's breath, sharp and ragged, almost loud enough to drown the way my heart hammered in my chest, death's knuckles beating on the door, demanding to be let in. I wiped my damp palms on my trousers, wishing I'd wound tape around the butt of my gun for a better grip. I needed a piss as well. Too late now.

Twenty minutes before the rendezvous, so I knew they'd be here in the next five.

Saltanat reached over and squeezed my hand.

'This is the bit I hate,' she whispered. 'Waiting. Always have done.'

I squeezed back, then stroked the back of her hand. The bones felt thin, fragile, unable to pull a trigger and blow a man's life into a memory. Appearances deceive.

As I sat there in the darkness, preparing for chaos and death, I remembered Chinara quoting one of her favourite lines of poetry, by some foreign poet, how love was what would survive of us. I wasn't sure it was true. Because love isn't the only emotion to linger after we die. Let's not forget despair and his best friend, hate. And since the cancer devoured Chinara, they'd both visited me several times to offer their sincere condolences.

It was Saltanat who spotted the headlights, growing larger, throwing the trees into light and shadows that spun away, parting before the black people carrier as it prowled the street.

The car pulled up outside the Kulturny, Lubashov snapping to attention. Regular customers obviously, or big tippers. The expected no-necks bailed out of the car, clutching those nasty little Micro Uzis, looking around for potential targets. After a moment, the front passenger door swung open and a giant emerged. He must must have been two metres from army boots to watch cap, so he would stand out in most places.

The Voice was a Western man, in his mid-forties, burly but not fat, shoulders threatening to split his jacket apart. His shaven head glowed almost white under the Kulturny's single light. Simply standing there, he exuded power, strength, ruthlessness. His mouth was wide, determined, like a shark hunting down its prey. His eyes were black coins in his face. We couldn't have chosen a worse foe.

The Voice looked around, head up as he'd scented our presence, reached for his mobile. I covered the iPhone with my hand, not wanting its glow to betray our position, sliding down in my seat, out of view.

'You're at the Kulturny?' I asked.

'Yes, where are you?'

'Never mind that, do you have the money? All thirty thousand dollars?'

'Yes,' the Voice answered, emotionless, deadly.

'Take ten thousand and go into the Kulturny. Alone. Walk down the stairs, go into the toilet, stuff the money behind the cistern. Don't look around, don't talk to anyone. Come back outside.'

'What the fuck?'

I broke the connection.

'What the hell are you doing?' Saltanat asked.

'Don't worry,' I said, worried. 'I have a plan.'

'A plan you're planning to share with me?' she asked. 'Or do I get killed so you can show how superior you are?'

'Saltanat,' I said, hissing the words into a whisper, 'trust me, I know what I'm doing.'

The indignant snort from the driver's seat didn't say a lot for my powers of persuasion. So instead I watched until the Voice emerged from the Kulturny. Lubashov walked towards him, maybe to ask if there was a problem, if he needed some help. Without breaking step, the Voice backhanded Lubashov across the face, once, twice, not looking to see if the young man fell or not. Lubashov stumbled back, then held up his hands in submission, a clear indication death by gangster wasn't on his agenda. The nearest no-neck nodded approvingly as the Voice clambered back into the car.

I switched the iPhone back on, and pressed redial.

'Drive to the junction of Ibraimova and Toktogul. There's a *shashlik* stand there, with a rubbish bin in front of it. Place ten thousand dollars in the bin, then drive one block down and wait outside Dordoi Plaza, the big supermarket. You'll be contacted there.'

'If you're fucking me around, I'll have your carcass dripping from a meat hook by tomorrow night,' the Voice said, menace sharp as a switchblade.

'We're both sensible men, businessmen, we take precautions to secure our interests. I just want your money, you want your secrets back. It's business, that's all.'

The people carrier drove off east towards Ibraimova, and as the headlights faded from view, Saltanat rounded on me.

'What the fuck are you doing, Akyl? You want to go and retrieve that ten thousand dollars? You're crazy.' Spitting out her words.

'I don't give a damn about the money,' I said. 'The first *alkashi* to stumble in there for a piss can have it, for all I care.'

'Then what are you doing?' she asked.

'The bleating of the sheep attracts the wolf,' I said.

'Very poetic. So?'

'Well, I'm just changing where the sheep's tethered,' I replied. And now we'd better get going.'

'Where?' Saltanat asked. 'Dordoi Plaza? They'll be waiting for us there.'

'I hope so,' I replied. 'That's why we're going to his house.'

Chapter 29

'It's like this,' I explained, as Saltanat drove us back towards Frunze. 'While he's chasing us all over Bishkek, we can do a spot of breaking and entering, try and get ourselves some evidence.'

'We've got the videos on the iPhone,' Saltanat said.

'Circumstantial. All we can prove is that someone who had the phone called him. And living where he does, the kind of money he must make, he's going to have enough clout to close down any questions. If he even gets asked any.'

I reached under my seat, found a bottle of water, swirled some around my mouth to clean out the fear, spat out of the window. On either side of the street, tree branches clutched at the moon. It wasn't the ideal night for burglary, but then it wasn't the ideal night for anything except being several hundred kilometres away.

'I think the film clips were used to find potential customers for the DVDs. A sales promotion kit, if you like. And you can bet the salesman isn't going to be found any time soon. Not with the back of his head intact. Dead men don't betray bosses. So no use looking for him.'

'What do you think we'll find at the house?' Saltanat asked.

'They've got to make these films somewhere. Somewhere private, secluded, soundproofed. You don't film this kind of stuff in your bedroom. And there's one other thing you need access to.'

'What's that?' Saltanat asked.

I drank some more of the water, feeling it hit my stomach, wondering if I was going to vomit.

'Raw material,' I said. 'Children.'

We parked a couple of blocks away from the American's house, and walked towards it, on the far side of the street, holding hands, just another couple taking a romantic midnight stroll. If you consider two people dressed entirely in black and clutching high-powered weapons romantic. All the trees had been painted white at their bases, as if the wind had managed to partially uproot them, so we weren't as invisible as I would have liked. We'd stuffed our ski masks into our pockets; no point in advertising. I kept an eye out for guards, for cameras, but saw nothing. Saltanat had linked her arm in mine, and I was very aware of the pressure of her breast against me. It didn't help my concentration.

Just before we reached the house, I turned to Saltanat, stroked her cheek, and then kissed her, her lips soft against mine. That way, she could stare over my shoulder and check out any possible trouble. Her hair smelt of cigarettes and shampoo, her mouth tasted of coffee. I just smelt of sweat and fear.

'All clear,' she whispered, her breath hot in my ear. 'But how do you plan we get through the gates? Levitate?'

I tried to ignore the effect of her body pressed against mine.

'If you look past the gates, there's some kind of access doorway. You don't want to fuss with opening the gates every time you want to go out for a litre of *moloko*, do you? There's always a weak spot, a way in – the trick is finding it.'

136

I put my hand in my jacket pocket, felt the cold metal of my lock picks.

'The Great Borubaev. With his magic, no lock is impregnable.'

'I'd prefer it if you had a key,' Saltanat murmured as we crossed the road, her head on my shoulder, looking up adoringly at me.

I turned to her and smiled, stroked her hair as we reached the narrow wooden door.

'I'll need you to keep watch; it shouldn't take me more than a minute.'

Five minutes later, I was still twisting the slender pick in the lock, sweat trickling into my eyes, as I failed to open the door. The longer I took, the greater the odds of being spotted, by the bad guys or some concerned citizen with the police on speed dial. Either way, we'd be in deep shit.

'Are you doing this deliberately?' Saltanat hissed, fury in her voice. I looked over at her, back to the wall, gun down by her side, head turning through a hundred-and-eighty-degree sweep.

'Of course,' I said. 'More exciting this way. Like a movie.'

'Shut up,' she suggested, taking the pick out of my fingers and pushing it into the lock.

Thirty seconds later, we were inside.

Chapter 30

'Ever thought of turning professional?' I whispered, as we stood in the shadow of the trees.

I put my arm around her shoulders, kissed her again, this time for real. I could feel her breasts against me, fear intensifying my desire. Saltanat abruptly pushed me away.

'Focus. Concentrate. This was your idea, remember?'

I looked around, across the perfectly manicured lawn towards the house. No lights, no sign of life. I'd banked on the Voice needing to keep the lowest of profiles, since even the Circle of Brothers wouldn't approve of his trade. No ostentatious guards carrying Kalashnikovs, no watchtowers, just the home of a wealthy recluse. The security he would have was probably travelling with him in the people carrier, waiting outside the Dordoi Plaza, impatient for my call. It seemed a shame to disappoint him.

'Sorry to keep you waiting,' I said. 'You could always grab a burger, you know. Good American cooking.'

'I want—' the Voice snarled.

'It's what I want,' I corrected. 'And what I want is for you to drive to the Russian Orthodox Church on Jibek Jolu and wait for me there. With the rest of the money, naturally.'

I ended the call and took a deep breath. The air tasted of grilled *shashlik* and fresh leaves, the scent of Bishkek in the spring. I pulled the ski mask back over my face, watching as Saltanat followed suit.

'He'll have left someone back at both the pickup points, to cover all the possibilities, and to recover his money,' I explained. 'So he's travelling light, on the back foot, his troops spread out.'

Saltanat nodded.

'Doesn't mean he won't have left anyone behind to guard the house,' she said.

'So we go quiet, in and out,' I answered.

We ran across the lawn and around the side of the house, guns ready. I'd once raided a drug den which turned out to be guarded by Dobermanns, mute because of their vocal cords being severed. That time, my gun had been holstered, which is how I got one of the more interesting scars on my left arm.

A side door led into a kitchen area. I tried the handle.

'Locked.'

'That's why you need me,' Saltanat said, using the pick. With the faintest click, the lock gave and we were inside. She produced a small flashlight from her pocket.

'What sort of detective are you?'

'The cautious, breathing kind,' I said, watching as she cast the light around the kitchen. The room smelt of damp and neglect, of faded spices and ancient meals. The house was silent, but I had the feeling it was simply lying in wait, that terrible things had happened here.

'What do you think?' she asked. I pointed to a wooden butcher's block as answer. Perhaps two dozen knives of differing sizes rested together on top, next to a large meat cleaver. The shallow curve in the surface of the block showed where hundreds, perhaps thousands of blows had whittled away at the wood. I picked up the largest knife, the sort butchers use, took a practice swing.

'An awful lot of knives for one house,' I said, and felt the hairs on my arms rise. Saltanat didn't answer, headed for the inner door. We walked along a narrow hallway, stairs rising at the left-hand side. A recess under the stairs held a small wooden door. I tried the handle. Unlocked.

'A cellar?' I said.

Saltanat looked at me. I knew we were both thinking the same awful thing.

'Only one way to find out,' I said, and opened the door.

I've always disliked basements, like the interrogation room at Sverdlovsky station, or the Kulturny. Too many opportunities for pain or punishment, too many chances to wound or maim in the darkness and the silence. I suspected this was going to be just such a place.

Saltanat used her torch to show the wooden treads of the stairs, leading away into darkness. I gripped the handrail and made my way down. Suddenly the room was filled with blazing light. I stumbled and almost fell. A bare light bulb dangled from the ceiling. I looked round at Saltanat, saw her finger on a switch.

'You want to give me a heart attack?' I snarled.

Saltanat shrugged, smiled.

'No windows, so why not use the light?' she asked, as the smile on her lips faltered and died. I looked round, saw why.

A large table stood in the middle of the room, thick leather straps attached to each leg. Two narrow runnels ran lengthways towards two rusting buckets. They were stained black, the same black that spattered the whitewashed brick walls. In one corner, a couple of professional lights stood next to a video camera and tripod. A shelf along one wall held various lenses and photographic equipment. This wasn't a basement, it was an inner chamber from hell.

The room stank of blood and sweat, semen and terror. I could imagine being dragged down the stairs, knowing this would be the end, struggling against remorseless hands that buckled straps to wrists and ankles. And then the sounds of the knives being sharpened.

'We need to get out of here,' Saltanat said, her face white with shock and nausea.

'Give me your phone,' I said, heard the tremor in my voice. 'We need pictures, otherwise they can clean this place up and we've got nothing.'

I spent ten minutes making a comprehensive record of the blood spatter on the walls, the straps stained from scraped and torn skin, wood darkened from tears and spit and vomit. I forced my mind to ignore the horror of what we had found. I needed evidence. And after that, I wanted revenge.

I looked at the lenses on the shelf. Nikon, expensive stuff, nothing but the best for child pornographers. Next to the chisels and scrapers and pliers, some of them bloodstained, there was a screw-top glass jar. I held it up to the light, gave a gasp of disgust, almost dropped it. Instead, I put it back on the shelf, wiped my fingers on my trousers. But I couldn't wipe away the sense of having touched something vile, corrupt and corrupting.

'Fingernails,' I said, my throat sour with bile, 'and fingers.'

I gave a final look around the room, saw a waist-high cupboard in the far corner. A heavy chain and padlock secured the two doors. I rapped a knuckle on the top, heard something move inside.

'Saltanat,' I whispered, my heart performing a manic tango. 'There's something inside. Something alive.'

I aimed my gun, as Saltanat used the picks on the padlock. After what seemed several days, she pulled the chain away and opened the cupboard.

A small boy, about eight years old, cowered away from us as far as he could, eyes wide with terror. His face was bruised, or dirty, and his clothes looked ragged. As he stared out at us, he started to cry, doing his best to stifle the sobs. Something about the rough haircut was familiar, then I realised. Otabek, from the orphanage.

Saltanat reached out a hand, and he flinched. She smiled, spoke softly, words of comfort, what a brave boy he was, we were the police, he was safe now. I put my gun away, smiled as best I could.

'We need to get out of here,' I said. 'We haven't bought ourselves that much time.'

She paid no notice, continued to reassure the boy, calming him, asking if he was hungry, if he was tired, would he like a nice bed of his own to sleep in.

Slowly, a kind of trust replaced the fear in his eyes, and he took Saltanat's hand. She helped him out of the cupboard, never taking her eyes off his face. As he stood up, I could see dark bruises on his arms and legs, and pity and anger made my head spin.

I stood at the bottom of the stairs, listening for a car engine, hoping we would be able to leave before then, hoping they'd return so I could kill them.

Saltanat crouched down, her face at a level with the boy's, speaking softly. He whispered something in her ear, and she turned to me, her face feral with anger.

'He says his name is Otabek,' she told me, with a voice of sharpened steel.

'*Privyat*, Otabek,' I said. 'Do you remember meeting me at the orphanage? Director Shokhumorov's friend?'

He stared at me, nodded briefly, a single jerk of the head, whispered something to Saltanat, never letting go of her hand as they walked towards the stairs. Her face was that of a goddess, vengeful and merciless, carved from stone. Only God could help whoever had done this.

'He wants to know,' Saltanat said, and at that moment, she was terrifying, 'are you going to kill the bad men?'

I nodded, never taking my eyes off the orphanage identity band on his left wrist.

Chapter 31

The three of us left the basement, went back outside, stopping only to snatch up a pile of papers on the kitchen table. I stuffed the papers into my jacket pocket, wondered about exploring the rest of the house, but we'd spent too much time in there as it was. And I had no stomach for whatever might be tucked away in the other rooms.

Saltanat locked the outer door as efficiently as she'd opened it, and we made our way back to the door in the wall. We were only just in time; as we reached the cover of the trees, the steel gates slowly swung open, powerful headlights illuminating the house and throwing long shadows across the wall.

'Don't move,' I whispered, but Saltanat had already dropped to the ground, her face turned away, pushing Otabek to the ground. The people carrier trundled through the gates, which closed behind it. Two no-necks got out and looked around. Basic security, but we were still trapped. I knew our best chance of remaining undetected was to stay still. It's movement that catches the eye of someone looking around, and it was dark enough under the trees for me to think we had a pretty good chance of getting away.

The Voice was still in the people carrier, and I saw a flash of light, as if someone was making a call on their mobile. Then the iPhone in my pocket started to ring.

The response of the bodyguards to the sound of the mobile

going off was immediate. Unable to locate the exact source of the ringing, they dropped to the ground, unslinging their guns from their shoulders. I knew we had maybe two or three seconds before the Uzis opened up, and emptied their magazines in our direction.

'Run for the door,' I told Saltanat, 'and leave it half open.'

She nodded and ran in a half-crouch, clutching Otabek's hand, hardly visible but enough to turn the bodyguards in our direction. I scuttled to the cover of the nearest tree, not very dignified, but a lot better than being perforated. I looked down the barrel of my gun towards the people carrier, and started firing. I didn't aim for any particular target, but with any luck the heavy calibre bullets slamming into the car would buy us a few seconds.

Almost at once, the Uzis began their horrible staccato cough, like watch dogs with bronchitis, and fragments of brick from the wall behind me spattered the back of my jacket and neck. But in their surprise they were aiming high, and the only casualty was the tree in front of me. That couldn't last though, and I had to move.

I rolled over, cursing as the stitches in my shoulder tore. There was a pause and relative silence as the Uzis ran out of bullets, and I took advantage by scrambling through the door and away from my new role as target practice.

Saltanat was driving towards me, headlights rising and falling as she rode up onto the pavement. I dived towards the passenger door and hauled myself in as the Uzis started up again. I was out of bullets, and Saltanat thrust her Makarov into my hand. I emptied the clip through the open doorway and then we were halfway down the road.

I looked back to see if the people carrier was following us, but a quick left then a ferocious right hid the house from view. Saltanat swerved into a narrow alleyway and a half-skid, sending me slamming into the windscreen. Two more sharp corners and then we were running parallel to Chui Prospekt.

I sat back and fastened my seat belt. In the side mirror, I could see the dark smudge of a bruise already beginning to form on my forehead. Together with the blood ruining my jacket, I looked like shit. Saltanat was as cool and collected as ever, though her hand gave the slightest of tremors as she changed gears.

Finally we parked by the side of the Metro Bar.

'I want a drink,' Saltanat said, 'and you're coming with me.'

We reloaded our guns, walked into the bar arm in arm, an innocent couple out for an evening stroll with their son.

The Metro used to be a puppet theatre a long time ago, the high ceiling and elaborate glass-panelled bar a testimony to more affluent days. The foreigners who came here when it was known as the American Bar have mainly gone home to count their tax-free earnings, leaving only a few eccentrics who are on the run either from their country's police or embittered ex-wives.

Saltanat disappeared to the toilets downstairs with Otabek, and I waited until they emerged, his face now clean but still scared and distrustful. A pretty Kyrgyz waitress with bleach-blonde hair and a crop top showing her navel ring came over to serve us.

'What would you like to drink, Otabek?' Saltanat prompted. 'Moloko? You like pizza?'

The boy said nothing, but nodded, never letting go of Saltanat's hand. Saltanat ordered milk, a Baltika Nine, the strong stuff, for herself, and pizza. I asked for coffee. When it came, it was lukewarm. We're really much better at making *chai*.

Otabek sipped at his milk, eyes wary, saying nothing.

'Close call,' I said, stirring my coffee, the spoon rattling against the cup as my hands shook. Saltanat said nothing, rummaging through her bag for a pack of cigarettes. She lit up, snorted smoke through her nose, watching as it dissolved into nothing. Her eyes looked across the bar, but I sensed she saw nothing but muzzle flashes, heard nothing but gunfire that clattered like pebbles on a tin roof. And beyond that, a vision of the Voice, sprawled on the gravel, executed with a bullet in the back of his head.

'You'll need to stitch me up again,' I said. 'Sorry.'

Saltanat nodded, showing as little surprise as if I'd asked her directions to the bus station. I reached into my jacket to find my own cigarettes, but instead found myself holding the papers I'd liberated from the house.

They were crumpled and spotted in places with blood I sincerely hoped was mine, but still legible. I spread them out and started to read. I pushed the top page towards Saltanat, but she ignored it, continuing to stare out at her recent brush with mortality.

It looked like a bank statement, but in English, so all I could understand were the figures. Pretty impressive numbers, almost four million in some unstated currency. Great if it's in dollars, even better in pounds, not to be sniffed at even in *som*.

'You wouldn't know what this means, would you?' I asked Saltanat. She broke away from her reverie just long enough to scan the top page.

'It's a bank statement, Akyl, even you must have seen one before,' she said.

'Never with so many noughts in it,' I replied. 'Do you know what currency it's in?'

'Euros, most likely, since it's from a Spanish bank,' she said. 'What does it matter? It's not like you have the ATM card to go with it.'

'No,' I said, annoyed by the sarcasm, 'but there's a clue right there, at the top of the page.'

Saltanat looked at it, then over at me, and smiled.

'You must be a detective.'

'It's a name. It's just a shame I can't read it, with it not being in Cyrillic. English was never my strong point at school, so I never learnt the letters.'

'Did your mother never tell you to study hard?'

I gave a bitter smile, and lit another cigarette, stirred the lumps in my coffee into submission.

'Not when she was away working in Siberia. And no one at the orphanage gave me much encouragement either.'

Saltanat gave me an appraising look, sensing the pain, the resentment I carry with me like a hunchback with his bent spine. I'd like to think I'm not bitter about some of the cards I've been handed out. But that doesn't mean I don't have the scars. Only one person ever gave me the support I'd wanted, needed, and she was dead and buried in a grave I'd helped dig. There's no statute of limitations when it comes to mourning and missing someone you loved, and still love. And if there's one thing I've discovered, it's that sorrow never leaves you.

'I was a good girl, top of the class, I know my letters,' she said.

'And?'

'The name of the account holder?'

'Yes.'

Saltanat studied the letter again, taking her time, keen to make the most of my impatience.

'The very rich gentleman is called Graves. Mr Morton Graves.'

I shrugged.

'Never heard of him,' I said.

Saltanat tapped the bank statement.

'I have,' she said, spacing her words for extra effect. 'And he's very rich. Very powerful. And very dangerous.'

I had no answer to that, and no idea what to do next.

Chapter 32

I looked over at Otabek, who was concentrating on his pizza.

'So?' I said, once again unsure if Saltanat shared everything she knew, or if I was just a useful sidekick. 'You know about this all-powerful pervert?'

'Let me tell you about Morton Graves,' Saltanat said, 'and then you'll have some idea what we're up against.'

She screwed up the bank statement and placed it in the ashtray in front of us, using her lighter to set fire to one corner. I watched as the paper started to char, smoulder then burn, the flame eating the numbers, until black ash remained. Otabek stared at the flames, drank the rest of his milk, taking huge gulps. The pizza had vanished, so I guessed feeding him hadn't been a priority for Morton Graves.

Saltanat ground the ashes into powder, and looked across at me.

'We don't want to be caught with any evidence of breaking and entering, do we? And it's not as if having a bank account is illegal.'

'Even a rich man's bank account?'

'Especially one of those,' Saltanat replied.

'So who is this man?'

Saltanat sipped at her beer, lit another cigarette, offered me her pack. For the ten thousandth time, I decided I was going to give up and shook my head.

'Morton Graves is an American citizen, although he hasn't

lived in the States for over twenty years. He's been here in Bishkek for the last ten years, and his visa application describes him as a "businessman and entrepreneur".'

'And you know this, how?' I asked.

Saltanat looked at me with the pitying glance she saved for my more foolish questions.

'Telepathy? Astrology? Educated guesses? If your ministry had any more leaks, you'd run out of buckets. And we like to keep a friendly eye on our neighbours.'

I nodded. Central Asia isn't noted for principles before payments, and most upright citizens would dip their beaks if it meant a few *som* in their pockets.

'He has businesses here?'

'And Almaty, Tashkent, even Dushanbe; he's a big player in the region. He's a major investor in telecoms, cotton in Kazakhstan, a private bank in Uzbekistan, hotels, supermarkets, a couple of restaurants, precious metals, anything that wets his palm.'

'Drugs? Heroin, *krokodil*?'

Saltanat shrugged, took another mouthful of Baltika, watching the bubbles simmer in the glass, tracing the condensation with a single scarlet-tipped finger.

'Rumours, but no one's ever proved anything. And if he's connected to the drug trade, then it would have to be with the consent of the Circle of Brothers. Pay-offs, a quiet word in the right ear at the right time.'

After the collapse of the Soviet Union, a lot of the criminal gangs in the former 'stans' grouped together in a loose collective called the Brothers' Circle. Each of the countries has their own crime boss sitting at the table with their foreign counterparts, doling out territories, alliances, joint operations in information, not just in Central Asia but in Europe, Africa, Latin America and the Middle East, the UAE in particular. Drugs are the big money-spinner, but they branch out into robbery, prostitution, counterfeiting, smuggling, anything else that can make money and isn't legal. Devotion is absolute: break the rules and the only question is just how long it will take you to die, and how painfully. Even the Russian gangs admit to being lightweight in comparison.

The Circle's possible involvement wasn't the best news I'd ever heard, especially since I'd been involved in the assassination of Maksat Aydaraliev, the local crime boss in Bishkek. If Graves was linked to the Circle, he probably wasn't a very nice man.

I looked over at Saltanat, felt the weight of the iPhone in my pocket, the weight of its contents heavy on my conscience.

'I suppose Tynaliev knows who he is,' I said. 'Maybe even does business with him?'

'You think you're being set up by him?' Saltanat asked.

Now it was my turn to shrug. I thought about the films I'd seen, gaping mouths with screams torn out of their throats, the eyes filled with dread, knowing there was no help or hope left. I saw how the knives filleted slices of flesh, rivulets of blood spilling over the chains and leather straps that held the children down. The weeping, the pleading, and then, finally, resignation, eyes filming over as death approached.

'It doesn't matter. Only one thing does.'

I wasn't surprised at the anger in my voice. I could see the masked man smiling, enjoying the degradation, the terror, the despair. The glint of camera lights off the blade, and then the blood.

'I want the bastard who did all this. Not to send him to court so he can buy his way out. Not to a comfortable cell with three meals delivered a day.'

I paused, wondered about another cigarette, decided against it. I stood up, wincing at the pain in my shoulder. Somehow that didn't seem important. In fact nothing seemed important, except for one thing.

'I want him under the ground. And I want to be the one who puts him there.'

'How are you going to do that?' Saltanat asked. 'He's got connections from here to Moscow, maybe even further.'

'First of all, I'm going to put a bit of stick about, give our Mr Graves something to worry about. Push a few buttons, stir the shit, watch what happens.'

I took the iPhone out of my pocket, dialled a now-familiar number.

'He'll kill you,' Saltanat warned.

'Not if I kill him first,' I said, rewarding her with a smile that stopped somewhere south of my cheekbones.

The phone rang, and was answered.

'I imagine that so far this evening has cost you some time,' I said, 'trouble, and perhaps even a little expense.'

There was only silence at the other end of the phone. The silence when the wolves are about to attack the sheep, when the farmer's finger tenses on the trigger.

'We've both learnt something tonight. You've learnt I'm not in this for the money, and I'm not an amateur.'

'And what have you learnt?' The Voice, dark, menacing, storm clouds looming over the Tien Shan mountains.

'I've learnt who you are, Mr Graves. Where you are.'

I paused for effect. Saltanat stared at me, perhaps wondering if I'd lost my senses.

'And most worrying for you, what you are.'

And I listened as the phone went dead.

Chapter 33

I held up the phone, then passed it to Saltanat.

'Can we leave this with your friend, Rustam?' I asked. 'There isn't anyone I can trust, not even Usupov.'

Saltanat thought about it, then nodded.

'Rustam doesn't say much, but if he likes you, he'll always be there for you. If he thought Graves had anything to do with the heroin that killed Anastasia, he'd go up there with one of his boning knives and gut the American himself.'

I wondered what it would be like to lose a daughter. All the hopes and ambitions you'd cherished for her, memories of those first staggering steps, the school prizes, the graduation ceremony. And the events you'd never see, the wedding, your first grandchild, the eternal circle starting again. Worse than losing your wife to cancer? Loss is loss, and it comes to live with us all.

Saltanat touched me on my arm and I came back from my reverie.

'Let's get back to the hotel, and I can stitch your shoulder up again,' she said, and I was touched by a tenderness I heard in her voice.

I placed my hand on hers, the slender fingers warm and alive against mine. I wanted to tell her I cared for her. But the words wouldn't come. So instead we each took one of Otabek's hands, and with him secure between us, walked out into the night.

As before, we parked inside the hotel grounds, the high steel gates hiding us from view. Carrying our bags, Rustam led us through the kitchen and up a flight of narrow stairs to the first floor. Without saying a word, he nodded as Saltanat explained about Otabek. Rustam pocketed the iPhone, crouched down so as not to frighten the boy, said there was a special bedroom with lots of toys for brave boys. Otabek looked at Saltanat for reassurance, worry clear in his eyes. She nodded and took his hand. Rustam handed me a key to one of the rooms, and then the three of them climbed up the next flight of stairs.

The room was fairly basic, twin beds set against one wall, a small bathroom, a wardrobe big enough for one person's clothes. I waited until Saltanat returned, closing the curtains, pushing the night away, a circle of light from the bedside lamp soft in the darkness.

'Poor child,' she said. 'He was asleep in seconds. He must have been terrified.'

'Maybe when all this is over,' I said, the words thick in my mouth, 'we can get him some help. See he doesn't have to go back to the orphanage.'

I wondered if Saltanat guessed the thought in my mind; a ready-made family created out of terror and love. Regaining what I had once lost and never thought to get again.

'You should shower,' she said, 'and clean your shoulder before it gets infected.'

I started to peel off my clothes, wincing as the dried blood on my shirt tore at my skin, and the wound started to bleed once more. I looked in the mirror, saw a face as worn and creased as my clothes. Stains like black eyes on my face matched the bruise on my forehead, weariness deep in the lines around my mouth. Maybe I was coming to my end, but right then I was too tired to care.

The hot water in the shower did a little to wake me up; it's never easy to feel good in clothes you've been wearing for three days. I was letting the water wash over my shoulder when I sensed movement behind me.

Saltanat was naked, dark nipples erect, her hair pinned up to avoid getting wet. She took the soap from my hand and started to wash my back. I began to turn but she put her hand on my good shoulder, to stop me. She rinsed the soap off my back, sliding her hands across, down, and then around my waist. I could feel the weight of her breasts against my back, small and firm, her thighs against mine, and I felt my heart surge.

'This is going to hurt, Akyl,' she said, washing my shoulder, fingers probing the wound. 'You really need to get this stitched properly, but I suppose going to a hospital isn't really very practical. How about your friend Usupov?'

'Have you seen the stitches he puts in corpses?' I said, wincing as she cleaned my shoulder. 'You'd swear he does it with his eyes shut. Mind you, they don't ever complain.'

I shut my eyes and gave myself up to the simple sensation of hot water, smooth skin, hands stroking my waist. Saltanat's fingers barely grazed my hips, light as cobwebs, circling, moving down towards my thighs. I heard a groan, almost silent as if from a great distance, and wasn't sure whether it came from her or me. And then, shockingly, I remembered a winter afternoon, in the apartment where Chinara and I lived when we were first married, a dismal studio down in the concrete depths of the tower blocks in Alamedin.

The building's heating had broken down, so we spent the

entire day in bed, getting up only to run to make *chai*, our breath white in the bitter cold. Her long hair spread out on the pillow, her eyes closed, smiling with pleasure and contentment as we kissed. In our first bed, where we conceived the child that was never to be born, the centre of our universe on that distant endless day. And I remembered another bed, the final one, where the morphine took her from me, piecemeal. Where Chinara had sometimes groaned in her sleep, waiting for nothing more than the ending of pain. An ending I gave her, with my hands and an embroidered cushion.

I felt Saltanat's hands take hold of me.

'What's wrong?' she asked.

'Nothing,' I lied, despite the evidence. I wondered what I could say. I could hear the hesitation in her voice, knew that even ice maidens have fears, insecurities. As do Murder Squad inspectors.

'I'm just tired, I've got a shoulder that looks like it's been chewed by wolves, an entire police force looking for me, and I've been to Jalalabad and back without any sleep.'

I sensed her pull away from me, felt a wave of guilt mingled with irritation.

'I'm also not twenty-one any more,' I added, just to reinforce an already obvious conclusion.

I looked round to see her already wrapped in a towel. Her face was set, stubborn.

'I'm aware of that, Inspector,' Saltanat said, her words clipped and impersonal, spat out like bullets. 'And I may not be twenty-one either, if you ever decide that you are.'

She stalked out of the bathroom and shut the door, in the way a braver man than me might call angry. I turned off the water and tried to dry myself on the handkerchief-sized towel Saltanat had been kind enough to leave for me. For the ten thousandth time in my adult life, I realised I knew nothing about women.

I waited until it was likely that Saltanat was dressed, aware no woman likes being seen half-naked while in the middle of a quarrel. I emerged to see her in yet another all-black outfit, reloading her Makarov.

'I'm sorry,' I said, and I was. 'I'm confused, happy you're here, worried I'm putting you in danger.'

It wasn't even close to the whole truth, but when has that ever helped explain things? Memories can betray the present just as easily as providing something to cling onto.

Saltanat sat back on the bed, lit a cigarette and watched as I pulled on my socks. I felt less than graceful, but at least she wasn't pointing a gun at me. The way she cocked her head as she looked at me said I was partially forgiven, but she wasn't going to say so right away.

'Sit down and I'll stitch that shoulder. Again,' she said. It didn't hurt any less than the last time, which surprised me, since she'd already made the holes. Perhaps she took a little extra time to pull the thread tight. But I knew better than to complain.

'You've got a plan, I hope,' she said, helping me button my shirt.

'Let's look at the situation,' I replied, meaning I didn't. I went through the motions of lighting a cigarette to buy myself a little time.

Saltanat raised an eyebrow, to show she was ready and waiting.

'Our strength lies in what Graves doesn't know. Right? If

he knew there were just the two of us, a soon to be ex-cop and a member of the Uzbek security services, he'd just laugh. He can stomp us out whenever he wants; nobody is going to stop him or protect us. He puts the word on the street, and one spring morning, some *govnosos* we've never seen before walks up and puts three .22s in the back of our heads.'

I drew deeply on the cigarette, feeling the nicotine hit me hard.

'Nothing we can do about that. But if he thinks he's up against a rival gang, then we have a chance. Are we trying to take over his heroin routes? Or muscle into the bars and clubs he owns? Or maybe we just want a nice healthy pay-off? We're using the snuff films as our leverage.'

I paused, thinking I sounded quite plausible, even to myself.

'The point is, he's confused. He doesn't know where the attack is coming from, or why. He's on the defensive. Any of his allies might be his enemy, and he doesn't know it. Who can he trust, who might betray him?'

'That's all very well,' Saltanat interrupted, 'but what are *we* going to do?'

'When you don't know what to do next, you get a very big stick, whack it everywhere, see what emerges from the shit you've caused.'

I reached for my bag, rummaged through it until I found what I wanted.

'Time to give our friend a very big whack.'

Saltanat looked scornful.

'And how do you propose to do that?'

'With one of these,' I said, then showed her the hand grenade nestling snugly in my hand.

Chapter 34

I'd pretty much passed out on the twin bed nearest the door, my Yarygin on the bedside table, a chair under the door handle. Saltanat took the other bed, and when I woke up, went into the bathroom to get dressed. Still not forgiven, then.

Breakfast was hot meat *samsi* at the hotel bar, served by Rustam with his usual charm and conversation. Otabek was still upstairs, asleep. Ten minutes later, we were driving back into the centre of the city, roads crowded with traffic, pavements dense with people on their way to work. A blue cloudless sky proclaimed everything was fine, harmless. Saltanat drove, while I cradled the grenade in my lap. A bottle of vodka weighed heavy and dangerous in my jacket pocket.

'Where did you get the *limonka*?' she asked, using the nickname that comes from the grenade's lemon shape.

'Back when I was still a lowly uniformed police officer, I arrested a dealer with a weight of *travka* and a couple of these. The weed made it as far as the station evidence custody room, but I thought it might be dangerous to store explosives down there. And more dangerous once they found their way back onto the street. Custody officers don't get paid a fortune. So I kept them.'

'Do they work?'

'Well, you can't really do a test firing. I hope so. But it

doesn't have to make a big bang to let Graves know we're serious. Like the Makarov bullet you once gave me. It's the thought that counts.'

'While you're playing at being a hero of the Great Patriotic War, I'm going to take Otabek to my embassy. I have a colleague, Elmira, who'll make sure he's safe until we've got this sorted out, one way or another.'

I nodded agreement. The kid deserved a lot better than life had dealt him so far. And I couldn't help remembering the way he'd looked when we went back to Rustam's hotel, any spirit beaten out of him, like a sheep to a ritual slaughter.

We were close to the house, so we pulled over. It didn't make sense for the Lexus to be spotted, and the number plate noted. We arranged to meet at the far side of Ala-Too Square, and Saltanat drove off. I pulled an ornate black and white felt *kalpak* hat over my ears, turned the collar of my jacket up, did my best to transform myself into one of the down-at-heel men with no job or purpose that wander around every city. It wasn't hard.

I wondered if I'd see Saltanat again, then stripped my mind of all irrelevancies and crossed the road. The concrete walls were just as high as I remembered, and the broken glass on top still as evil-looking. The metal gates were shut, and no sound of life from the house inside. There would be guards on the lookout, so I dawdled along, bottle of vodka in hand, faltering a little, just another *alkash* who drank his breakfast.

I drew level with the gates, pulled the pin on the grenade, tossed it over the gates. Nothing fancy, no movie-style dramatics, the way you might throw an empty cigarette packet aside. I lurched forward as if I'd caught my shoe on the edge of an uneven pavement, caught my balance the way drunks do, walked on.

One, two, three, four . . .

The explosion wasn't particularly loud and it didn't blow open the gates. But it was noisy enough, and I heard shrapnel clatter and bang against the metal. A thin smudge of blue-black smoke trickled uncertainly over the gate, and I heard shouting and curses. From the sound of it, I'd managed to cause some major damage to the bodywork of the car, maybe even to a no-neck or two.

I turned the corner, crossed over the street and up an unpaved alleyway, doubled back towards Chui Prospekt. I put the vodka down on the ground, a present for the next drunk who woke with a thirst and wondered where his next glass was waiting.

'How did you get on?' Saltanat asked, an hour later. I'd taken off the *kalpak*, adjusted my collar, but as I looked in the rear-view mirror, a no-hoper still stared back out at me. I gave myself a jovial wink I was very far from feeling, grinned at her.

'I imagine the car took the worst of the blast,' I said. 'It's a start, but we can't sit here chattering. Places to go, people to fuck up.' And then I told her to drive east, towards the bus station.

On the way, Saltanat explained she'd handed Otabek over to Elmira, a junior colleague at the embassy. She was right in thinking Otabek would probably be frightened of strange men.

'Right now, he's safe. Perhaps the best thing is if I organise an Uzbek passport, get him out of the country and away from Graves. What do you think?'

I nodded; it was a plan, and I couldn't think of a better one.

After half an hour, the bus station loomed ahead, depressing in its ugliness. Most cities put their public transport in the less expensive parts of town, and Bishkek is no exception; our bus station is where lots of minivans and *marshrutki* congregate, as well as shipping containers, clustered together as if shipwrecked on the shore of a long-dried-up sea. Saltanat had made a couple of calls while waiting for me, bought some bits and pieces I'd asked her to get.

We parked near a container with the initials MG stencilled in Cyrillic on the sides and doors. I took the five-litre can of petrol Saltanat had bought, together with a couple of towels, and sauntered over towards the container. As I reached it, as I'd expected, a guard turned the corner and glared at me. Cheap trainers, dirty jeans and a greasy leather jacket straight out of Osh bazaar. But the Makarov in his hand was the real thing.

'What the fuck do you want?' he asked, not unreasonably, I thought.

'Message for Mr Graves,' I said, holding my hands wide to show I posed no threat. 'It's about this can.'

'Yes?' he said, and then recognition made his jaw drop. I'd last seen him watching us drive away from Jalalabad, and I was willing to bet his Makarov had already fired at us once before.

He grunted as I swung the petrol can in a wide arc into his face. The trick is to aim behind the person you want to hit, so the can is travelling with maximum impact when it hits. To say the blow caught him by surprise was an understatement. There was a sound like a meat hammer pulverising a juicy steak, and the man's jaw moved about fifteen degrees up and out of true. His eyes crossed, rolled up in his head, then he fell backwards, giving himself a second concussion as he slammed against the side of the container. I liberated his Makarov, poured some of the petrol onto one of the towels. I stuffed it under the container, near the bricks that supported it from the ground, poured the remainder of the petrol into one of the ventilation grilles. I threw the can away, lit a match to the corner of the remaining towel. Once it was fairly alight, I threw it to join its cousin under the container. The petrol caught, and I made my way back to the car.

'What about him?' Saltanat asked, pointing to the unconscious guard, his jacket already beginning to smoulder.

'What about him?' I asked, giving her the hard stare. 'He might be one of the guys in the videos. Maybe the one who fucks the little girls. Or truncheons the boys into a pulp. He'll wake up. Or not. I don't give a fuck about him.'

She gave me a look I couldn't fathom. Maybe impressed, maybe worried. She got out of the car, pulled the thug away from the side of the container.

'I'll tell you who he is,' I said. 'And then maybe you'll push him into the flames yourself.'

'You know him?'

'Knew him. At the orphanage when I was a kid. You remember I told you about Aleksey Zhenbekov? The bully who beat up the little ones?'

'This is him?'

'A lot older, a lot uglier, a whole lot more dangerous. He was the one who shot at us in Jalalabad.'

Saltanat thought about it for a few seconds.

'How did he know where we were?' she asked.

'A leak in Tynaliev's staff? Or maybe Tynaliev himself. The high-ups will always fuck you one way or another. We're little people, pawns, of no importance. But now it's my turn to fuck someone up.'

'So no more Mr Nice Guy, Upholder of Law and Order?' Saltanat said, turning the ignition and steering the car back towards the market.

'He's on vacation. Maybe permanently,' I said, glaring out of the window. The sky had become jammed with rain clouds, black and oppressive.

Chapter 35

'Who are you? And what do you want?'

The Voice. Snarling, filled with anger, incredulity that anyone should dare to challenge him.

'You don't need to know. What do we want? The folding stuff, of course.'

'You're not Circle, I know that. They've all filled their beaks from me.'

I laughed, making the sneer evident. Nothing annoys a *pakhan*, a big man, more than thinking someone would have the temerity to fuck them over, think they could get away with it. The big man becomes angry, and that means reckless. Then you have him.

'Times change. People get hungry, prices go up.'

'Not when I make a deal.'

'Who said you'd made a deal with us?' I asked.

Silence on the other end of the phone.

'Think about what you've got. Think about how much you're prepared to lose. Not just containers stuffed with dodgy goods, but staff, bodyguards. Once they think you're losing control, they're out the door and you're all alone. Keeping that has to be worth something, don't you think? So think; we'll be in touch.'

Saltanat looked across at me as I switched off the phone. It was one of a dozen pay-as-you-go mobiles I'd bought at an internet café near the railway station, onto which I'd copied

Graves's number. I didn't know if Graves had the muscle to get them tracked, but I've never been a one for unnecessary risks. I could see she wasn't happy. The hotel room had never seemed more cramped.

'So what exactly is your master plan?' she asked, her voice like a steel bar hitting a table. 'I'm assuming – hoping – you've got one?'

'This Graves; he's got businesses, restaurants, shops, and not a big enough crew to protect them all. Petrol bombs, drive-bys, we can keep him hopping from foot to foot, until he doesn't have the muscle or money to keep himself protected.'

I slapped my hands together, the way you do when you squash a fly.

Saltanat shook her head in disbelief.

'You want to start a war? A one-man war, I might add, because I'm not going to take part in it,' she said.

I looked at her, shrugged as if to say it was no concern of mine.

'I thought Gurminj was your friend. My mistake, I guess,' I said. 'The identity band on the kid's wrist links Gurminj's killers with the rapes and murders. All we have to do is hunt them down.'

'I know you can be a bastard, Akyl,' she said, and I heard both anger and pity in her voice, 'but I never thought you'd be a stupid one.'

She lit a cigarette, blew smoke at the ceiling.

'This isn't about revenge for Gurminj. Or justice for all those dead children. This is about you wanting to die, taking as many of the bad guys with you as you can.'

'You're being ridiculous,' I said. 'Why would I want to die?'

She stubbed her half-smoked cigarette out, jabbed her finger at me.

'Because your wife is dead and you're not. Because your friend died and you couldn't protect him. Because of tortured and murdered children, and you can't give them justice. Because you can't work out whether you want to fuck me or leave me. Because you think you've failed and there's nothing left.'

All of this delivered in a flat, impersonal tone, the more wounding because of it.

There was nothing I could say.

I stared at my reflection in the mirror above the small desk. Eyes empty as bruises on a corpse's face. Was there any way back to feeling anything other than despair and anger?

'You've struck at him three times now. He's not stupid. You think he won't be waiting for you to pull another hit? You'll walk into a trap, and you won't ever know what's hit you when someone gets a .22 to whisper in your ear.'

'What do you suggest, Saltanat? I'm the one on the run from the police,' I said, 'the one with nowhere to go. You want to drive me over to Sverdlovsky so I can hand myself in?'

'You really want my advice?' she asked. 'Or would that just be the ideal excuse to storm out and get yourself blown away?'

I looked at Saltanat, drawn in by her anger, her crystal-hard intelligence. The sudden thought of living without her was almost intolerable, like having a limb amputated without anaesthetic. And, as always, I wondered if there was anything she could find to enjoy in a man like me.

I sighed, nodded, offered a cigarette, lit hers and mine.

'I rely on you,' I said, 'more than I should.'

If I was expecting her to melt into my arms, I was mistaken. She squinted at me through the smoke that coiled between us, her eyes determined, suspicious.

'I don't need bullshit, Akyl,' she said. 'I don't need lies. Not from anyone. And especially not from you.'

She reached over, stroked my cheek in the gesture of a friend rather than a lover, took her hand away, sat upright on the bed.

'This is what we're going to do,' she said, 'and listen to me. Otherwise, you're on your own.'

Chapter 36

For the next half-hour, I listened while Saltanat outlined her plan. It made sense as far as it went; she countered every objection, answered every question. When she finished, I looked at her, not pretending to hide my admiration.

'Pretty impressive,' I said.

She gave the smile that had always captivated me.

'It's the obvious course of action. Or it would be if you weren't so keen on getting shot.'

I nodded, as if agreeing with her. But I also wanted to put Graves in the ground, preferably after an unhealthy dosage of pain and blood.

'When do you want to get started?' I asked.

'Let's go and see the adoption people. Who knows, they might even think we'd make wonderful parents,' she said and smiled as if scenting prey.

The ministry building where the bureaucrats in charge of adoptions huddle is yet another tribute to the glories of Soviet architecture. A depressing stained fake-marble entrance conceals a rarely working lift that judders to a halt at floors hiding endless narrow corridors. Every second light bulb is missing or burnt out, and those that work don't dispel the gloom. A shoulder-height smear of dirt reveals where people stand in line for hours, leaning against the wall before closed doors that rarely open. The building smells, unaccountably, of smoked fish, old sweat and drains. As a place supposed to offer new hope and fresh beginnings, it doesn't show any enthusiasm for the task.

I followed Saltanat until she stopped at a door rather less battered than the others we'd passed. A piece of paper taped to the door read *K. Sakataev, Director*. Saltanat rapped sharply, and opened the door. An overweight silver-haired man sat behind a conspicuously bare desk, looking up in outrage as we strode in. Before he could open his mouth to speak, Saltanat flashed a credentials wallet, stuffing it back in her bag before he could read what it said.

'Director Sakataev?' she said, her voice hard with authority. 'Irina Shaikova, Senior Investigator for Child Welfare. This gentleman is Inspector Akyl Borubaev of Bishkek Murder Squad.'

I handed Sakataev my credentials, hoping he wouldn't know I was on the run from my colleagues. The red-faced man turned white, wondering what crime of his we'd discovered. Even the innocent feel uneasy when two policemen arrive to question them. And in this city, there aren't many innocents.

'I don't know what—' Sakataev started to stutter, then shut up when Saltanat held up her hand.

'This isn't about you, Director. At least, not yet,' she threatened. I looked at Sakataev, wondered if he was in the early throes of a heart attack.

'Just a few questions, that's all. For the moment,' I said, and gave my least pleasant smile as I did so.

'Naturally, of course, if I can help in any way,' Sakataev said, eagerness to please evident.

'As you know, families are the first to suffer during periods of, shall we say, instability? Which all too often leads to families breaking up, and the children being housed in orphanages,' Saltanat said.

Sakataev nodded, looking relieved that the conversation wasn't aimed at any scam he might be undertaking.

'When the moratorium on foreigners adopting children was lifted back in 2011, my post was created to protect our children from the risk of trafficking, sex abuse, or organ sales,' Saltanat continued. 'I'm sure you agree this was the right policy.'

'I ensure very strict vetting of all foreigners who apply to adopt,' Sakataev said, 'and of foreign agencies, naturally.'

Saltanat nodded her approval. I simply folded my arms, leant against the wall, gave Sakataev the benefit of a policeman's hard stare.

'The system works very well,' Saltanat confided, 'but human nature being what it is, and with foreigners willing to pay huge amounts, there's always a risk that some under-the-counter deal goes through.'

Sakataev replaced his look of fear with one of sorrow; I didn't like either one, or the way he kept sneaking a look at Saltanat's breasts.

'I can assure you no one in my department would ever consider such a thing.'

'However, you understand we have to investigate any cases reported to us,' Saltanat said. I kept my mouth shut, and simply stared at Sakataev a little harder.

'The inspector here has a personal commitment to such cases, and doesn't leave any aspect unexamined.'

Sakataev opened his desk drawer and started to rummage around. The Yarygin was in my hand at once, not pointed at him exactly, but not in the opposite direction either.

'Slowly, *tovarich*, slowly,' I said. 'Let's not make any mistakes we might regret.'

His look of sorrow turned into one of terror, the way a rain cloud suddenly scuds over the Tien Shan mountains. His hand shook as he took out a bottle of vodka and three small glasses.

'I thought we might . . .' he started, and then fell silent.

I replaced my gun, and shook my head.

'Thank you, but no, Director,' Saltanat said. 'But please, if you feel you must have a drink, then by all means go ahead.'

Sakataev poured himself a more than generous shot, threw it back, spluttered, and waited for the alcohol to hit.

'I don't normally make a practice of this,' he said, voice hoarse from the vodka.

I raised an eyebrow, the cynical, suspicious cop who disbelieves everything he's told on principle. Sakataev noticed, and poured himself another, smaller drink. I walked over, looked through the open drawer, knowing he wouldn't have the courage to object. There was the usual detritus of pencil stubs, paperclips crusted with earwax, a few scribbled notes with first names and phone numbers. I also noticed a set of car keys, on a BMW fob. A framed photograph showed Sakataev posing proudly beside his car in front of an elegant *dacha*.

'Let me tell you what I'm looking for, Mr Director,' I said, injecting a tone of menace into my voice. 'A list of the foreign adoption agencies here in Bishkek, and the names of your contacts in each one.'

'Of course, they're all very reputable, vetted by the ministry,' he said. 'That won't be a problem.'

'I'm not so sure about that,' I said. 'What about the ones

who help you afford a BMW and your lovely *dacha*? The ones who work off the books, pockets stuffed with more money than you've ever earned in your life.'

To reinforce my point, I let my hand fall against the Yarygin's butt.

'I don't know what you're talking about,' Sakataev mumbled, but his heart wasn't in it. 'I've done nothing wrong.'

'Director, we're not accusing you of anything,' Saltanat said. 'But if the inspector here doesn't get the answers he wants, he can become rather emotional. And while you're discovering just how much a police interrogation can hurt, I'll be making an anonymous call to the authorities.'

Saltanat paused, lit a cigarette, the smoke doing nothing to mask the stink of sweat and fear in the room. Her smile, when it came, was no sweeter than mine, and twice as dangerous.

'After I make that call, once the people you deal with hear about it, I don't think you'll be working with them any more.'

She paused, ground the cigarette out on the fake leather desktop.

'I wonder who'll inherit the *dacha*.'

Chapter 37

'You're really not going to blow the whistle on that shithead?'
I asked. We were driving back to the hotel while I looked
through the folder Sakataev had thrust into my hands.

'Of course not,' she said. 'A promise is a promise, right?'

'If you're sure,' I replied.

Saltanat looked over at me, then laughed.

'You can be trustingly naive at times, Akyl, you know that?
Of course I'm going to burn the fat fucker as soon as we get
this sorted. He'll either end up in the pen or in the ground, I
don't really care which.'

'He did offer us the *dacha* and the car, though.'

'I've got a car, and I'm allergic to the countryside,' she said.

'Pollen?'

'And animals and trees and outhouse toilets.'

'City life it is, then,' I said. 'But how did you know he was
the guy to question?'

Saltanat stared at me as if unable to believe what I'd just asked.

'Akyl,' she said, her voice pitying, 'why wouldn't he be?'

The way it works in Bishkek, you bribe an official to do
what you want. He takes the money. Then you blackmail
him for ever after, just to make sure he keeps quiet about the
first time. The amazing thing? They fall for it every time.

Sometimes you have to decide how you want to live your life,
and if you're lucky, you find someone to share it with. I'd

loved Chinara, and lost her. I didn't know if Saltanat and I had a future to share. One part of me hoped so, if we managed to get through this alive.

We parked outside the hotel; Saltanat hit the horn to summon Rustam to open the gates. We waited for a couple of moments, sounded the horn again, but the gates remained shut.

'I don't like the look of this,' Saltanat said, taking out her Makarov from the glove compartment. She backed the Lexus against the gate, and we scrambled onto the car roof.

I peered cautiously over the top of the wall. There was no sign of Rustam, or any of the other staff. I swung my leg over the gates, dropped to the ground, Saltanat covering me from above. Yarygin in my hand, I opened the side door, and Saltanat joined me. Her face showed she felt as uneasy as I did.

I ran up the steps, looked through the glass panel of the door leading into the kitchen. In the hallway beyond, I could see a pair of legs, a woman, one shoe on, the other lying nearby.

I put my finger to my lips as Saltanat joined me, and we cautiously made our way into the building. I recognised the body, one of the hotel maids, a young Russian girl called Alina, pretty, with long black hair and a shy smile. She wasn't pretty any more. Her body sprawled on the floor, her head pillowed on a mat of blood from where a bullet had split her forehead. Her dress had been pulled up to her waist and her underwear lay twisted around one ankle. She stared up at the ceiling, searching for a rescue that wasn't ever going to arrive.

I quickly checked the room, then Saltanat and I searched the rest of the hotel. Urmat, the Kyrgyz cook, lay on the first-floor landing, his head twisted at an impossible angle, the fingers on both hands broken, blood leaking from the bullet wound in his temple.

We found Rustam in the last of the bedrooms. Saltanat stared at the turmoil of his body while I turned away and retched. As always, when you believe you've seen the very worst that human beings can do to each other, someone prepares you a fresh horror to populate your nights and make you wish for dawn.

Rustam had been crucified to the wardrobe door. Thick steel spikes through both wrists held his arms high above his head. His bare chest had been repeatedly slashed and scored, with gobbets of meat scattered around the floor. Where his eyes had once been, deep caves were smeared with congealing blood and matter. He stank of blood and shit and meat on the turn.

I felt my legs go weak, sat down on the bed.

'Saltanat . . .' I started to say, realised I had no words. My hands were shaking, and I put the Yarygin down on the duvet, worried I might pull the trigger by mistake. With the strange clarity that comes with shock, I noticed the duvet was patterned with red roses on a white background. Like the wounds on Rustam's body. I managed to make it as far as the bathroom, gripped the bowl's cool porcelain, resting my head against the mirror.

I rinsed my mouth and spat, vomit and bile sour in my throat. Saltanat stood in front of Rustam, her face expressionless, looking at him with the same intense scrutiny you might give a famous painting, as if deciphering a hidden code or a private symbolism.

'We need to call this in,' I heard myself say. 'A massacre. We can't just leave them here to rot.'

Saltanat shook her head.

'Not yet,' she said. 'They're dead. Past all pain. But whoever did this, they're not.'

'They will be,' I heard myself saying.

Saltanat looked at me as if she was seeing a new person, one she didn't like or admire. There was no way she would allow anyone to take this case away from her. I knew she felt guilty about not being able to save Rustam's daughter, Anastasia. And now she and I had led Rustam to his death. I'm not the only one who believes in justice for the dead.

'Akyl, we know who did this.'

She reached over and handed me back my gun. I tucked it away, nodded. I was beginning to recover some composure.

'And we know what to do about it, right?'

I nodded again. The woman was a force of nature, a hurricane, a winter blizzard, ice cold and unstoppable.

'But first,' and the break in her voice was so slight, I could have sworn I imagined it, 'first we have to get him down.'

I shut the door and we stripped to our underwear to avoid bloodying our clothes. I held Rustam's body in place in a bizarre imitation of a waltz while Saltanat pulled at the spikes that held him aloft. Finally, they came free with a disgusting squelch, and I took the weight of his broken body in my arms. Together, we laid Rustam's body on the bed, and covered it with the duvet. At once, fresh roses began to blossom on the cotton.

'What do you think happened?' I asked, as we got dressed. Saltanat stared down at the mound on the bed for a moment or two, before replying.

'The iPhone. I think Rustam must have switched it on,' she said. 'Just curious, or maybe wanting to see how it worked, what was on it. And they were able to trace the signal.'

I'd forgotten about the iPhone, but it was nowhere in sight, and I felt sure Saltanat was right. So not only had we lost our one piece of evidence, but we'd brought a world of shit upon our heads, and death upon Rustam and his staff.

'That means some high-powered equipment. Or a source within the phone company,' I said. 'Expensive. Connected.'

Saltanat looked at me, and I could see a savage anger in her face.

'Or in the police force or state security,' she said, turned, stared out of the window. I made no move to hold her, comfort her. Outside, the world continued, the uncaring song of birds, the random hiss of leaves upon the wind.

And then we heard footsteps in the hallway.

Chapter 38

I stepped behind the door, gun held up by my cheek, ready to shoot. The footsteps stopped, and there was a moment's silence. I could hear breathing, or rather, gasping, together with a noise I realised was weeping. There was a light knock on the door.

'Rustam?'

A woman's voice, terrified.

I pulled the door open, took aim at chest height, to be greeted by hysterical screaming. The woman who stumbled and fell to the floor was one of the hotel's chambermaids, Rosa. The bag she was carrying split open, onions and potatoes rolling around my feet.

I got my breath back under control, holstered my gun, offered the girl my hand. She only screamed louder when she saw Rustam's blood smeared up to my wrists. The crotch of her jeans turned a darker blue as she raised her arm to cover her eyes, then she fell and scrabbled back towards the stairs. The reek of urine mingled with the stink of blood.

'Rosa, it's all right, you're safe,' Saltanat said, her voice calming, soft. 'You know us, we're friends.'

But the girl kept screaming, her eyes clamped shut, her palms tearing at her cheeks, pressing herself against the wall to make herself as small a target as possible.

I looked at Saltanat, gestured towards the stairs. Someone

would have heard the shots, the screams; we had very little time before the police arrived. Or the killers returned.

'We can't just leave her like this,' Saltanat said, touching the girl's shoulder, watching her flinch.

'You want to bring her with us?' I asked, already heading down the stairs. 'That puts her in a lot more danger than she's in now. And us.'

'What's wrong with you, Akyl?' Saltanat snapped. 'She needs help.'

I sighed and turned back up the stairs.

'Take her other arm,' I ordered. 'We can at least get her away from the bodies.'

Between the two of us we helped the weeping girl stagger down the stairs into the hotel dining room. Saltanat opened a drinks cabinet, poured a glass of vodka. Rosa choked as she drank it, but her tears slowed and she grew slightly calmer.

'Now can we go?' I asked, and started for the door. Saltanat gave me a look that would melt snow off Mount Lenina, but followed me. I unlocked the gates, while Saltanat made a call.

'Murder Squad?'

'Ambulance. For Rosa,' she said, and pushed past me towards the car, her shoulder slamming into mine. She climbed into the driver's seat, started the engine. As the car pulled away, she used her phone to take a photo of the hotel sign; I had to scramble to get into the passenger seat.

'What the fuck? Were you about to leave me?' I snarled, grabbing at the dashboard to prevent myself going head first through the windscreen.

'The arsehole you seem to have become, I can well live

without. I can be over the border in a couple of hours, and then you can get yourself killed without my help.'

I stared out of the window, lit two cigarettes, passed one to Saltanat. I wound down my window to let the spring air cool me down.

'Sorry,' I said, tried to make it sound genuine. Saltanat took the cigarette, took a long draw. The adrenalin was starting to slacken off, and I felt as if my shoulders had been beaten with iron bars.

The Lexus bounced around on what was not much more than a potholed track, pushing forward between one-storey shacks with corrugated-iron roofs hiding behind mud-brick walls and tumbledown gates. I had only the vaguest idea of where we were, somewhere north and east of Ala-Too Square, but Saltanat clearly knew where we were headed.

'Sorry,' I repeated, and this time put a little sincerity into it. Saltanat gave me a suspicious glare, then seemed to relent slightly.

'The hotel's blown, and we can't go to your apartment, obviously,' she said, hurling the car into a ninety-degree turn that lifted two tyres off the road. 'We'll use my safe house, at least for a couple of days while we decide what to do next.'

I remembered the safe house from the Tynaliev affair. We'd taken a *pakhan*, a mafia boss, there, threatened to torture him and have his granddaughter raped, then sent him on his way, promising his revenge. That never happened though, because twenty minutes later one of Saltanat's Uzbek security colleagues put two bullets in him. One in the back of the head to denote an execution, one in the mouth to say he'd talked beforehand. I'd not been back since, and the thought of returning didn't ease the gloom.

The safe house was on the eastern edge of Bishkek, three storeys surrounded by a two-metre wall and blue ornamental sheet-metal gates. Saltanat unlocked the heavy steel door and we entered. It was no more cheerful than I remembered it, though not quite as bitterly cold. Unfurnished rooms, stained wallpaper peeling in places, spots and blisters of mould seeping through damp plaster, bare wooden floorboards. And beneath us, the cellar and furnace room, with everything required to make a man betray his family, his friends, anything to stop the pain. Simple things for the most part: coal tongs, a hammer, chisels and screwdrivers, kitchen scissors, boiling water. It doesn't take much to persuade someone of the righteousness of your cause.

Then I remembered Graves's cellar, the blood-soaked butcher's slab, the thick leather belts, the straps, and video equipment to capture every scream, every spasm. For a moment, my head was spinning, I thought I was going to vomit again and rested one hand against a clammy wall.

Saltanat saw my distress, helped me slide down the wall until I sat on the floor, knees drawn up towards my shoulders, my hands shaking as if I had a fever.

'Sorry,' I said, for the third time in an hour, as if apologies could ever change things, ever heal the sick or bring the dead back to life. Sorry means clutching at hope the way a man swept away by a raging river tries to grasp an overhanging bough. Sorry sounds good, but it changes fuck all.

'You want some water?' Saltanat asked. I shook my head, then reconsidered. My throat was too dry to speak, so I simply nodded. Saltanat returned from the kitchen with a bottle of water. It was warm, and flat, but I emptied the bottle in a few desperate gulps. I rinsed my mouth, spat out the last of the water, looked up at Saltanat. The words I wanted to say were trapped in my throat, handcuffed by sorrow and fear.

She stared down at me, pity in her face, for what I had once been and what I had now become. I knew what I had to do, knew it would change everything.

'I want you to go back home, Saltanat, back to Tashkent. This isn't your battle, the dead aren't your people, there's no reason why you should risk your life on our behalf.'

Saltanat opened her mouth to speak, but I held up a silencing hand.

'This is hard enough for me to say, without you making me change my mind and keeping silent. I'm a coward, you see, and by not telling you the truth, I'm betraying how I feel for you, how you might feel for me. So I have to speak.'

I looked up at her, remembering my past which lay between us like a river in full flood between two banks.

'Believe me, Akyl, I know you're not a coward. I've seen that over and over, ever since I first met you. You care too much for other people ever to be that.'

'You mean I care too much for the dead,' I said.

'You care about justice, not just for the dead, like Gurminj and Rustam, Alina and Urmat and Yekaterina Tynalieva, but for everyone without a voice. Justice for everyone who wakes up wondering what new pain will appear when the sun rises,' she said, and I felt my heart splinter against her words.

'Let me tell you about being a coward,' I said, making my voice ugly, harsh. 'It's about hiding from the truth, doing anything to avoid being confronted by something that terrifies you. It's about doing something wrong because you can't bear the situation you're in to continue.'

185

I stopped for a moment, trying to put the words together in my head that would force her to abandon me.

'When Chinara was in hospital for the last time, and we both knew there was no hope of her ever coming back home . . .'

I paused, unable to speak.

'I know what you did, Akyl,' Saltanat said, with a gentleness I'd never suspected of her. 'I guessed it almost from the moment I met you. You demand justice for the dead, but you also want mercy for the living.'

I was silent, my palms sweating, my heart the loudest thing in the universe.

'I know, because when I was raped, you didn't blame me, you didn't agonise about what you could have done to prevent it. You got me medicine, you gave me clothes and shelter. You helped avenge me.'

Saltanat put her hand on my shoulder, the way you comfort a child newly frightened out of a nightmare. I felt her breath warm and sweet on my cheek.

'It must have hurt like hell to see me wearing your dead wife's clothes. I remember the hope on your face when I walked into the room, and the pain when you saw I wasn't her. And how we sat in silence watching the moon pick out the snow on the mountains.

'You eased Chinara out of her pain and onto her journey. And now you hate yourself for it, and blame yourself for living when she died.'

Saltanat slid down beside me, placed her arm across my shoulder, held me, while I thought of nothing. We listened to the silence of the house, and I hoped that would bring some kind of grace and absolution.

Chapter 39

By silent consent, neither of us discussed what turned out to be a confession, perhaps even a declaration of sorts. We shared a mattress on the floor of an upstairs room, Saltanat sleeping with her head on my shoulder while I lay awake for hours, staring at the faces that emerged from the stains on the wall.

We spent the next day discussing what to do. I voted for a quick headshot and a high-speed exit over the border into Kazakhstan. Once there, we could work out what to do next. My desire for revenge was fierce, on behalf of Gurminj, Rustam, the dead children. At night, I dreamt of seeing the sudden terror in Graves's eyes, heard the half-uttered scream and watched his brains spatter grey and viscous against a bloodstained wall. I could almost taste his fear. And if a bullet came my way, perhaps that made a suitable end for an endless struggle.

Saltanat was calmer, more rational. She wanted to see Graves punished, but, smarter than me, she thought ahead, wanted to prove me innocent of the child pornography charges. Hour after hour, we debated strategy, tactics, but all the time I could feel the tension on a trigger, imagined my finger tightening and then the recoil. The muscles in my jaw pulsed with the need for sudden blood.

'Listen to me, Akyl, killing Graves isn't the answer. We

haven't even proved it's him,' Saltanat argued, pounding one fist into another for emphasis.

'He's dirty, and you know it. You saw the films.' My voice flat.

'Yes, but I didn't see him. Maybe he wholesales the porn, buys it in, that makes him guilty of a lot of things. But maybe not murder.'

'I don't give a fuck about proving it. He doesn't know what goes on in the cellar of his own house?'

I heard my voice getting angrier, didn't bother to rein it in.

'When you scoop shit off the street, do you care whether it's from the arse of a dog, a cow or a horse? It's still shit, and needs to be cleaned up.'

Saltanat sighed in frustration, sat back on her heels.

'If you're looking for a gunfight, one in which you die heroically, gun blazing, the bad guys falling dead, that's up to you. I can't stop you. If you don't mind everyone remembering you as a man who peddled the worst kind of filth for money, again, your call.'

I shrugged, as if I didn't care one way or the other.

'First of all, we have to appear to back away. To convince Graves the slaughter at the hotel made us realise we were in too deep. Amateurs. And with him having the iPhone evidence of his involvement, we're just going to disappear.'

I had to admit it made a lot of sense, even if my anger and pride made it hard to swallow the truth.

'So what do you want us to do?'

'We call him,' Saltanat said. 'We tell him we got the message, we're crossing the border, he has nothing to be concerned about.'

'He won't believe that,' I said. 'He's made a lot of dirty

money, dirty friends, dirty enemies. He won't be happy until we're in the cellar starring in his next home movie.'

'That's why I'm going to make the call,' Saltanat said. 'He hears an Uzbek accent, we're a gang from over the border. Especially when I tell him you're dead. And send him the photos to prove it.'

'I take it I'm not actually dead,' I said.

'You're face down, shot in the back, somewhere up in the mountains where it's still snowy,' she said.

'I hope it was quick,' I said.

'You never knew what hit you,' Saltanat said.

It's as good a description of love as any I've ever heard.

Chapter 40

The following morning, we drove out of the city, up to Ala Archa, the national park that climbs up into the mountains. It's a serene, beautiful place, with rowan and birch trees sheltering under the steep slopes of the valley. At weekends in the summer, it's always busy with walkers, tourists and people who just want to get out of the heat and dust of the city. Hike to the far end of the park and you might spot wolves, bears, perhaps even a snow leopard, while eagles and hawks patrol the sky. Saltanat parked in front of the small hotel marking the end of the road, and we started to walk.

The air was crisp, the remnants of the winter still white underfoot, and the music of the river created a swirling soundtrack as we climbed up into the treeline. The snow got deeper, its chill creeping through the soles of my boots. I was out of breath, out of condition, but Saltanat strode ahead, making no concessions to my lack of speed or the leather case she was carrying

Finally, we stopped, in a natural clearing, where birch trees clustered around us, like onlookers at a road accident. Or perhaps witnesses at an execution. Saltanat put down the bag, looked around.

'This is as good as anywhere,' she said. 'Take off your jacket.'

I felt a cold breeze brush across my chest. The upper

branches of the trees quivered, and I felt a faint drift of snowflakes on my face.

Saltanat opened the case, took out a glass jar and a plastic bag. A medium-sized raw steak glistened inside the bag, streaked with blood, marbled with fat. The jar was half full of a thick red fluid that was all too familiar. I decided not to ask where she'd acquired the blood.

Saltanat unwrapped the steak, laid it on the snow, poured a little of the blood on and around the meat, then covered it with my jacket. I shivered and realised I should have brought a sweater. At least, that's why I thought I was shivering.

Saltanat pressed her Makarov against the bulge caused by the meat, and fired a shot. My jacket jerked as if I'd still been inside it, and some blood oozed out of the bullet hole, its edges blackened by powder burn. I could see charred flesh, smelt burnt meat. I felt slightly sick.

'Now the fun part,' Saltanat said. 'Put your jacket back on.'

I did as I was told, and waited for instructions.

'Fall forward, and don't use your hands to break your fall,' Saltanat said. 'We need this to look convincing.'

I was convinced she was enjoying this rather too much, but I fell forward, my face buried in the snow, arms flung out. Saltanat placed the steak under the bullet hole, and I could feel a clammy sweat on the back of my neck. Saltanat spattered some of the blood by my side, and I could taste its rich scent in the back of my throat.

'Stay still,' she commanded. I didn't move for four or five minutes, until she told me to get up.

I lumbered to my feet, brushing snow and dirt off my face, out of my hair.

'My jacket's fucked, I suppose,' I grumbled, wiping the worst of the blood against a clean patch of snow.

'Not at all,' Saltanat said, scrolling through the photos she'd taken. 'A bullet hole, what could give you more street cred than that, a Murder Squad inspector who survived an assassination attempt?'

It would be all too easy for someone to repeat the exercise, next time for real. I'd seen too many bodies sprawled out on pavements, in fields, under birch trees, to think the same fate could never await me.

'Won't they want to see my face?' I asked. 'Find out who I am, I mean, was?'

'The last thing we want is for someone to recognise you,' Saltanat said. 'Better to say we decided to turn you into food for the crows. By the way, you make a lovely corpse.'

'That's what I'm afraid of,' I said, started back down the hillside towards the car, until I slipped and landed on my arse, felt the snow seeping wet into my trousers. Saltanat's laughter followed me all the way down.

Chapter 41

The Voice at the other end of the phone was guarded.

'Yes?'

'Mr Graves?' Saltanat said.

Silence.

'You spoke to a former colleague of mine the other day.'

'Did I?'

'Regarding a series of financial transactions that, in the event, never happened,' she said. Her tone was officious, impersonal. Saltanat could play the ice queen to perfection.

'And?'

'There was a series of cancellations at a local hotel. Perhaps you read about them?'

'Perhaps.'

The voice was noncommittal, giving nothing away, not even confusion or misunderstanding.

'The colleague who spoke to you is no longer with our organisation, ever since we discovered he was acting on his own, without our authority. His employment was terminated. And so was he.'

More silence.

Saltanat continued, the frost in her voice amplified by the formality of her language.

'As a gesture of our commitment to an amicable solution, we're sending you photographs of his resignation. We hope this ends any unpleasantness between our two organisations. Please accept our apologies.'

After a moment, the Voice spoke.

'Damage was done, costs incurred. I would expect some form of compensation.'

Discussing death, violence, crime, in the language of the boardroom. Not for the first time, I wondered if the entire world was greedy and corrupt. The biggest thieves sit at boardroom tables discussing takeovers and share options. And the only handcuffs they ever get to put on are golden.

'I quite agree, Mr Graves,' Saltanat continued, 'but my superiors feel the quickest way to deal with this problem is to simply let the matter drop, and we both continue to go about our respective businesses as before.'

The Voice started to speak, but Saltanat abruptly broke the connection. She handed the mobile to me.

'You might want to have a look at your corpse,' she said. 'That's not something you get to do every day. And then take a hammer to the phone.'

I thumbed through the images of my dead body in the snow. They looked pretty convincing, and it wasn't as if I'd never seen such things before. The close-up of the bullet hole with the charred meat and powder burn was particularly effective.

'So Graves gets these, and decides the problem's over. Then what?'

Saltanat took the phone back from me, and started to dial a number.

'His problem is just starting, whether or not he believes it's been sorted. Once I send a photo of the hotel, together with your holiday snaps.'

'Sending them where?'

'To your old colleagues at Sverdlovsky station. Together with a text that the very dead body in the photo is yours, that the hotel massacre is involved, and our friend Mr Graves knows something about both. Let's see what they do then.'

You can only admire such deviousness.

An hour later, we were parked a couple of hundred yards away from Graves's mansion when the first squad car arrived. An officer got out of the passenger seat, adjusted his uniform, squared his peaked cap, said something into the gate intercom.

After a couple of moments, the side gate swung open and the *ment* went inside.

'This is your version of stirring the sewage and seeing what floats to the top?' I asked. Saltanat shook her head.

'Nothing so direct,' she answered. 'We watch what happens, and that tells us just how well protected Graves is. He's got to be giving a lot of beaks something to drink; maybe this will tell us whose.'

'Sverdlovsky's going to be very happy the missing inspector is going to stay missing,' I said, 'but I hope that's only going to be temporary.'

I tried a light-hearted voice, but Saltanat looked at me, concerned perhaps I was losing my edge, my fire.

'You know, Akyl, if you wanted to get out of Kyrgyzstan, we could go to Tashkent. New papers, a new identity, you could start over again.'

I took her hand, squeezed it.

'I'm touched you'd do that for me,' I said. 'Honestly.'

I looked around and waved a hand in the general direction of the mountains.

'But this is home. Not much, I know, but . . . '

I shrugged, then leant forward and kissed her cheek.

'This is where I am, this is what I do. Without it, I'd be nothing.'

Saltanat raised an eyebrow.

I smiled, then stiffened as a black limousine turned the corner, parked behind the squad car. Tinted glass prevented us from seeing who was inside. The uniformed driver opened the rear door and an elegant middle-aged blonde woman emerged. Dark glasses covered her eyes, but even at a distance, I saw she was attractive, slim, head held high, full of confidence. Her hair was piled up in a French plait, and her clothes were expensive. From GUM in Moscow, or Bond Street in London. A lot of Russian oligarchs live there now, and they like their mansions expensive, their cars high-end and their women stylish. Why steal billions of roubles from the Russian people if not to enjoy the fruits of your labours?

'You know who she is?' I asked, flicking through the filing cabinet in my mind, not coming up with any immediate answers, although there was something familiar about her. Saltanat frowned, said nothing.

I did recognise the man who got out of the car and walked with the woman towards the gate. I'd last seen him just a few days before, drinking *pivo* at a market stall in Jalalabad.

Mikhail Ivanovich Tynaliev, Minister for State Security.

Chapter 42

'So now we know,' I said, lit a cigarette, my hand trembling. I'd expected Graves to be connected, but hadn't imagined it would be so high up.

'We could have guessed Graves and Tynaliev would know each other,' Saltanat said, 'but we don't know how close the connection is. Graves has legitimate businesses. It could be Tynaliev is involved in those, but not in the porn.'

I understood Saltanat's logic, even agreed with it. But doubts nagged in the back of my head, like blisters from a pair of new shoes.

'I can't imagine Tynaliev would approve of Graves's cellar activities, not after the murder of his only daughter,' I said, 'but as Minister for State Security, a dog can't bark in Panfilov Park without it being reported to him.'

'Then why would he fly down to Jalalabad to see you, tell you to solve the case, tone down the police hunt for you?' Saltanat asked. 'Surely if he was involved, he'd be more interested in you taking the fall for everything?'

I shrugged.

'Maybe he fancies a press conference where he can announce "Rogue Inspector Shot Dead Resisting Arrest". And then everybody can get back to the cellar work, cutting and raping and killing and piling up the money just like before.'

Saltanat didn't look convinced, although the logic seemed pretty plain to me.

'So who killed Gurminj? And the buried children? And why the false identity bands?'

I didn't have a reply. I wasn't even sure I wanted one. All I knew was my gun had the solution. Or rather, seventeen of them. Sixteen for the bad guys and one for myself.

Saltanat must have seen what I was thinking in my face, because she reached over, put her hand on the butt of my gun.

'Not an answer,' she said. I thought of Lubashov's brother, bleeding out on Chui Prospekt outside Fatboys, three of my bullets taking refuge in his chest. I remembered Chinara's uncle, Kursan, dead at my feet, his brains spoiling the pattern of the carpet. Men I'd killed.

'Sometimes it is,' I said, stared out of the window.

It was Saltanat's turn to shrug. I looked over at her. Something was off, out of kilter.

'That woman, the one with Tynaliev?' I said. 'You know who she is?'

Saltanat paused for a moment, nodded.

'Not good news,' she said. 'Not for you. And especially not for me.'

'So who is she?'

'She's called Albina Kurmanalieva. She used to be in the Uzbek security service. But now she's freelance, a specialist.'

I didn't like the sound of that. I've known too many specialists who let their work get out of hand.

'Specialist in what?'

Saltanat said nothing for a moment, her mouth set fierce.

'We call it "spilling", sort of an office joke,' she said. 'But not really a funny one.'

'Spilling what?' I asked, already guessing the answer.

'Blood. Brains. Whatever needs taking care of, or who-ever. She's an assassin, Akyl.'

I lit another cigarette, trying to put together an under-standing of a situation that seemed to swirl and drift and go out of focus, as ungraspable as smoke, fragmented as ash.

I'd heard of Kurmanalieva, though I'd never encountered her. She was supposed to have been responsible for *mokroye delo*, the old KGB phrase, 'wet work', down in the south near Osh, where the riots started back in 2010. Only we don't call them riots, or civil unrest or even revolution. The politically correct phrase is 'events'. The KGB weren't the only ones good at euphemisms.

I'd heard Kurmanalieva had crossed the border, taken down two of the principals behind the troubles, one Kyrgyz, one Uzbek, handcuffed them back to back, and gave each of them an unseeing third eye. She left them propped against each other in the centre of Osh, then drifted like smoke back to wherever she came from. A message to both sides to stop fucking around.

It wasn't the only story I'd heard about her. She'd spent time in Chechnya, working with the Spetsnaz, Russian Special Forces, hunting down people the Russians called terrorists and who called themselves freedom fighters. You could use her name to frighten young would-be police officers at the academy. Screw up, and Albina would pay you a visit.

'She's good with handguns, rifles, unarmed combat,' Sal-tanat said. 'Better than me. Better than you. And what she's best at are knives.'

'So why is she here with Tynaliev?' I wondered. 'And why would he take her to meet up with Graves?'

'My guess?' Saltanat answered. 'You spooked Graves with

that hand grenade and arson play. He knew his crew weren't up to dealing with whoever you were. So he called his good friend, Minister Tynaliev, asked for a specialist to help him out with his problem. For a price, of course.'

I nodded. It made a kind of sense, like reflections in an old mirror where half the silvering has rotted away and the frame is buckled.

'So you don't think your call made any difference?' I asked.

'It didn't do any harm,' she said, 'but men like Graves don't get rich and powerful by taking other people's word as the truth.'

'Have you had dealings with this specialist, this Albina?' I said.

Saltanat looked away, as if pulling bitter memories out of the sky. She touched the thin white scar that bisected her left eyebrow. I'd always wondered how Saltanat had been cut, and now I had a vivid image in my mind. I pictured a Chanel-clad beauty wielding a switchblade, then decided, as with so many parts of Saltanat's life, to leave the question unasked.

'We have a history,' she said. 'We're never going to go shopping for shoes and make-up together, put it that way.'

She didn't volunteer the rest of the story, the violence it surely contained. I thought of Chinara, her gentle soul, teaching the laws of the universe at school, and at the same time trying to decode human beings through poetry. A woman who'd never come close to violence, let alone been the cause of it, until the cancer attacked her, savaged her like a rabid dog. Show me the poem that can make that go away.

'So now what do we do?' she asked, the intensity of her gaze searing.

'I've already told you this isn't your fight.'

'Akyl, this is where I want to be. Even if you don't want me here. If I'm not here to look after you, who knows what trouble you'll get into.'

Then she smiled, and my head and heart turned like distant planets around the sun.

Chapter 43

We sat and watched Graves's mansion for a couple of hours, before Saltanat turned the key in the ignition and started to pull away.

'You don't want to wait and follow Kurmanalieva?' I asked.

Saltanat shook her head, her hair cascading across one cheek. So beautiful, so deadly. I could smell her skin, cool, delicate.

'She won't stay with Tynaliev,' she explained, turning right towards Chui Prospekt. 'That would put him in jeopardy if things didn't work out, and she was caught or killed. And if she's here to protect Graves, why would she leave his side? I'm sure he's got a couple of guest rooms.'

'I'm sure he won't take her on a tour of the cellar,' I said, then wondered if that might not be something they would have in common.

'Kurmanalieva isn't a sadist,' Saltanat said. 'It's always strictly business with her. Unless it's personal, of course. Then all bets fall by the wayside.'

I cleared my throat. I was always on dangerous ground whenever I asked Saltanat about her past. I knew she was divorced, but I didn't know where she lived, if she had brothers and sisters, if her parents were still alive. Shit, I wasn't even sure if Saltanat was her real name. Smoke and mirrors; no one wants to fall in love with a reflection, a mirage.

'The history you have with her. That was personal?'

Saltanat's face tightened, and once again she touched the scar that ran through her left eyebrow. Not a good memory. 'Yes.'

It was obvious she didn't want to tell me any more so I rolled down the window, lit the last of my cigarettes, watched the girls on Chui in their pretty spring dresses as they laughed and chattered and believed they would live for ever . . .

An hour later, we were back at the safe house, having stopped on the way at Faiza on Jibek Jolu for takeaway *shashlik* and *lagman*. The food was rich and warming, and I felt more confident with my belly full. I looked at the bustling waitresses with their white headscarves and long maroon skirts, watched the ease with which they took orders, brought piled plates of food, envied them their calm and professionalism.

Saltanat took a long swallow from a bottle of beer, poured a little more *chai* into my teacup, the sign of an attentive hostess.

'We can't hide out here for ever,' she said. 'Kurmanalieva will still have plenty of contacts back in Tashkent, and sooner or later she might want to use this place, or bring people over the border on a mission.'

Saltanat pulled a sour face, drew her forefinger across her throat.

'So we have to find out why she's here?' I asked.

Saltanat nodded agreement, finished her beer. The alcohol had gone slightly to her head, and she gave a smile that was friendlier than her usual impassive stare. I was sober, but it was still encouraging.

'The way I see it, there are various scenarios,' I said. 'One:

Tynaliev, Graves and Albina are all in this together. Two: Albina is here to do a job for Graves that isn't connected to the murders. Three: Tynaliev and Albina are lovers, and he's introducing her to a powerful local businessman.'

'Do you think Tynaliev and Albina might be lovers?' Saltanat asked.

I weighed the idea up, shook my head.

'He's known for liking young women; that's why his wife lives at their *dacha*. Albina's well-preserved but about twenty-five years too old for Tynaliev.'

I ran the alternatives through my head once more.

'I can't see Tynaliev being involved in the porn and murders,' I said, shaking my head. 'He doesn't fit the profile. And too much to lose.'

'Well, we know Graves is involved,' Saltanat stated. 'You don't think Tynaliev is. So we need to lean on Albina, find out why she's here.'

'How do you propose we do that?' I asked. The thought of facing a knife-crazed virago at some point didn't have a great deal of appeal.

'We have to give her something she won't be able to resist,' Saltanat replied.

'Which is?'

'A rematch with me, with knives.'

The smile she gave would have frozen Lake Issyk-Kul in high summer.

'You're going to call her?' I asked. 'Won't that let Graves know that we're still out to get him, despite your earlier promise?'

'You think Uzbek security service agents contacts each other using another country's phone system?'

The scorn in her voice was light, but still there. As usual, I realised I was out of my depth when it came to the way the invisible ones worked. Give me a badge and a gun and I could sort most things out. In a world of whispers and false information, I was a novice.

Saltanat took pity on my ignorance.

'In our tradecraft,' she explained, 'we use pay-as-you-go mobiles to send text messages to a secure encrypted website. We have a second cut-out by using code numbers, the way you police do when calling in. But our code numbers change every day, again encrypted on a personal basis. So even if I read what another agent wrote, I wouldn't be able to make sense of it. Only when I get a message back can I use my private codes to decipher it.'

'Wouldn't it be easier to just make a call?' I joked.

Saltanat didn't smile.

'Only if you're not bothered about ending up underground if it all goes wrong,' she said.

So I stopped smiling as well.

'I've learnt not to trust anyone, Akyl,' she said, and the pain in her voice snatched like a thief at my heart. 'Not when it comes to work.'

I leant forward, placed my palm against her cheek.

'Let me tell you a story about trust,' I said, sent my memory back a quarter of a century . . .

I'd been in the orphanage for only a few months when we were all told we had to make our dormitories spotless; an important visitor was coming to see us. It's not that we didn't keep the place clean, but we spent two days sweeping every corner, scouring the kitchen pots and pans until they gleamed, washing windows free of the past winter's stains.

A few of us had nice clothes in the battered cardboard suitcases we'd brought with us, so we paraded in our idea of finery. I was almost thirteen, still small for my age, and I used to stare out of the window up towards the mountains for hours, waiting for my *mama* or my *dedushka* to come and take me home, back to hugs and kisses and streaming, over-flowing bowls of *plov*. I still had hope, a trust that everything was only temporary, that it would all turn out for the best.

On that day, I stood on tiptoe, my chin resting on the win-dow ledge, nose pressed up against the glass. I was watching for the cloud of dust in the distance, down the road, that would announce the arrival of the important visitor. I won-dered – hoped – it might be my *mama*, rich from her time away in Siberia, coming in a big black limousine to take me away. For two hours I stared, until my head began to spin. And then I saw it, the big black car I'd been hoping for, a Zil Classic, the kind the president rode around in. I watched it get closer, sunlight flaring on the tinted windows, before it finally turned through the gates that led to the orphanage's main entrance.

I could see the orphanage director, a tall, too-thin man called Zenish who stared suspiciously at the world as if it was determined to do him down, with a hand all too quick to clip an offending ear as it passed by him. But today he wore a smile that fitted as badly as his clothes. I watched as the car came to a halt beside him, noticed how he polished the toe of one shoe on the back of his leg.

A uniformed driver hurried round to the rear door of the car, opened it. A woman got out, and tears burnt in my eyes as I saw it wasn't my *mama*. An elegant young woman, slim, stylishly dressed in clothes that had obviously never seen the inside of a Bishkek shopping mall. I knew nothing about fashion but I could recognise the sheen of money and power.

From the way Zenish rushed forward and shook her hand, I could tell she was important. He started to say something, but she cut him off in mid-sentence with a nod of her head. She walked towards the entrance, and Zenish followed, with that odd crabbed gait tall people use to keep behind someone they don't want to offend.

Zenish clapped his hands in the hallway, to summon all the children. We ran into the hallway, formed a ragged line, staring at our visitor with unconcealed interest. She was probably the richest, most sophisticated person any of us had ever seen.

Seeing her close to, I could tell she was only a few years older than me, her late teens or very early twenties perhaps, with Slavic features and blonde hair tightly coiled onto her head. I wondered if perhaps she was a famous film or television star, looking for children to be in her next production. We all watched as the woman walked slowly down the line, inspecting all of us. From time to time she stopped in front of a child, boy or girl, held their faces up with a hand under their chin, staring to see if they flinched from her gaze. Her eyes were black, cold, and her mouth was tightly closed, as if holding back an insult or a curse.

The little girl standing next to me started to whimper from nerves, twisting the threadbare material of her ill-fitting dress, a hand-me-down from an older sister. The woman heard the noise and crouched down in front of the child. Her eyes were cruel, probing for weakness, fear. The little girl started to sob, and I smelt the sudden reek of urine as she wet herself.

I don't know why I did it, but I pushed myself in front of the little girl, shielding her from the woman's eyes. A flare of surprise crossed the woman's face for a fraction of a second, before she stood up. Zenish was immediately beside her to apologise, clouting me hard across the face with an open hand.

'Such insolence to our important guest, you'll—'

'Director, this one at least has some courage,' the woman interrupted, 'and defending his little girlfriend does him some credit, does it not?'

Zenish clearly didn't know whether to keep kissing her arse and risk losing the power he had over us.

'As you say, but we must have discipline, don't you agree?'

The woman took my chin and wrenched my head up. I summoned up my most defiant stare, the one that had always angered my grandfather's new wife.

'What's your name, boy?' she said, and I could hear the menace in her voice. I said nothing, staring harder, trying to ignore the pain as she squeezed my jaw tighter. I was determined I would not cry, would not let tears betray me. The heavy scent of her perfume was strong and sickly like dying flowers in week-old water. I sensed the curve of her breasts under the tight-fitting dress. I was attracted, the way boys turning into men sense the power of a woman, any woman. But I was also repelled, imagining her as a spider, a vampire, hovering, waiting to strike. I felt my knees tremble, but I made sure my face remained expressionless, my mouth closed. Finally, Zenish could no longer stand the silence.

'Borubaev, Akyl,' he said, spitting the words out like a bad taste in his mouth. 'Dumped here by his stepmother as a bad job.'

The woman continued to stare at me.

'Akyl,' her voice almost caressing, 'would you like to come and live with me in my big house? Ride in my big car? Go to a good school and grow up to be somebody important, famous?'

I kept my silence. The thought of escaping the orphanage was overwhelming, the sense of potential freedom intoxicating. But I sensed the cruelty of the woman, her need to control and hurt. And I loved my mother. So I said nothing.

The woman let go of my jaw, taking a handkerchief out of the pocket of her skirt and wiping her hands on it, as if I were something dirty that had soiled her skin.

'You should watch this one, Director,' she said, the steel in her voice a lash on my back. 'Believe me, he'll either kill you or take your job. Or both.'

She started back towards the door, but turned and looked at me.

'Let me tell you something about life, Akyl,' she said. 'It's all about trust. That bit's easy. The hard bit is knowing who to trust. And when.'

Her voice was softer, somehow caressing, and for a few seconds, I actually wondered if I'd misjudged her, if she was someone kind, someone to trust as the nights drew near and the shadows lengthened. But then I remembered the way she squeezed my jaw, the cruelty in her eyes. Four-legged wolves can't sheath their claws, but the two-legged variety can. And they're the kind you must never trust. So I shook my head, afraid to speak in case a tremor in my voice betrayed me.

She shrugged, turned, shook her head at Zenish as he

approached and walked away, her heels tapping on the concrete floor, the sound of nails driven into wood. I stood there for a long time afterwards, wondering if my instincts had been wrong, if she really wanted to adopt me, if she might have been the promise of a new life. Questions I've never been able to answer . . .

Chapter 44

Saltanat went off into the centre of Bishkek to send a message to Albina Kurmanalieva, from another Uzbek safe house, I assumed, one I didn't know about. Trust, or the lack of it, playing its part as usual. Personally, I thought the whole spy tradecraft exercise was nonsense, an over-elaborate hangover from the days of the USSR, when everyone was so busy watching each other no one noticed the country collapsing around their ears. Easier just to make a phone call, grab a pocket full of bullets, and take your chances.

When Saltanat returned, I didn't bother asking her where she'd been, who she'd spoken to, what she'd said. It was as if a sheet of glass had been thrust between us, like visiting a convict in prison. Except I didn't know which one of us was the prisoner. We sat in silence, and smoked too much, for two days that felt like two months, the minutes slouching along on crutches of fear and boredom.

I was beginning to wonder whether anything was going to happen, and on the morning of the third day, I decided I'd had enough.

Saltanat was asleep when I left the safe house, walking for half a kilometre to where the morning *marshrutka* minibus was waiting to take people from Tungush into the centre of Bishkek. The bus was already crowded, so I stood for most of the journey, hanging onto a seat back as we jolted and bounced over potholed tracks. The early morning sun bathed the Tien Shan mountains with a soft golden light that high-lighted the year-round snow-covered peaks and shone through the branches and budding leaves of the trees lining our route. The air was crisp and clean, defying petrol fumes and the smoke coiling out of chimneys. As always, I thought of the beauty of my country, how it deserves better people than the ones who live here. But perhaps that's true of everywhere.

Finally, we reached the smoother roads of central Bishkek and as people got off the bus, I managed to snag a seat, keeping my hand on my wallet in case of pickpockets. When we reached the public sauna baths on Ibraimova, I squeezed my way to the front, paid my nine *som* to the driver, and alighted. From there, it was a ten-minute walk south to my apartment block. I wanted to see if the place was still under police observation, and, if not, to collect a couple of items I'd stashed away there. I bought a meat *samsi* at the stall on the corner of Ibraimova and Moskovskaya, eating it as a cover for staring at the entrance to my *Khrushchyovka* block. The prefabricated concrete sections at the front were worn and stained from years of scorching summers and brutal winters, and some teenage wit had spray-painted his girlfriend's name across the metal entrance door. But the apartments inside were solid and warm; better than living in a yurt, that's for sure.

I checked my watch. Just before seven o'clock. By now, Saltanat would be awake and cursing me. But every day we did nothing, I was in greater risk of being caught by my colleagues – I still thought of them as my colleagues, and knew Tynaliev's instructions to downgrade the case against me would have set many people wondering if I had been framed. And more importantly, every day's delay meant some poor soul might be in Graves's basement, suffering the torments of the damned while a video camera captured every last drop of blood and every plea for mercy.

I couldn't see any police cars parked nearby, and I was pretty sure no average *ment* was going to be standing out in the cold. I wiped the last of the grease from the *samsi* on my sleeve, spat out the inevitable piece of gristle, strode up to the entrance door.

The trick is always to appear confident to anyone watching, show the world you have nothing to fear and even less to hide. Look furtive or worried, and even if the law doesn't spot you, some sharp-eyed *babushka* with nothing better to do than spy on her neighbours will call it in.

I keyed in the four-digit number on the electronic lock installed after one of the tenants on the third floor was found stabbed to death, pushed open the door. Security might have been tightened since then, but half the light bulbs on each landing were still either dead or missing, and the lift was the same cramped and stinking toilet it had always been.

I took the lift up to the floor above mine, and walked down the stairs to my front door. A thin ribbon of crime scene tape was still attached to the frame, but there was no sign of anyone guarding the place. I knocked on the door, just in case some *ment* was hoping to earn promotion, and when no one appeared, let myself in.

Chinara would have been horrified at the mess, but it was nothing more than I'd expected. Chairs overturned, drawers emptied out onto the floor and left open, the bed tipped to one side, with a couple of diagonal knife slashes across the mattress for good measure. Maybe with all the porn they'd found, the crime scene officers had decided to mark the spot with an X.

The poetry books Chinara had loved, had scrimped and saved to buy, littered the floor, spines twisted or broken, pages bent or torn out. I remembered the consolation she had sought and found in these poems, wondered how poetry could save the world when it couldn't even save itself. I picked up a book at random, looked at one of the final poems.

Dying: nothing new there these days,
But living, that's no newer.

Written by someone called Esenin, apparently. I wondered if he was still alive, if he'd be interested in meeting up one evening. With that attitude, I thought we'd get on just fine. Then I flipped to the frontispiece, and learned young Sergei had hanged himself at the tender age of thirty, in the Hotel Angleterre, St Petersburg, back in 1925. So no meeting of minds then.

I picked the books up off the floor, put them back on the shelf where Chinara had always kept them. I wasn't going to bother tidying the rest of the apartment. As far as I was concerned, the place where she and I had made our home no longer existed.

I looked around for the framed photo I'd kept of her, laughing, her hair caught in the wind as we rode the Ferris wheel in Bosteri, on the shore of Lake Issyk-Kul. It wasn't in its usual place, but then I spotted it, face down, half-hidden under a pile of clothes.

The frame was intact, but the glass was broken, and someone had ripped Chinara's photo in two. Checking to see if anything was hidden behind the picture, I guessed. I held a piece in each hand, and brought the ragged edges together, trying to make her whole, hoping to bring her back to life. But some things are impossible; life pins you down, picks your pocket of all the happiness and comfort you'd ever hoped for. Life had made my wife die, and made me her murderer. And knowing I'd simply brought her inevitable end nearer didn't make me feel any less guilty.

I put the two pieces of the photograph in my jacket pocket, remembering why I'd come back to the apartment, went into the tiny kitchen. As I expected, the cooker and the refrigerator had been searched, and the doors left open, which accounted for the sweet aroma of decaying food. But no one had bothered to search properly under the sink. Years before, I'd constructed a false back with a space of five centimetres between it and the concrete wall. You never know when you might not be able to get to your major arms dump. I'd painted over the cracks on either side, so only the closest inspection would spot it. And nobody had.

I used a screwdriver to prise the false back away, and reached inside. My fingers found the thin plastic-wrapped package inside, surprisingly heavy for its size. My knees creaking to remind me I wasn't getting any younger, I stood up and slipped the package into my pocket. I checked my watch; half an hour since I'd arrived. It was time to get out of the apartment; I'd been there too long already. I listened at the door before opening, but the landing outside sounded deserted. I pulled the door shut after myself, the click of the lock sounding as final as anything I'd ever heard. An end to my old life, I told myself. The only question was if there would be a new beginning.

I took the stairs two at a time, managing to avoid the piles of litter that had accumulated at each turn. We Kyrgyz are houseproud when it comes to inside our apartments, but communal space is a different matter altogether. Maybe that's why the light bulbs are always missing.

I was in a hurry, and the stairwell was dark, which was why I didn't spot the empty Baltika bottle until I stood on it. It rolled away under my feet, taking me with it. I staggered and waved my arms about like one of those Soviet circus clowns that used to make holidays so miserable, then smacked my head against the wall.

I was only unconscious for about three minutes, but apparently that was enough. Because when I came to, and tried to touch my head where I'd attacked the wall, I found I couldn't move my hands. And I was blind.

Chapter 45

Somehow in the fall, I'd managed to lose my shoes and socks, and pull some kind of sack over my head. I'd taken two of those little plastic ties that hold computer cables together to attach my thumbs together. I'd also done the same with my big toes. I must have looked as if I were practising a particularly strenuous yoga exercise. Except I wasn't.

'You always have to be careful just how tight you make those restraints,' a woman's voice said, so close to my ear I would have jumped, had I been able to move.

'Too loose and your captive might just be able to wriggle your way out of them,' she continued. 'Too tight and the blood gets cut off and after a few hours, it's amputation time. Just be grateful I didn't put one around your dick.'

'They don't make them in that big a size,' I said.

'If you're going to mouth off, then I've got some other toys I like. You won't, but that's the least of your problems,' the woman said, her mouth against my ear. I could smell her scent, floral, powerful but somehow reminding me of decay. Her voice rasped, as if she'd been kicked in the throat a long time ago and never quite recovered. She didn't need to whisper threats to sound terrifying.

'Have you ever noticed how someone walks when they've had their toes cut off?' You wouldn't think it would make much difference, such small bones, with hardly any meat on them. And it takes very little effort, it's like trimming your toenails, only a little further down. But, believe me, it does. People shuffle as if they're drunk, or they've only recently learnt to walk. They walk round obstacles rather than over them, they can't manage stairs, and they'll never play football again.'

I said nothing.

'You must think us very simple, Inspector Borubaev. Or is that ex-Inspector? Haven't you become one of the little people now? Looking over your shoulder in case some *ment* keen on glory spots the wanted child pornographer, puts two between your shoulder blades and gets a quick promotion?'

I could feel her staring at me, imagined her head cocked to one side.

'Sometimes people like you just make it all too easy. Like filling in all the hard answers in a crossword puzzle. I knew you'd come back here sooner or later. We put a little locator on the top of your front door. When you opened it, the connection broke and told us you were back. Fifteen minutes later, we were here, parked outside, about to come up when we saw the lights go out. You had your little stumble in the dark, we picked you up and dusted you off.'

I felt hands pick me up, heard the slam of the apartment block's metal door as it clanged shut, then I was being carried face down. A car boot opened, and I bounced off the spare wheel as they dropped me inside. I felt the vibration as the car doors opened and closed, and the grunt of the engine as it turned over and fired.

The journey was uncomfortable, but at least it was on roads, which gave me a faint hope I wasn't being taken to the mountains for a quick scenic tour followed by a bullet in the back of my head. Or worse.

I did my best to shift my weight off the spare, tried to get more comfortable. But comfort is a relative term when you're tied up. I could feel the rim of the wheel pressing against my knee, and heard my trousers snag and tear as I levered myself backwards. I moved around a little more, and rolled forward slightly, until I could place my thumbs against the wheel rim. Cold metal, a sharp jagged edge maybe a centimetre long, where a stone or rock must have hit it. One of the unexpected benefits of living in a country with potholed roads. I rubbed my thumbs against the cold metal, felt it scratch and tear at my skin, drawing blood. It wasn't much of a chance, but it was all I had.

I shifted position once more, until I was lying face down, arse up in the air, my thumbs against the metal. I started to saw at the plastic restraint tying my thumbs together, wondering how much time I'd have. Every time the car took a corner, it threw me backwards, and I had to scramble back into position and start again.

In the darkness, it was hard to guess the exact spot, and after a few minutes, the metal was slick with blood. The pain was a fire biting into my flesh with each stroke of the metal against plastic. But I carried on sawing away. Maybe I'd lose the use of my thumbs, but that was the very least of my worries. God only knew what I'd done to my toe, but then I wasn't planning on playing football anyway. But I sawed on for what felt like a couple of hours, until I felt the restraint suddenly fall apart. I sucked at my thumb, my tongue running along the length of the gash, my mouth filling with blood and skin.

With my hands free, I pulled off the hood, took out my cigarettes and matches. I resisted the temptation to light up, struck a match instead.

It took a couple of matches before my eyes got used to the sudden flare, and I was worried about setting fire to a petrol can, so I made sure each match was safely out before I lit another.

I'd never taken a ride in a car boot before, and it wasn't anything anyone would want to write to relatives about. The usual debris lay in a heap to one side, including a couple of blankets. I was a little pissed off no one had thought to spread them out to make my journey a little less uncomfortable. I was definitely going to complain to the tour operator. A tyre lever looked like a suitable way to make my point, but I quickly decided against that. Whoever opened the boot wasn't going to be standing there, wondering what I was doing, as I clambered out, tyre lever in hand, and took my best shot.

Instead, I reached for the package I'd strapped to my calf back in my apartment, started to pick at the tape I'd used to seal it. What was inside was going to get me out of that car. Not a lockpick, not a saw. Two knives, but not just ordinary kitchen knives.

These were Uighur knives.

Chapter 46

For those who don't know, Uighur blades are the Central Asian knife equivalent of the Japanese Samurai sword, the ultimate combination of precision steel with age-old craftsmanship. They say if you hold an Uighur knife up in the air, and let the wind blow a silk scarf across the blade, the silk falls into two pieces. If it doesn't, the knife is broken up and the long process of manufacture begins again.

I don't know if there's any truth to the story, never having had a silk scarf to try it out, but they're fearsome weapons all the same.

The Uighurs live on the other side of the Torugart Pass which leads from Kyrgyzstan to China, and knife-making is one of their proudest traditions, one that goes back for centuries. Every Uighur carries at least one knife, to use for everything from halal slaughter to preparing fruit and vegetables. The craft is usually handed down from father to son, and the Uighur take great pride in the beauty of their knives, as well as their practicality, with handles decorated with inlays of shell, bone and semi-precious stones. But mine were different, very different.

Some years ago, I'd helped out an elderly Uighur man. He'd lived for years in a tiny apartment in one of the older, more decrepit blocks in Alamedin, but the landlord was threatening to throw him out. A couple of heavies tried to persuade the Uighur to seek new lodgings. One of them lost a thumb and index finger when he discovered just how sharp the Uighurs make their knives.

He returned the next day, this time with a Makarov, presumably having practised with his other trigger finger. I took his gun away from him, and broke his remaining index finger in all three bones while doing so. I didn't feel bad about it: he wasn't planning on typing his memoirs.

The old man was grateful, said so in broken Kyrgyz. I was puzzled when he took hold of my hands, judging the length of my fingers, the muscles in my palms, the flexibility of my wrists.

Six months later, the old man appeared at Sverdlovsky station and with a great deal of broken-toothed smiling pushed a thin package into the inside pocket of my jacket. I started to reach for it, but he looked worried and shook his head, his gold teeth catching the light. Our little secret.

Once he'd left, I went back to my office, opened the package. Two knives, but not traditional decorated Uighur knives. There were brutal-looking unornamented throwing knives, handle-heavy, obviously handmade. They were made for fighting, for killing, nothing else. They fitted perfectly in my palm, and I understood why the old man had taken so much time inspecting my hands. I took one, weighed it, threw it at my office door. The thud as it hit could have been heard in the street, and the quiver it made as it spun through the air set my teeth on edge.

I bought a couple of dartboards, glued them together, fastened them to the back of the bedroom door, practised my knife-throwing routine until I got pretty good, at least from about eight feet away. At first, Chinara would ask when I was going to run away to join the circus, but that joke got old very quickly. Then she started to complain about the noise, and why didn't I get a quieter hobby.

I said I'd get rid of the knives. Which I did, after a fashion, stashing them away in their hiding place, hoping I wouldn't ever need them.

If only life were that peaceful. But it rarely is.

I used one knife to cut through the remaining restraint, and stretched as best I could in the confined space, while the car moved forward towards what promised to be the end of my life. I found a roll of duct tape and strapped one of the knives against my back, under my shirt, and held the other ready for a forward throw. A lot of the skill lies in the wrist, the sudden snap and release that triggers the blade forward. I'd practised long enough on the dartboard, but never on a person. I wasn't worried I might freeze when the time came to throw; self-preservation does away with all that nonsense. I was only afraid I might miss. Of course, once you've thrown your knife, you've effectively disarmed yourself, so I clutched the tyre iron with my other hand. The blood from my thumb made it slippery and difficult to grip, but it was better than getting out of the car trunk with nothing more deadly than a smile.

Squatting in the dark, waiting to kill or be killed, memories reeled past me, as if to remind me of the times I felt immortal, when the world was mine. Pulling Chinara towards me for a long kiss in the cold waters of Lake Issyk-Kul, dazzled by light reflected from the mountain snow. Joy that never seemed to end, pain that never seemed to stop. The livid scar that commemorated Chinara's cancer. The corpses that showed how bottles and blades and bullets can drain the life out of anyone. And the taste of fear in my mouth, sour like cheap wine and copper wire.

Then the car turned, slowed, the clang of gates closing behind us.

Time to die seemed the most likely option. I would have liked more years, children to scold, grandchildren to pamper. But we all get what's coming to us, in my case, sooner rather than later.

I guessed we were back at Graves's compound. I held my breath, waited for the boot to open, hoping I'd catch someone off guard, if only for a few seconds.

With luck, it might even be Kurmanalieva herself, and I could sort out Saltanat's problem with her there and then. The catch snicked, then daylight poured in.

To his credit, the thug who peered down at me had quick reflexes. He was almost fast enough to step back and shout that I'd somehow got free. But I was faster. I felt as if I were moving in slow motion, with all the time in the world to take aim, register the surprise in his eyes, watch his mouth open to cry out. The knife left my hand with the same snap of the wrist I'd practised so often. Sunlight caught the blade, like a sudden flash of summer lightning, moving with the effortless grace of an eagle swooping on its prey.

The lightning turned scarlet as the blade hit the man's neck, just below his left ear. Even as the first arterial spray jetted a thin stream into the air, I was pushing myself forward, feet on the boot's rim. The man's hands grappled with the blade, as if pulling it out would somehow stop the pain, darkness already spilling into his eyes. I snatched the handle, twisting and pulling sideways, and with my other hand brought the tyre lever down between his eyes.

His blood splashed warm and sticky down my face. I was in a moment that lasted for hours, now bringing the tyre lever down on the hand holding a gun glimpsed in the corner of my eye. Bones splintered, the impact jarred my arm, and as if from miles away, I heard a scream of anger, realised it was mine.

And then everything snapped back to the present, as I felt the unmistakable bite of a gun barrel pushed into the back of my head.

'That's quite enough, Inspector,' a woman's voice said, harsh and brutal as a raven's cry. 'I've no wish to kill you. Yet.'

I paused, getting my breath back, feeling adrenalin rush through me. I dropped the knife and the tyre lever. They lay beside the corpse of the man they'd just killed, almost as if I'd had nothing to do with his death. A few feet away, another man clutched at his shattered hand, bent double, face grey with pain and shock. After the boot, the air tasted fresh, vital. I wondered how long I'd be around to savour it.

'You have the advantage of me,' I said, in my best tough Murder Squad voice, feeling my knees tremble as my heart slowed.

'I do,' she said, and the gun pressed harder against my skull. 'And I intend to keep it that way.'

'Albina Kurmanalieva,' I said. It wasn't a question.

'You've been busy, you and that bitch,' she said. 'But she was never stupid, that one. You? Like all men, the merest sniff of *pizda* and you lose what brains your mother gave you.'

I shrugged, very slowly, so as not to give her the opportunity to pull the trigger.

'So where do we go from here?' I asked. Suddenly, I felt sick to my stomach. The blood smearing my face felt like a mask I'd assumed as a disguise, only to discover I couldn't peel it off. The stink of too-strong perfume was cloying, and I could taste bile rising in my throat. When she spoke, it was all I could do to stand still and not vomit.

'I'm sure you're an ambitious man,' she murmured, her voice making my flesh crawl. 'I thought we might make a movie star of you, Inspector.'

Chapter 47

I've spent a lot of my working life in cellars, one way or another, and the experience has never been a good one. All too often, a cellar has seemed like a prelude to being permanently underground. I've been beaten, tortured, threatened with death in cellars. I've watched people die, helped them die. I've stood by in basement interrogation rooms as a burly *ment* beats a confession out of a suspect. Cellars are not my favourite places. But as somewhere to die, they're almost unbeatable.

Nothing looked to have changed in the cellar since Saltanat and I broke into the house what seemed like years ago. No fresh bloodstains on the floor, the hooks and knives still in their racks, ropes and chains coiled on shelves. Not that I could see much, since leather straps held my head, wrists and ankles securely in place against a semi-upright wooden table that stank of dried blood.

I took comfort in the thought that no one else had stared into the unwinking eye of the camera since we'd started our hunt. A small boy kicking his football against a wall with a goalmouth chalked on it, a little girl singing lullabies to her favourite doll; they were safe, if only for the moment. If I was the price to be paid for their safety, that goes with the territory every policeman signs up for, the day they pin on their badge and strap on their gun.

I was under no illusions about my bravery. I'd seen too

many people broken in cellars to believe that. The toughest guys loosen their tongues if you push a needle under their fingernails or a lit cigarette against their eyes. The Circle of Brothers might take an oath of silence, but where are your brothers when you watch someone pouring a cup of hot oil into a funnel or whetting the edge of a kitchen knife? It takes so little to make a man talk, sometimes just the thought of the pain to come is enough.

'I apologise, Inspector, for not having anywhere more congenial to chat to you,' Kurmanalieva said, her voice hoarse and menacing. She came into my line of view, her blonde hair tied back in a ponytail, her suit immaculate. When you've something very special to sell to collectors, you can afford to buy the very best for yourself.

'I thought this was one of your favourite places, Albina,' I said, using her given name to show my contempt. 'The only place in the world where you can reveal your inner nature.'

Kurmanalieva smiled. This close to her, I saw the generous lipstick did little to hide thin, bloodless lips. Her skin looked stretched, waxy. I wondered if it was vanity that had inspired the plastic surgery, the nips and tucks, or simply to avoid being captured in the field. Her face was that of a woman in her early thirties, I guessed, but her hands were old, compact and brutal, veins like blue strings under the skin. Early forties? It didn't really seem to matter. I didn't think she would want to fuck me before killing me.

'I want you to know, Inspector, I don't enjoy the things I'm about to do to you. Not like some of my colleagues. They sometimes get carried away in their enthusiasm, with tragic consequences. Tragic for the individual, of course, but also tragic because one may not get all the information required. Then there's all the mess and fuss involved in disposal.'

She reached forward and drew a fingernail across my forehead, pausing to hold it against my right eye, its touch as light as a spider's web.

'Me, I know exactly what I'm doing. When to start. When to stop. When to let someone consider the error of their ways in trying to be brave.'

She pressed her fingernail ever so slightly harder, and I could feel the edge hard against my eyeball. Three millimetres more and she would blind me. Then, almost coquettishly, she pulled her hand back.

'And that, Inspector, is why I am the best. Unfortunately for you.'

She turned and strode out of my sight. I heard the creak of a chair, the rasp of a match, the quick breath in and the satisfied exhale.

'It's a cliché that people enjoy a cigarette after sex, don't you think? Personally, I like to smoke before I get down and dirty, before I set to. It's the ritual, you see. And control. Smoke and fire and death, all in that one little white tube of passion. You've heard people say they'd die for a cigarette? Sometimes I make it come true.'

I sighed, as if I'd heard it all before.

'Just what is it you want, Albina?' I asked.

'Well, I'd appreciate knowing where I can put my hands on Ms Umarova, for a start.'

'I don't know where she is,' I said, glad Saltanat and I hadn't arranged to meet at the apartment. 'And I don't see how finding her helps you, to be honest. There's too much information out there now, about you, about Graves.'

She simply laughed.

'You'd be surprised at how little people hear when you stuff their ears with *som*, Inspector. Everyone looks the other way for the right price.'

'You're asking me to betray her?'

'I'm asking you to save yourself a lot of unnecessary anguish. If she were here now, strapped next to you, maybe even holding your hand in some sickly sentimental pact, whose eye would you rather I took out? Hers or yours?'

I was silent. Kurmanalieva stood in front of me, blew a cloud of smoke into my face, and smiled. But it was more like a grimace than a smile, making her look both human and insane.

'I rest my case, Inspector,' she said, inspecting the glowing tip of her cigarette as if solving a puzzle, before stubbing it out on my left hand, the one with the scar tissue I'd acquired during the Tynaliev affair. A lot of the nerves in my hand had been damaged and the scars were thick enough to lessen the pain, but it was still enough to make me cry out.

Kurmanalieva threw the butt onto the floor, grinding it out with her shoe. Elegant scarlet stilettos, I noticed. If I was going to be tortured, it might as well be done with style. She reached up again towards my face, my eye, and smiled as I flinched. She patted my cheek, and her fingernail scratched against the stubble on my jaw. I felt beads of sweat slide down my back.

'Back in the good old days of the USSR,' she said, 'I was seconded to the Lubyanka in Moscow for two years. The Kremlin was keen to ensure its distant territories stayed loyal, or at least quiet. So it made sense to have some Central Asians batting for the team.'

As she spoke, she walked towards the shelves with the knives, hooks and whips, testing the point of a boning knife with her fingertip, running her thumb against the edge of a narrow blade, choosing how to inflict pain. She hesitated, selected a pair of pliers, old and rusted.

'I imagine you're thinking "Traitor", or some such nonsense,' she said, her back towards me, so I was unable to read her expression. 'But times were different. The Russians offered stability, peace. Casualties? There always are. But the people who bleat about democracy are always the ones with a passport and money for a ticket out.'

She turned back towards me, stood in front of me, her eyes drilling into mine.

'No comment, Inspector?' she asked. 'You spent a few years in an orphanage, you know how turbulent things were then.'

I said nothing, unwilling to provoke her, to risk further pain.

'Did you know the Lubyanka was originally the headquarters of an insurance company?'

She laughed, that horrible false laugh again, charming as a scar.

'If you think about it, in one way, that's what it stayed as. Insurance for the elite, for the country.'

She shrugged, resumed pacing around the room.

'I learnt the virtues of patience. Rush in too quickly with the pliers or the electricity and you either kill your subject or they defy you, tell you nothing. The way I work, you'll tell me everything, I'll be a mother confessor to you. Your words spilling out, tripping over your tongue, unstoppable.'

I remained silent, shut my eyes, wished I could do the

same for my ears. The awful thing was I knew she was right. I'd talk, sooner or later. Her voice continued, cajoling, wanting me to see her point of view.

'Normally, I'd take my time. Mix a little pain with a lot of sympathy and understanding. I don't want to do this, any more than you want me to. But what choice do you give me?'

I bit the inside of my cheek, focusing on the pain rather than her hypnotic voice. A standard anti-interrogation technique, only a matter of time before I broke. Hours, days, weeks; none of it matters if you're dreading the next few minutes.

'As I recall, you didn't say anything the last time we met. Or don't you remember?'

I remembered her perfume, the scent of dying lilies, the curve of her breasts, the cruelty in her eyes. The woman in the orphanage. I'd sensed her malevolence even then.

Without warning, Kurmanalieva knelt down and took hold of my foot. I tried to pull away, but the leather straps held me firmly in place.

'Ticklish?' she asked, drawing her fingernail lightly across the sole of my foot. She looked up at me, winked, as if we were in some conspiracy together.

I watched as she held up the pliers.

'Haven't used these for a while,' she said brightly, snapping the jaws open and closed, open and closed. 'I do hope I haven't lost the knack.'

She placed the pliers against my little toe, and squeezed, just hard enough for me to feel the cold steel.

'Start off small, that's always been my motto,' she said, cheerful, as if giving a toast at a birthday celebration. 'The trick is not to damage the root bed; that way, your toenail grows back. Eventually. Of course, there's a certain amount of initial discomfort, live and learn, eh?'

The last thing I wanted was a lesson in anatomy, but I could only listen.

'The nail plate, the bit you trim, that's just dead, compacted cells, the stuff that rhino horns are made of. But underneath, at the back, that's the matrix, the living tissue that grows the nail. Very sensitive.'

And with that, she jerked her arm back.

A bolt of white fire screamed up my left leg, turning me sightless for a few seconds.

I opened my eyes, wondering if I'd pissed myself, looked at my torturer. Kurmanalieva held up the pliers, my blood-stained toenail trapped in their jaws.

'There, all done, that wasn't so bad, was it?' she asked, in a terrible parody of maternal feeling, as if taking a splinter out of my finger or cleaning a cut on my knee.

'Just be glad it wasn't your big toe, that really does hurt. Or so I've seen.'

She held the pliers close to my face. I could smell the blood, see the gleam in her eyes. I managed not to vomit, although messing up her designer suit was a temptation.

'It's not the sort of wound you can put a bandage on, but as long as you keep it clean and dry, the nail will grow back, and you'll be fine in eighteen months.'

Kurmanalieva reached into her bag, took out her cigarettes, lit one, placed it between my lips. I inhaled, dizzy as the smoke filled my lungs. She looked down at my foot, a worried expression carving lines in her forehead. She looked at the lit tip of her cigarette, and softly blew on it, until it flamed a rich orange.

'I don't think you can keep your toe clean and dry, Akyl, not being tied up and in this damp cellar. So it's probably best if I cauterise the wound.'

She knelt down again, and with a single stabbing movement, stubbed her cigarette out on the bare raw flesh where my nail had been.

This time, I fainted.

When I came round, Kurmanalieva was scrubbing the pliers clean with a cloth she soaked from an unlabelled bottle.

'Vodka,' she explained. 'I keep things hygienic. No point in questioning people if they're going to die from blood poisoning first.'

She held the bottle up in front of me, raised one eyebrow, held the thumb and forefinger of her other hand a couple of centimetres apart.

'Just a small one, raise the spirits, loosen the tongue? Oh, of course, you don't drink, do you?'

She turned away, then splashed some of the clear liquid over my bare foot. I didn't pass out, but I did vomit. Unfortunately, only on myself. Music suddenly filled the cellar. 'Dies Ira', 'Day of Wrath', played in the cheap tinny tones of a mobile phone. Kurmanalieva rummaged in her bag, produced a smartphone, turned away to take the call. She listened without speaking for a moment, then spoke.

'Thirty minutes. Don't be late.'

She ended the call, placed her phone back in her bag, turned to me.

'I know it's very rude of me to leave you, the sign of a poor hostess. But that was your delightful friend, Ms Umarova. She wants to meet with me, maybe reminisce about when we worked together. And wants to make a trade for you. True love, Inspector?'

She stared at me, at her handiwork. I stared back.

Kurmanalieva shook her head at Saltanat's taste in men, smiled, waggled her fingers in farewell. There was something I had to know before she left the room.

'Why haven't you killed me?'

She stared at me, one foot on the stairs, before giving a slow smile that highlighted the crow's feet around her eyes.

'Because you're not top of my list. Yet.'

Then she switched off the light.

Chapter 48

I don't know how long I was in Graves's cellar, moving between a state of dazed half-consciousness and moments of simple terror. Pain gnawed at my foot, as if rats had emerged into the darkness to chew on my flesh. I never knew fear had a scent until then; a woman's perfume strong with the ripeness of lilacs, the tang of rusting steel, the singe of burnt meat.

The leather straps binding me to the table made movement impossible, and cramps tore at my shoulders, back and legs. As my muscles spasmed, the straps bit deeper into me, reminding me of my helplessness.

The darkness was endless; my eyes saw nothing but the splashes and stains of pure colour caused by the pain that consumed me. I was going to die in that cellar, swallowed up in blackness. And part of me welcomed that.

I heard death fumbling with the door at the top of the stairs, his key twisting in the lock, the tumblers falling into place. Presumably using a skeleton key. Heavy boots clumped down the wooden stairs. I didn't know any prayers; that time was long past for me. I remembered my dream, falling into Chinara's open grave, joining her in the long waltz, realised it wasn't a dream but a prophecy.

The brutality of the light dazzled me, but the room slowly swam back into focus. A burly man stood in front of me, a scowl tattooed on his face. We'd never met, but I knew his name.

Morton Graves.

'You've caused me a lot of trouble, Inspector.'

'I'm pleased to hear it,' I said, the words raw from my dry throat.

'Trouble is perhaps an exaggeration,' Graves said. 'I probably shouldn't rank it higher than an inconvenience, a nuisance.'

Graves's face was oddly asymmetrical, as if steel plates had been inserted under his skin and badly welded together. His eyes were the dark blue of a winter dusk, with all the warmth and compassion of an ice cube. His left eye had a slight cast, as if even he was unable to look at his handiwork without squinting.

'Albina give you a hard time? Make you all sorts of promises and nonsense about how this hurts me more than it hurts you? We're all in this together?'

I would have shrugged, if I'd been able to.

'I've had worse,' I said, thinking back to that other cellar, where my hand had been sandwiched between the hotplates of a portable grill.

'Heard you were old-school tough, told Albina her usual methods would be wasted on you.'

'You should have whispered it louder,' I said. 'She might have heard you,' then winced as a fresh bolt of pain shot through my foot. I knew it would be worse later on, when the throb of infection kicked in, but right now it was just about bearable.

Graves looked down at my bare foot. His expression didn't change as he saw the burn.

'If you're going to stub out your cigarettes on the floor, best keep your shoes on next time,' he said, gave a mirthless smile at his own humour.

He reached out towards my forehead, and I shut my eyes in preparation for the slap or punch. But instead, I felt his fingers working at the buckle of the strap around my head. Graves swore under his breath, but continued to pull at the strap until suddenly I could move my head.

'Easier, eh?' he asked, and turned my head from side to side. I felt the muscles and tendons pull and stretch, heard my neck bones creak. For a moment, I wondered if he was going to snap my neck, but he seemed to have other plans.

A few moments later, he'd undone all the restraints, held me up by my armpits, helped me slide down to the floor when my legs gave way. I slumped there for a while, gingerly flexing my arms and legs. The burn on my foot throbbed like a bad toothache. My shoes were on the floor beside me, and Graves gestured at me to put them on. That made the throbbing considerably worse.

'I don't understand,' I said, and I didn't. 'Why are you letting me go?'

'Who said I was doing that?' he asked.

'Then what are you going to do with me?'

'Kill you, of course. Stamp on you like an insect. One not worth wasting shoe leather on.'

My hands were still numb, but my knife pressed against the small of my back. Maybe I'd be flexible enough to show Morton Graves just how skilled an Uighur craftsman can be.

'So why untie me?' I asked. Graves leant forward, crouching so his face was almost level with mine. I smelt mint toothpaste on his breath, expensive cologne on his skin. I knew I smelt like an outside long-drop shithole, with an undernote of charred meat.

He looked at me, his gaze intense, unblinking. It suddenly

occurred to me this must be how madness looks at the world, distorted, invincible.

'You're a Muslim, right?'

I shook my head. I wasn't anything. I'd given up on faith and belief and salvation with the first murder scene I attended, an old man beaten to death by his nephew, smashed on vodka, arguing over some forgotten nonsense.

'Well, you've been in a mosque? Or a church? Somewhere sacred?'

I nodded, to break the monotony of shaking my head.

'Well, this place is my church, if you like. This is where I do the things that matter to me. The rites, you might say. These walls,' and his arm swept in a grand gesture, 'these walls hold the essence of everything that's important to me.'

I watched his mouth move, noticed how spittle gathered in the corners, saw a rivulet of sweat worm its way down his cheek.

He stood up; his knees didn't creak, the way mine would.

'I wouldn't taint them with your blood, with your death. You see, what I do here protects the young, the innocent by keeping them innocent, for ever young. After I've finished with them, no one can rob them of that. I'm not a hunter, but a saviour. And I get to fuck them as well. You understand?'

I looked up at his eyes, realised he was quite mad, as he gave a smile that was almost angelic. Listening to this drivel, I decided enough was enough, and fuck the consequences.

'If you could hear yourself mouth off, Graves: "keeping the innocent innocent". By terrifying them, by raping them, by killing them? You've got a very odd idea of protecting the young. And I don't suppose the money hurts either, when you sell your shit on to other lunatic perverts.'

He scowled again, one corner of his mouth turning up in a sneer. His contempt was like a blow to my chest.

'Inspector, I'm a very rich man. Richer than you could imagine. I don't do this for the money. Small minds like yours always think it's about money; that's because you don't have any, and you envy anyone who does. I could buy this shitty little country with the change I've got in my pocket. I own the police, politicians, lawyers, I can do whatever or whoever I want, with no one to stop me. Especially not a minor policeman from the sticks who's about to meet with an accident.'

'All part of your master plan, is it? Power, terror and a few free fucks thrown in?'

'I wouldn't expect a dumb *ment* like you to have a clue.'

And with that, he cuffed my hands in front of me, reached for a large hessian sack from the nearest shelf, dropped it over my head.

Chapter 49

'If you're going to kill me, why bother with the bag?' I said as Graves half-pulled, half-dragged me up the stairs. I stumbled over a couple of the treads, and he tugged at my arm in irritation. I caught my thigh on what I assumed was the kitchen table, and Graves swore again, as if not being able to see where I was going was my fault, not his.

'Because I don't trust you,' he said, as if stating the merely obvious.

Then we were outside, clean air biting into my lungs, refreshing after the damp claustrophobic cellar. My feet scuffled across gravel, and I was thrust against the side of a car.

'Get in,' Graves ordered. I fumbled with the door handle, scrambled into the passenger seat, banging my shins as I did so. If they ever found my body, it would be a mass of bruises, scars and wounds. I realised I was in the people carrier I'd seen earlier.

'Don't worry, Inspector, an accident en route is the least of your worries,' Graves said, hitting the ignition and the gate opener at the same time. 'And besides, the air bag will save you. Which may prove not to be a good thing.'

The metal gates scraped across the drive, then we were moving forward, turning left, picking up speed at a rate that would get us stopped if the car didn't have diplomatic plates.

'I liked the photo of you lying dead in the snow,' Graves said. 'Very imaginative, I thought. And it gave me a few ideas of my own. After all, if you're already dead, who's going to be looking for you now? And in a couple of years, there won't be anything left to identify you anyway.'

I didn't care for the way the conversation was turning, so I stayed silent.

'You know, Inspector, when I'm in my church, I often notice how my congregation changes at the end. They've gone through fear then terror, to pain beyond anything they've ever imagined. They've been humiliated, shamed, helpless. For some of them, if they come, well, that's just another way their bodies have betrayed them. Sperm first, blood later. Pleasures of the flesh, and so on. But there's a moment, just before the end, when I see their hopes fade. Resignation takes over, maybe even a wish for a swift ending. Their eyes glaze over, ready for the final extinguishing of the light.'

Graves's voice took on a new tone, a preacher delivering a sermon, a politician offering promises he would never intend to keep.

'You expect me to do the same, Graves?'

'Why should you be any different, Inspector? You saw your wife die, didn't you? I'm sure she went into darkness the way we all do. In pain and afraid.'

At that moment I hated Graves with an intensity so great I wanted to grab the steering wheel, force us off the road or into the path of another car. I didn't mind dying myself if it took him off the planet.

He must have guessed what I was thinking, from the mocking tone when he spoke.

'No heroics, Inspector. Remember, I'm the one with the seat belt, and I don't think you'd enjoy a flight through the windscreen.'

'I'll sit still, if you'll take the bag off my head.'

His only answer was a laugh.

'One thing I'd like to know, Graves, before you shoot me. Just to put my mind at rest. The identity bands from all those orphanages. What was that all about? I already know they didn't match the dead bodies.'

Graves laughed.

'Do you know anything about magic, Inspector? I don't mean spells and incantations, I'm talking about conjuring, illusions, tricks.'

'No,' I said, shaking my head, although maybe that wasn't apparent under the hood.

'Virtually all magic relies on misdirection, making your audience look in the wrong place while you perform the trick. Deceiving their eyes while stealing their wallet, you understand.'

'So the bands were there to divert our attention, to go off on a search that wouldn't take us anywhere?'

Graves laughed again.

'Only partly, although that was a welcome side-effect. It's really to help us in selling the films. Obviously, what we were offering wasn't your average fuck and suck film. What you might call a specialist interest. And an expensive one. The collectors of such material are rich, able to spend big money. And for that, they want discretion, reassurance their local police force isn't going to break down the front door of their mansion with a search warrant.'

'So?'

'So we reassure them by pointing out all our movie stars are orphans. No family to worry about them, demand an inquiry into their disappearance.'

'And your customers' desire for this shit makes them all too happy to believe your explanation,' I said. 'Little head ruling big head.'

'Exactly,' Graves said. 'And the beauty of it is, quite a lot of them really were orphans. And since you stop being an orphan at sixteen, officially, the bands also provided evidence that even the older boys and girls were still under age when they made their cameo performances.'

'And the bodies up in Karakol?' I asked.

Graves paused before answering.

'A bit of a mistake, I suppose. We were offered a great deal of money to make a one-off film, one customer only, to be shot outdoors over a period of a few months, up in the Jeti-Oguz valley, with the red sandstone rocks as a backdrop. I couldn't attend the shoot myself, I was in Moscow, but I gave very precise instructions about the disposal of the bodies. Scatter them all over, I said. Instructions that weren't followed, which is why you found them all together. Annoying, but the client still paid.'

Seven infants slaughtered for a rich man's whim. And all the other deaths that followed on.

'I understand; you're a paedophile, a murderer, a rapist. You're insane. But Graves, you're rich, why risk everything by selling this shit?'

Graves paused, and his voice was subdued when he spoke.

'Of course I could have given the films away for free to other collectors. But it's a law of nature that we only value something if we've had to pay for it. And the more we pay, the greater its value. So the more extreme the material, the more it costs. Surely that's obvious?'

I said nothing in the face of such twisted logic. I wondered why I didn't grab the wheel, strangle him with my bare hands as the car rolled over and slid off the road. And then the answer came to me.

Fear. Of pain, of falling into dark nothingness. I could imagine a tiny part of the terror of the children led into Graves's cellar, perhaps enticed down steep steps with the promise of food, toys, a warm place to sleep.

I reached up, managed to pull the bag over my head. Fuck it; what could Graves do that wasn't already going to happen to me?

I blinked, saw we were travelling east out of the city, back towards Karakol. Plenty of deserted spaces, overgrown cemeteries filled with the inhabitants of villages that had long since dwindled and died, fields no longer cultivated, paths no longer trod. This was where my life had led, my body left to the mercies of rain, sun and snow. I felt nothing, knew it meant nothing.

The car picked up speed, and I placed my hands on the dashboard to brace myself in case we braked suddenly. The road was deserted, and I wondered why Graves didn't just pull over, drag me into a field and put a bullet in my ear.

'Don't worry,' he said, as if he were reading my thoughts. 'I've got just the place in mind for you – think of it like going on holiday. Quiet, no one will disturb your bones.'

We passed a farmer's wooden cart, a sour-looking donkey trudging away at the front. Graves hit the horn, but the donkey plodded on, the farmer giving us a sideways scowl as we passed. The donkey didn't even do that. A motorbike overtook us, its rider anonymous in leathers and a full-face helmet, revving the engine and disappearing into the distance.

We drove on for three or four kilometres, and then,

rounding a bend, we saw the motorcycle lying on its side, wheels still slowly spinning. The rider lay face down a few feet away, one arm thrown out above his head, the other folded beneath his body. The only way we could pass was by driving into the ditch on either side of the road.

Graves swore, and applied the brake, so we slowed to a halt about five metres away.

'You stay here,' he ordered, opened the car door. As his foot touched the ground, the motorcyclist rolled over, producing a gun from underneath his body, aiming it in our direction.

Graves scrabbled underneath the driver's seat and came up with a Makarov. I ducked down as a bullet shattered the windscreen and embedded itself in the driver's headrest. I managed to twist around and grab the door handle. Graves crouched behind his open door, returning fire, but by now the assassin was shielded by the cover of his bike. I heard a bullet thud into the door; time to go. Another bang, and the car lurched forward and sideways; the gunman must have hit one of the front tyres. I threw myself out of the passenger door, landing and rolling onto my bad shoulder. I struggled to my feet, ran for the safety of the ditch. It was only a few feet away, but my shoulder blades tensed, waiting for a bullet to rip through my spine. A lifetime later, I was face down in mud and sheep shit, wondering how to get the handcuffs off.

I didn't know whether the gunman was out to get Graves, or me, or both of us, so I decided my best plan was to stay where I was and hope they'd forgotten me in the turmoil. I risked a quick look, saw Graves pull the trigger on an empty magazine. As he reached inside the car to reload, I seized my moment, levered myself up onto my feet, ran towards the shelter of some birch trees.

I looked back to see the motorcyclist jump up, pull the bike back onto two wheels, and race in hot pursuit. Graves was back behind the wheel of the car, the engine stalled, or maybe hit by a not-so-stray bullet. There didn't seem much point in trying to outrun a motorbike, so I tried to make myself invisible behind the trees. If that didn't work, maybe I could throw my remaining shoe at him.

The motorbike came towards me, rider crouched over the handlebars, weaving from left to right to be less of a target.

'Climb on!' the rider yelled, twisted the throttle. I stood still for a few seconds, and then ran forward and hoisted one leg over the pillion. Even before I was properly balanced, we set off over rough ground that had me bouncing up and down. We didn't stop until we were well out of range, braking so suddenly my nose slammed into the leather jacket in front of me.

I watched as gauntleted hands removed the helmet.

'Do I have to do everything for you, Akyl?' the voice demanded. Honey spilt over vanilla ice cream.

Chapter 50

'I was really pissed off with you when I found out you'd gone,' Saltanat said, sipping at a cup of hot *chai*. We were sitting in a small coffee shop in Tungush, on our way back into Bishkek.

'I was pretty sure you would have gone either to the Ibraimova apartment or to keep watch outside Graves's house. So I borrowed a motorbike, well, stole it, arrived at your apartment just in time to see Kurmanalieva supervising two of her thugs dumping you in the boot of her car. I couldn't tell whether you were dead or unconscious, so I followed them back to Graves's house, waited outside.'

Saltanat took another sip, then lit a cigarette, watching the smoke rise upwards.

'I wasn't going to storm the house. I had no idea where you were, how many people were there. So I waited, put in the call to Kurmanalieva. I saw her drive away, waited some more. Then Graves drove out, so I followed you. You know the rest.'

Saltanat had snapped the linking chain of the handcuffs, but I was still wearing fancy bracelets. The waitress had noticed them as she brought us our tea, and I'd made some joke about a bet gone wrong. She didn't laugh, simply looked at me as if I was crazy, slapped down the *chyoht* and walked away. Saltanat didn't laugh either.

'I'm beginning to think you're a liability, Akyl,' she said, staring at the tip of her cigarette, her eyes refusing to meet mine. I felt my heart stop, kick-start and turn over, my throat suddenly parched and sore.

'That sounds like the start of a familiar song,' I said. 'One of those traditional songs about parting lovers, and eternal tears and all that stuff.'

'No,' Saltanat said, and I could see she was choosing her words with great care, 'I'm not saying that. But we have to end this, Akyl. I don't just mean nailing Graves for the murders, avenging Gurminj. But we go two steps forward, one step back, one step forward, three steps back.'

It was as close to a declaration of sorts that I'd ever heard her make.

She paused, stubbed out her cigarette, started to reach for another, then put down the pack.

'Give me your wallet,' she said. I picked up the *chyoht* and looked at the total.

'I was going to pay,' I said, starting to count out a handful of *som* notes.

'No, give me your wallet,' she repeated, and then plucked it out of my fingers.

'This is what I'm talking about, Akyl,' she said, flipping past the slots for my non-existent credit cards. She pulled out a passport-sized photograph, and held it up for me to see. Chinara, on the Ferris wheel.

'I won't compete with a dead woman,' Saltanat said, and I could hear the determination in her voice.

I took the photo from her and started to tear it up, but Saltanat reached over the table to stop me.

'Nice gesture, I appreciate you making it,' she said, 'but you need to decide what is important to you.'

'What do you want me to do?' I said

'You're the detective, solve the mystery,' she said. 'And anyway, it's not about what *I* want you to do, it's what *you* want to do. I'm not looking for a lapdog.'

I nodded, afraid words would fail me if I tried to talk about her, about Chinara, what they both meant to me. Can you love two people without betraying each of them with the other, even after death? I didn't have an answer. I wasn't even sure there was one.

We stood up, and I put the money for the bill on the table.

'Just a couple of things; where are we going to stay tonight? The safe house is out, my apartment's out, the hotel's out. And more important,' and I held up my wrists, clanking the handcuffs together, 'when can I get rid of the jewellery?'

Chapter 51

'You're such a dead shot, why didn't you put two into Graves when you had the chance?' I said, pouring champagne for Saltanat, mineral water for myself.

'Wouldn't you rather he stood trial, be exposed for the monster he is?' she replied. 'I want him to know his empire and his reputation are crumbling around him.'

'Nice idea, but who knows how many judges and lawyers and politicians are on his payroll,' I said. 'So he has a dungeon in his basement? He's an adult. The films? He knows nothing about them, they're probably fakes anyway. The thugs he surrounds himself with? He's a rich man in a poor country, he needs security.'

I looked around at the suite Saltanat had booked at the Hyatt Regency, the best hotel in Bishkek, and the most expensive. I assumed Uzbek state security were picking up the bill; Saltanat had argued no one would expect a fugitive from justice to hide out in such a palace, that we were more likely to find anonymity here than in some backwater where the management were paid to make tip-offs to the police. I didn't know whether she was right or not but it had to be better than staying in Penitentiary One for fifteen years.

'So what now?' I asked.

'We wait,' Saltanat said. 'Albina is bound to get in touch with me. Graves will have told her you escaped, and that gives us an opening we can exploit.'

I would have liked to take the initiative ourselves, but sometimes it's better to allow the enemy to commit themselves. Then you can see an opening to strike back.

'Why don't you call her?' I said.

'There's nothing will aggravate her more than thinking I'm ignoring her,' Saltanat said. 'And if she's annoyed, she won't be thinking clearly. And that's to our advantage.'

I could see the feud between the two women had become Saltanat's main concern, but mine was still with Graves.

'Shouldn't we deal with Graves first?'

Saltanat shook her head.

'Graves with Albina is a lot more dangerous. Getting rid of her puts him on the back foot, removes some of his protection.'

'You're going to kill her?' I asked the question, but I already knew the answer.

'If I don't, then she'll kill me. And then you. You've already had a taste of what she can do. It's a matter of survival.'

'You realise that when she calls you, she'll be setting up a trap?' I asked.

'It's only a trap if we let it be,' Saltanat replied. 'It doesn't take much to make sure your opponent's foot gets snared, not yours.'

I looked around at the enormous flat-screen TV, the elegant table and chairs, the king-sized bed. Western businessmen must have used this room to plot fortunes, deals, lies and deceits. Upmarket working ladies earning in an hour what I made in a month. Caviar on a plate and mistrust in the air. It seemed a very odd setting to be discussing a woman's death, avenging rape and murder, but maybe not so odd after all. Suddenly, I felt restless, out of place, wanting to get back to the streets and grimy bars, where I understood what was going on, knew how to deal with it. The hotel suite was as alien to me as the far side of the moon.

Saltanat looked at me, sensed my mood, knew what I was thinking.

'The police are still looking for you; is it smart to go wandering about town?'

I shrugged.

'I'll wear dark glasses,' I said, hoping to make her smile. It didn't work. 'I'll go crazy, just sitting around here, I'm not going to shout my name outside the White House. I just need to walk around, decide what I'm going to do next.'

If Saltanat noticed I hadn't said what we'd do next, she didn't show it.

'I'll call you later,' I said, shrugging on my jacket. Then it was Saltanat's turn to shrug. It felt as if any possible relationship was doomed to capsize before it had begun. My fault, I imagined. Too much pain, too many memories, the fear of loving and losing again. I nodded, and walked towards the door. I didn't say goodbye.

As I walked down Chui Prospekt, the young women who worked in the parliament building were out in force, enjoying the spring sunshine and the chance to show off their summer dresses. I went past several groups, laughing, chatting, mobile phones held like talismans, charms to ward off the twin dangers of growing old and being alone. None of them noticed me; it's what happens to men when they see middle age staring at them like the barrels of a shotgun.

I tried to shake off my melancholy, strolled through the park, past the swings and rides, listened to children shrieking in their excitement. They sounded like birds returning in flocks to settle in the upper branches of the trees. I walked past the roughly carved stone statues that peered out from behind bushes or crouched down among long grass. They looked elemental, timeless, as if they had been here long before the city, and would be long afterwards, staring out across broken walls and burnt-out cars.

I sat down on a bench, stared up at the sun through the canopy of leaves. The light made everything dappled, camouflaged and mysterious. I felt as if I'd lost my way in a dark wood, the path uncertain, my journey pointless. I knew Graves was too well-connected, with money and contacts. They would keep him out of a courtroom, out of a cell. Before, the thought of him getting away with murder would have enraged me. Now, it simply seemed the way of a world that ignored all the ways of living in which I believed. Cynicism or realism? Perhaps they're both the same.

I sat there for an hour or so, trying to wipe my mind clean of the tiny bodies I'd unearthed, the films I'd sat through where blood splashed the walls, and eyes and mouths screamed silently for a help that didn't arrive. But if I was hoping for peace, it didn't come. Too many bodies, too much suffering. The pretty girls and old men and dancing children never see my world, if they're lucky. I'm the man in black who squats in the corner of people's lives, unnoticed, an undertaker for souls.

A cloud passed over the sun, wind shaking the leaves. Spring holds the promise of summer, but the memories of winter are never too far away. I walked back to Chui Prospekt and made a call on the way. I suggested a meeting place, then walked unseen past laughing children and their watchful mothers.

Chapter 52

The *banya* at the far end of Ibraimova is one of the better legacies from our not-so-glorious days as part of the Soviet Union. Recently renovated, it's a great place to relax, with two different sauna rooms, massage tables, and a circular ice-cold pool under a white tiled hemisphere. There's even a snack bar where you can buy horse-meat sausage and cold beer, and if you want to get a haircut, there's a small salon run by two women whose indifference to the naked men who use the *banya* suggests they've seen everything, from long and tall to short and small. It's the ideal place to meet if you want to make sure no one's hiding a gun or a tape recorder.

I undressed, put my clothes in one of the lockers, and making sure no one was looking, slipped some papers onto the top of the lockers. I walked into the shower room, where I paid a thickset middle-aged woman for a thin cotton sheet, wrapping it around my waist. She looked at my damaged shoulder, at the blood-crusted furrow whose edges were already starting to look inflamed, infected.

'You can't go in the pool, not with that,' she said.

'I'm only going to use the heat,' I replied. My answer seemed to satisfy her; I was only grateful she didn't look down at my foot.

'How did you get that, anyway?' she asked, nodding at my shoulder.

I shrugged, did my best to look browbeaten. It wasn't too hard.

'The old woman, she's got a temper on her. Tatar,' I explained. 'And maybe I'd had a couple of beers too many, got home late.'

The attendant pursed her lips.

'You'd have got worse from me if you were my husband,' she said, and turned away, convinced once more about the fecklessness of men. I nodded, decided not to buy a bottle of Baltika, in case she hit me with it.

I was early, so I took a long hot shower, then endured ten minutes in the hottest of the steam rooms, surrounded by naked men, most of whom were slapping themselves or each other with birch twigs. We have some strange customs in Central Asia. Some of the men were also wearing tall *kalpak* felt hats, which must have added to the heat. The wooden slatted floor was littered with leaves, and they stuck to my feet when I finally couldn't take the heat any longer. I was pouring buckets of cold water over myself when a voice behind me called my name.

'How are you, Akyl?'

'Well, you know,' I said, turning to face Kenesh Usupov, Bishkek's chief forensic pathologist. 'There's nothing I like more than getting myself into deep shit, then trying to get out of it. So I thought I'd give my old friend a call, arrange a reunion.'

'I didn't expect to hear from you again,' he said, wiping his face dry with a towel. 'Not until you'd sorted out all that business about child porn in your apartment.'

'I'm working on that,' I said, 'but things keep getting in the way. Like being beaten up, tortured, being hunted by my former colleagues, having old friends turn their faces away from me.'

To his credit, Kenesh looked ashamed for a few seconds.

'I have to think of my family first, Akyl. And how could I help anyway?'

I nodded; if I wanted Kenesh to help me, I had to show him I wasn't one to bear a grudge.

'I got the word, from someone very senior,' I said, not wanting to mention Tynaliev by name. 'They said the Be On The Lookout for me was being unofficially scaled down.'

'There's talk you were set up,' Kenesh said. 'Maybe by people who supported the chief before he went away. You know, revenge.'

I knew that wasn't the case; the people who'd backed the chief wouldn't have rolled him in a snowdrift if he'd been on fire. Those people move on, to the next deal, the next scam, the next arse to kiss.

'I want you to do me a favour,' I said, and watched as Usupov immediately looked cautious. 'Don't worry, you can see I'm not wearing a wire.'

'Not unless you've hidden it in a very uncomfortable place,' Usupov said, in a rare flash of humour.

'Well, if I was, you don't want to speak into the microphone,' I said, and the tension in the air seemed to ease. I scooped another bucket of cold water out of the tub, poured it over my head. The shock was like a punch in the face, but it gave me a moment to work out how to convince Usupov to do what I was about to ask.

'We should leave separately,' I said, 'but before you go, there's something I want you to collect from my locker.'

'What is it?' he asked.

'Nothing to worry about,' I reassured him, 'but I've done a lot of digging about the dead children we unearthed. I'm pretty sure I know what happened to them, and why. But in case someone's digging a hole for me, I've made some notes, and I want you to hang onto them.'

I paused, staring into Usupov's eyes to reinforce the seriousness of what I'd just said.

'Then if I don't turn up, or if they find me after someone's given me a Makarov kiss, send them to the editor of *Achyk Sayasat*. You know how anti-government they are; they'll publish straight away, and you can't close all the mouths. An anonymous tip-off. You won't be implicated.'

'I suppose I can do that,' he said. 'But why don't you just send the information to Tynaliev? You'd get rehabilitated, the porn charges would go away, you'd have the minister backing you all the way.'

I didn't want to let Kenesh know Tynaliev was possibly involved in the murders; he'd be out of the *banya* and down Ibraimova without stopping to get dressed. I told him where I'd hidden my notes, watched as he headed towards the changing room. I decided to give him ten minutes before leaving, just enough time for one more shower to ease some of the stiffness out of my joints.

That was when I saw the burly guy with a shaven head and a chestful of prison tattoos as he came into the shower room.

And when he noticed me.

Chapter 53

He started to move towards me. Naked, the slabs and sheets of muscle across his arms and chest were clearly visible. He could snap me in half with all the effort it takes to part a pair of chopsticks. The plaster cast on his hand was a souvenir of my hitting him with the tyre iron back at Graves's house, and his scowl suggested he wasn't in a forgiving mood.

He stood between me and the changing room, and I knew there was no other way out of the *banya*, or time in which to get dressed. I moved away from the steam rooms, towards the corridor that leads to the circular pool, pushing through the door as he followed me. He moved slowly, with the curious grace you sometimes see in burly, over-muscled men. He knew I was cornered, intended to relish the time he had in which to kill me.

In the pool room, he took hold of a nearby broom, jamming it through the door handles to prevent anyone else joining us. The pool was deserted, the water impassive, motionless. Light from the windows placed high upon the walls spilt down through the water, reflecting and shimmering off the blue tiles. It looked like a very good place to die.

I moved to the far edge of the pool, so we faced each other. For every step he took in either direction, I could match him, so we remained opposite each other. Theoretically, it was a dance we could carry out for hours, or until someone came to investigate why the pool room door wasn't opening. But I couldn't rely on him not having a colleague with him, still getting changed, who would spot his partner's absence, follow him, and then have me trapped as they closed in on either side. I had to act.

I walked slowly around the pool towards him, flexing the muscles in my back and shoulders. I got to within three metres of the man, his eyes never leaving my face. The light reflecting off the water gave him an almost unreal intensity. I could see every pore in his skin, every hair on his arms and legs, the heft of his belly. The blue-grey tattoo in the centre of his chest was of a Russian church with three onion domes: he'd served three prison sentences. The dagger piercing his neck told me he'd committed murder while in prison, and he was available for hire. It wasn't a hard guess to work out his latest assignment.

I knew that the plaster cast on his hands would be a weapon as long as he wasn't in the water, where it would become a liability. So I dropped my head, raced towards him, then dived into the water, dragging him in with me.

We both touched the bottom of the pool at the same time, my arms wrapped around his waist, while he tried to club at my neck with his cast. The cold water bit into my wounds like a starving wolf. I kept my head tucked into my shoulders, so they took the worst of his blows. The resistance of the water and the weight of the cast meant he couldn't really hurt me. I kept hold of his waist, punched his stomach as hard as I could. It was like hitting a side of beef, his muscles rock solid. I clenched my fist, hit him again. The air in his lungs exploded upwards in a giant bubble. Still holding my breath, I reached down and twisted his balls. His mouth opened in a silent scream and he started to panic. I let go of him, and pushed myself up to the surface. The pool is three metres deep, so I started to tread water, waiting to see him appear.

It was then I realised he couldn't swim. He broke the surface, eyes wide in terror, his legs unable to find the bottom, arms thrashing the water and sending waves over the tiled surround. I swam to the far side of the pool and clambered out. If I tried to help him, he'd probably drag me down in his panic, drown me with him. A result, even if it didn't work out so well for him. I stood there, water dripping down my body, hair plastered to my head, looking down.

His arms waved underwater, the way weed sways with the current of a river, quickly at first, then slower, losing momentum as his lungs filled with water. Finally, he lay motionless at the bottom of the pool, anchored by the cast on his hand.

I knew he would have killed me, choked the life out of me or held me underwater. I was sure he'd killed before, watching the life go out of his victim's eyes, replaced with nothingness. Perhaps he'd been the man who'd raped and murdered Alina back at the hotel. I imagined he would lie in bed and relive the taking of life with a pleasure that went beyond sexual feeling.

But none of that made me feel any better about standing by and watching another man drown.

Chapter 54

There was no sign of Usupov as I left the *banya*, which was encouraging, as long as he came through with releasing the material in the event of my death. The wail of a police siren meant someone had discovered the body in the pool and put in a call. I crossed the rough ground that passed for a car park, worked my way along behind a brick wall. Don't run, don't look worried or suspicious, just a regular citizen going about his lawful business.

I called Saltanat, arranged to meet her at the Metro Bar in an hour's time. That would give me the opportunity to walk across the city, to try to put the pieces together in some kind of order. I've always thought best when walking, often at night, when the streets are empty, and the darkness empties my mind of distractions. The routine of footstep after footstep, the pattern and rhythm, seems to create new links, fresh connections. It would also help me distance myself emotionally from the death in the *banya*. I told myself I hadn't killed him, that he would have killed me, that I shouldn't blame myself.

I took my own life in my hands, and crossed the road onto Chui Prospekt, ignoring the horns and shouts of the drivers trying to steer a way around the worst of the potholes. From there, I could walk through the centre of the city, invisible in the crowds. My gun was hidden in Saltanat's car, and I felt oddly naked without the reassurance of its weight. I've always believed you should never get too attached to weapons, because that's when they become the solution of choice, the easy option. But without even a nail file to fend off my enemies, I was wondering whether I should revise my opinions.

I wondered about going to see a doctor about my shoulder, which had more stitches in it than my jacket. The hot shower followed by the cold pool had cleaned the wound, but the fight had opened it up again, and I could feel my shirt sticking to the bloody edges. I decided against a doctor, at least for the moment. If I was on a Be On The Lookout list, then *som*, or maybe even dollars, wouldn't guarantee silence.

As I crossed Ala-Too Square, I looked up at the giant national flag as it flapped in the breeze, a crimson red broken only by a stylised yellow *tunduk* in the centre.

Our flag has always given me hope there is more to men and women than brutality and greed, lust and terror. But now I wondered if it was an empty promise, a passing illusion like headlights reflected on dark windows. The flag's halyard clattered against the flagpole in a jerky rhythm like distant rifle shots. I looked towards the monument in memory of the protesters shot during the last revolution, remembered the day when the square echoed with bullets ricocheting off buildings and into flesh.

Sometimes you despair, but you carry on. What else is there to do?

Saltanat was waiting at the Metro Bar, a Baltika already half drunk in front of her, clouds of cigarette smoke spilling and drifting above her head. She managed to look both incredibly beautiful and incredibly pissed off.

'You've eaten?' I asked, waved at the pretty red-haired

waitress to bring menus. I ordered *chai*, then we discussed the merits of various pizza toppings before agreeing to share a Diavolo.

As we ate, I told Saltanat about the drowning in the *banya*. She looked at me, sipped her beer, lit another cigarette before speaking.

'You know he would have killed you. He probably took part in all the rapes and killings. But you still feel bad about him being dead?'

I shook my head.

'Not exactly. But I feel bad about the way he died. That I did nothing to save him.'

Saltanat stubbed out her half-smoked cigarette.

'One of your great virtues, Akyl, is that even with all the death and violence you've seen, you haven't acquired a taste for killing. Of course, in your job, that's also your problem. A second's hesitation on the trigger, an impulse to try to wound rather than blast some shithead into eternity; that could be your biggest mistake. And your last one.'

'I joined the police to protect people from the bad guys,' I said, surprised at the slight shake in my voice, 'not to become one of them.'

Saltanat winced at what she saw as my naivety.

'Akyl, an exterminator isn't a bad guy because he kills rats. It's just something that has to be done. Let the rats live and they damage all of us. The rats do what they do because they're rats. We do what we do because there's no alternative.'

'It's a philosophy, I suppose,' I said, not wanting to get into the argument about my many shortcomings, as a policeman, as a lover, as a human being.

'For you, maybe,' Saltanat said, a hard edge to her voice. 'For me, it's a practicality.'

There didn't seem a lot to say, so after that I only opened my mouth in order to sip my *chai*.

'While you were at the bathhouse, I ran through the list of foreign agencies we got from that shithead at the adoption agency, Sakataev. Who ran them, if they had any directors or owners indirectly involved. And tucked away behind a holding company owned by a holding company, guess whose name was there in small print?'

'Our friend, Morton Graves?'

'Exactly. Registered to help find potential adopters from abroad, vet them, and then suggest potential adoptees. All legal, above board and fully signed off.'

I looked hungrily at Saltanat's cigarettes, decided to forgo the pleasure.

'And?'

'I went back to pay a visit to Sakataev. I caught him just as he was getting ready to drive his BMW to his *dacha*. Rewards for all his hard work. He was so keen to help me with my questions he managed to break two of his fingers in his desk drawer.'

'And?' I asked, picturing the scared and overweight bureaucrat, not wanting to linger too long on how such an unfortunate accident might occur.

'When I mentioned Graves's name, I thought he was going to piss himself. Stammered he couldn't possibly discuss confidential information, government regulations, all the usual nonsense.

'Graves runs a legitimate adoption agency, calls it Hoping For Love, highly recommended, testimonials from delighted parents in New York, San Francisco, Toronto. And the photos, some of them broke my heart, Akyl.'

I looked up, to see a hint of tears in her eyes.

'Little children born with cleft lips, terrible birthmarks, unloved, unwanted. Before and after photos, showing what money and surgery can do. Little boys showing off in their Spider-Man T-shirts, their cleft lips repaired so they smiled and it didn't look like they were snarling. Small girls in pretty frocks laughing, showing off the cheek they'd always turned away from the camera. Nice clothes, a warm house, toys, hugs and kisses from parents who couldn't have children themselves.'

Saltanat wiped her eyes, glared at me as if I'd somehow failed to help these children.

'All it takes is fucking money,' she said.

'And love, Saltanat,' I said. 'Don't ever underestimate love.'

Chapter 55

I bought Saltanat another beer, felt the rough wood of the table under my fingertips.

'So we know Graves has helped some children. Maybe part of how he conceals his other activities, looking like the noble benefactor. Does that change anything?'

'It's a good cover, and he's certainly in it for the money. Bribes, certificates, flights, medical checks, it all adds up. But nothing compared to the money if he sources illegal adoptions on the side.'

Saltanat blew smoke towards the ceiling, sipped her beer.

'Say the courts won't approve you as an adoption parent, but you're desperate to have a child. Well, Graves's agency can help you with that.'

'Follow the money?'

'Here's how it works. First of all, you get approval to run a licensed adoption agency. The certificate doesn't cost very much, but the bribe to get one is going to set you back fifteen to twenty thousand dollars. Then you set up a website, contact adoption agencies in other countries, let people who are desperate to have a child know you're in business. More time, more money.'

I nodded, scrawling some figures on a napkin.

'Each time you get a referral, that there's a child in the system that can be adopted, a couple of thousand dollars gets left in an envelope, as a "present". Getting the paperwork sorted out is another thousand. So the costs are rising. And then the foreigners enter the picture.'

Saltanat looked around, but all the tables nearby were empty, and I didn't imagine Graves's caution would extend to bugging the Metro Bar.

'Imagine you've been married for twelve years, trying for a child for the last ten. The tests can't point to a specific problem, IVF hasn't worked out for you, her biological clock batteries are almost exhausted. What do you do?

'You go to the adoption agencies in your own country. They say you're too old, you've been married before, there aren't any children available in your ethnic group. Come back next year, but no promises.

'You're spending your evenings arguing about this, you don't have sex any more, it's splitting you apart. Then you read an article about the orphans in Kyrgyzstan. Beautiful Asian children living in poor conditions, horrible surroundings you wouldn't keep a dog in, poorly fed, barely educated, often with physical or mental handicaps, no one to love them, care for them.'

'It wasn't like that where I grew up—' I started to say, when Saltanat held up her hand to silence me.

'Akyl, "poor conditions" to these people means not having Wi-Fi and a 42-inch flat-screen TV in every room. Their heart goes out to these orphans, of course it does. So they get in touch with an agency, like Hoping For Love, and are told to fly to Bishkek or Osh, to meet some of the children. And once they do that, they're hooked.'

'Once they've found a child, they can't walk away,' I said. It wasn't a question.

'Of course not. The smart ones, they find a lawyer to help

deal with the agency, to keep the bribes down to a minimum and to make sure the paperwork's legitimate.'

'How much are we talking about?' I asked.

'Maybe as much as fifty thousand dollars,' Saltanat said, rubbing thumb and forefinger together to emphasise her point.

Fifty thousand dollars. That's a lifetime's earnings for a lot of people in Kyrgyzstan, years of rooting up potatoes, growing fruit to sell by the wayside, slaughtering a goat or a sheep and hacking it up to sell in the market you set off for before dawn, with a cold wind coming down off the mountains.

'The thing is,' Saltanat continued, 'if you've paid that sort of money, you end up with a child to take back to your country. It's expensive, but you get what you paid for. And compare it to the cost of surgery if it's needed, school fees, university, it's not that much if a child is all you've ever wanted.'

I nodded. I didn't like the idea of children being taken from their roots, detached from their culture, never knowing their birth brothers or sisters, but I wasn't stupid enough, or patriotic enough, to not realise it could be a ticket to a better life.

'So everyone feeds their beak, everyone gets what they want?'

Saltanat stared at me, and shook her head.

'Say you don't have the fifty thousand? Or before you can lawyer up, someone says, we can cut out the paperwork, get things sorted faster.'

I knew I wasn't going to like hearing what was to come next.

'We know it's expensive, that's the government, but for thirty thousand, paid direct to us, we can get you a child from outside an orphanage, better looked after, healthier, yours to take home, no complications.'

I reached over, took the last cigarette from Saltanat's pack. Time to reclaim my gun; I wanted to be tooled up when I next met these fuckers.

'Imagine you're a family over in Karakol, or up in Talas or way down in one of the villages past Osh. Poor, but honest. The only crop you're good at growing is children. Too many mouths to feed, clothes, shoes, no money coming into the house.

'An agency approaches you. Chance of a new life for your new baby. Wealthy foreigners. They're looking for a handsome *malysh* or a beautiful *malyshka*. Boy or girl, whatever you've got. They show you pictures of the big white house outside Vancouver, the farm in upstate New York, places you've never even heard of, luxury you can't imagine. That's where your baby's going to grow up. Of course you'll miss them, but there'll be photographs, letters, maybe even visits over the years. How can you deny them that?'

Saltanat took the cigarette out of my fingers, inhaled, handed it back, waved her empty glass at the waitress for another beer.

'Of course, they want to compensate you for your loss. A thousand dollars, look, I have the money right here, clean new hundred-dollar notes, never even been folded. Pay off your debts, new clothes for the older children, maybe a new dress for the wife. What are you going to do?'

I could picture the father, hands roughened by years in the fields, the mother, worn out before her time by too many children and the endless battle against mud and hunger. I thought of my mother with her cheap plastic suitcase with the split handle leaving for Siberia, my grandfather unable to meet my eye as we arrived at the orphanage, the dormitory where I covered my head with a blanket and silently wept, night after night.

'The agency takes pictures of the child, sends them on to prospective parents. They always want a baby or a toddler, someone who won't remember their earlier life, never a sulky teenager. And one couple will say, yes, that's the baby for us, then the money changes hands and so does the kid. Probably handed over to Albina, pretending to be caring and maternal, to reassure the mother.'

There was a question I knew I had to ask, dreaded hearing the answer.

'And then what happens?'

'A lot of the time, it goes through, the foreigners get a cut-price baby, the parents have some spare cash for the first time in years. A couple of thousand buys the baby a passport and adoption certificate allowing it to leave the country, and we hope it all ends happily.'

I could follow the logic; if official channels were bypassed, that only meant fewer beaks got dipped.

'But?' I asked, certain there would be more to the story, and it wouldn't be pleasant.

'It often depends on the foreigners, how gullible they are,' Saltanat said. 'Sometimes the same baby gets sold to four or five couples; one of them gets the child, the other ones are told the child has died, or the parents have backed out at the last minute. Of course, it's impossible to offer a full refund, and, having broken the law, the couples can hardly go to Sverdlovsky station and lodge a complaint. They've heard too many horror stories about Kyrgyz jails to consider that.'

'So they fly home to an empty cradle and a bank account light by thirty thousand dollars?'

Saltanat nodded.

'But the worst if no one buys the child?'

Her face grew hard, and I waited for her to speak.

'Better not to risk returning the child. The parents are told all went well, and they keep the thousand dollars.'

'And the child?'

'You dug seven of them up in a field outside Karakol. And I shouldn't imagine that's the only dumping ground. If they're lucky, they get killed quickly. If not, they star in one of Graves's home movies.'

I said nothing, remembering the pathetic bundles in that cold field, the sun turning the mountain snow the colour of blood. I wanted to vomit, to blow the story to the newspapers and see *nomenklatura* heads on spikes. Most of all, I wanted to kill Morton Graves.

While we sat there in grim silence, the waitress brought over a fresh beer for Saltanat. She was young, pretty, and I couldn't remember her name.

'You're looking very serious, Akyl. Hope there wasn't something wrong with the pizza?'

'It was fine.' I smiled, and made sure I didn't watch as she walked back to the bar. However, that didn't stop Saltanat.

'Pretty girl,' she said, in a nonchalant tone that didn't lower my defences for a moment. 'You've known her for a long time?'

'She's a waitress. In a bar. That I used to drink in. She's seen us both in here before. I need a hard time about it right now?'

Saltanat was silent, but I knew that conversation wasn't over.

Her phone rang, startling us both.

She listened, then broke the connection. She looked over at me, her face betraying absolutely nothing, professional, a trained killer.

'Albina,' she said. 'With a time and a place.'

'You think she wants to give up Graves? I asked. 'Cut some kind of immunity? Do you trust her?'

Saltanat shook her head.

'Not a chance; I know what she wants. To kill me. As she always used to say, the hard bit is knowing who to trust. And when.'

Chapter 56

'What you just said about knowing who to trust? I just remembered where I'd heard that before,' I said. 'Albina was the woman who came to visit the orphanage. Those were her exact words: I thought she looked familiar.'

'You didn't recognise her from before?' Saltanat asked, never taking her eyes away from the traffic in front of us. We'd decided there wasn't time to go to the lock-up for more weapons; the Uighur knife would have to do.

'It was one incident one afternoon a long time ago, in a time I've tried to forget.'

Saltanat nodded, said, 'I can understand that.'

'Really?' I asked.

'I was brought up in an orphanage too, Akyl. You're not unique. But I did get adopted.'

Her voice told me it hadn't been an idyllic childhood, that questions would not be welcome.

'How soon after Albina saw you did you get to go home?' she asked.

'My grandfather came down to Karakol about three months later, and met me at the bus station. He bought two tickets to Bishkek, and we headed west in a beat-up old *marshrutka*. Nine hours until we arrived, and I don't think my *dedushka* said more than five words. He certainly didn't say why we were going to Bishkek. We walked for about half an hour – my grandfather wasn't one for spending unnecessary *som* on taxis – until we came to Panfilov Park, and sat down on one of the benches near the funfair.

'We waited for about an hour; grandfather bought me an ice cream with black cherry juice on top. I'd never had one before, and I tried to make it last as long as possible, until finally the ice cream started to melt and run down my arm and onto my shirt.

'I was licking the last of the juice off my fingers when I heard a woman's voice. "I can't leave you alone for a minute, Akyl Borubaev, can I? You think clean shirts grow on apple trees?" and I looked up and there was my *mama*. She looked tired, older, her shoulders more stooped, but it was her. I think my mouth fell open in surprise, and then she opened her arms, and I was hugging her waist and we were crying. Everybody stopped to stare, but I didn't care, and I thought my heart was going to burst with happiness.'

I sat still, remembering that day, how we'd stayed with one of her cousins until we could find a place of our own, in Ala-medin, just behind the market, so our three-room apartment always smelt of newly picked fruit and fresh vegetables. It was the last time my mother ever showed me any emotion, any clue to her feelings. Whenever I was cross or unhappy, she would scold me, saying, 'Don't show your character.' She watched without comment, without emotion, as my grand-father's body was carried out of our apartment, followed years later by that of my father, on one of his rare visits. She didn't approve of me joining the police force, a staunch sup-porter of the widely held belief that all policemen are on the take. My mother died not long after meeting Chinara. She approved of our marriage, said Chinara was too good for me. And when her time came, my mother fought her own death with an unwillingness to accept anything stronger than her own strength of will.

'That's a good story, Akyl, you were lucky, believe me,' Saltanat said. I knew any attempt to interrogate her would lead only to silence and a distancing that would take hours to break down. If she told me, I might understand her motives, her attitudes. If she didn't, she was still Saltanat, with all her mysteries.

'How dangerous is Albina?' I said.

'Hand to hand? The best.'

'Why don't I wait just out of sight?' I said. 'Then put her down with a single shot?'

Saltanat looked over at me, and smiled.

'One, you're not that good a shot. Two, you'd never get near her, her instincts for a trap are superb. She's relied on them for twenty-five years, they've never let her down. She's as cautious as a snow leopard. Three, you wouldn't see her coming until she'd brought death to your side. And four, this is between her and me, something waiting to be settled for a long time.'

'Personal stuff,' I said. She nodded.

'Very personal.'

We parked on Orozbekova, just beyond the statue of Lenin at the back of the Historical Museum, his new home since 2003. We don't deny his influence, we just don't give it the prominence it once had. His arm is still outstretched, pointing to the future, but his face is always in shadow, thanks to the tall trees that now surround him, trees that have lasted longer than his glorious revolution.

I looked across to the trees, but there was no sign of Albina.

'What makes you think she won't just shoot you the moment you step out of the car?' I said.

'She'd see that as a failure,' Saltanat said. 'She needs to show she's still the best at what she does.'

'She's pretty good at lots of things,' I said, feeling the burn in my toe, the tightness of the linen pad we'd bandaged it with earlier. 'I've got something for you,' I added, handing over my Uighur knife. 'Albina has its twin, and it's only fair you're as well-armed as she is.'

Saltanat took the blade, felt the heft, the balance, nodded approvingly.

'If I think she's getting the better of you, or she's going to kill you,' I said, reached for my gun under the seat, held it up, 'then I'm going to blow her fucking head off.'

Saltanat started to protest, but I put a finger to my lips. She leant forward, kissed my cheek, and I could smell the freshness of her perfume, the lemon shampoo of her hair.

Saltanat's phone rang. As she listened, her face changed from shock into anger. She put the phone back in her pocket and turned to me.

'That was my embassy. Elmira, the woman looking after Otabek? She's been shot, she's dead. And the boy's missing.'

And then she was out of the car, walking without haste towards the base of the statue. Albina emerged from the shadows, turned and beckoned Saltanat to join her. I got out of the car, following the two women further under the trees. Lenin ignored them, obviously dreaming about the irresistible rise of the proletariat.

Finally, we came to a spot away from the park paths, where carved stone statues stood in a ring, as if refereeing the fight.

Their faces in the shadows were cruel or uncaring, as if they'd seen it all before and remained unmoved. Albina held up a hand towards me, indicating I should come no further. I nodded my acceptance.

Across the far side of the clearing, Otabek stood, his arms wrapped around a slender birch tree, wrists tied together. Even from a distance, I could see the despairing slump of his shoulders, the dried tear tracks on his cheeks.

'Will you be able to carry this bitch's body back to your car on your own, Akyl? I imagine that foot of yours is giving you a little trouble?' Albina shouted. 'You'll need to make two trips if you're going to carry the boy's body as well.'

'We'll be leaving your body where it falls,' Saltanat said. 'Unless you'd like Graves to fetch you to star in his next major motion picture? A non-speaking role, obviously.'

'You always were a difficult child, Saltanat, you've grown up to be a troublesome woman.'

The two women, one blonde, the other raven-haired, both dressed in black, crouched and started to circle each other. What little sunlight came through the trees reflected off the blades of the knives, the way ice skates spark and dance on winter lakes.

The two women moved sideways, placing each foot down, testing the ground, as if treading barefoot on glass. I'd been present at the aftermath of several knife fights, but those had been drunken, messy, brutal affairs, more bravado than an intent to kill. This was different, like watching two ballerinas performing to music only they could hear. There was a grace and elegance about the whole thing, a ritual no one but the participants could understand. There was none of that non-sense of tossing the knife from hand to hand you get in movies. If the knife isn't in your hand, you're unarmed. Drop it and you're not just a bad juggler, you're a dead one.

Albina skipped forward, light on her feet as a cat, flicked out with her blade, before stepping back. Saltanat twisted to stand sideways, and I thought the blow had missed her. Then I saw the cut in her sleeve, blood rising through the dark material. I slid my hand inside my jacket, loosened the Yarygin. At that distance, taking Albina down would be easy. Taking her alive? Rather more difficult.

Albina raised one leg and aimed a Thai-style kick at Saltanat's hip, the knife as a follow-through aimed at the throat. Saltanat swayed backwards, stabbed down with her own knife. The blade's tip nicked the webbing of Albina's thumb and forefinger, blood hanging in the air like a shower of rose petals.

Albina fell back, her face a mask of anger and pain, raising her hand to suck on the wound. When she took her hand away, the blood that smeared her face and teeth reminded me of the wolf I'd once seen shot in the mountains. But this wolf's eyes were ferocious, alive with hate and bloodlust.

'You used to be good at this,' Saltanat taunted. 'Old age finally caught up with you?'

'Good enough to have killed your friend, the orphanage director. Good enough to have given you that scar,' Albina said, pointing at Saltanat's face.

The dance never stopped, a step forward, a step back, block, move, thrust, both women swaying from side to side to hide their next attack. Albina leapt forward two paces, catching Saltanat just below the earlier wound, deeper now, blood staining the grass. But the leap had caught Albina off balance and as she stumbled, Saltanat plunged her knife into the bicep of Albina's knife-arm. Even as Albina registered the shock of the blow, Saltanat twisted the blade and drew it down the length of the arm.

The dance was coming to its inevitable conclusion, as Albina dropped her knife and fell to her knees. With her other hand, she tried to pull the edges of the wound together, but blood continued to spurt, and I realised Saltanat had hit an artery.

I stepped forward, but Saltanat turned on me, enraged, raising her knife at my face.

'Get back,' she said. 'It's not over.'

Albina's clothes were drenched in blood, and I knew that even if Saltanat had let me approach, it would have been too late to save Albina. She knew she would bleed out in just a few minutes, but the expression on her face said she wasn't ready to submit. She intended to face death as it ran through the trees towards her, scooping her up and carrying her off to feast at its leisure.

'Saltanat,' I said, tried to put my arm around her. She pushed me away, lowered her blade, walked over to where Albina still knelt, upright by some miracle of will.

'We always knew it would end this way,' Saltanat said, 'ever since I was a little girl.' And there was a softness in her voice that sounded almost like love.

'You made me what I am, Albina, for good or bad. Good for me, bad for you.'

Albina's eyelids drooped, her head swaying. She started to speak, but only disjointed sounds emerged.

'I suppose you killed Gurminj when he caught you abducting Otabek,' Saltanat said. 'A decent man, who only wanted to help children. Even if I could, I wouldn't help you. Now all that's left for you is to rot in the earth.'

Saltanat spat onto the ground, wiped her mouth with the back of one bloodstained hand, walked towards Otabek.

I watched as Albina's face went slack, and death began to flood her eyes. She made one ineffectual grab for her knife, missed, tried again, and then fell forward onto her face.

And then Saltanat was walking back to me, carrying Otabek, who clung to her neck as if nothing could ever break his grasp. They passed Albina's body without sparing it even a glance as I picked up the knives. I saw Saltanat's face was filled with a haunting mix of love and sorrow. Perhaps mine was as well.

Chapter 57

The three of us managed to sneak through the hotel lobby and up to our room without attracting too much attention. I'd managed a makeshift bandage for Saltanat's arm, and her dark clothing hid the blood fairly effectively. I bathed the cut, shallow and just above the elbow, poured the remaining hydrogen peroxide over the wound. I remembered how much it had hurt when Saltanat had done the same for me and couldn't help smiling.

'Revenge?' she said, gritting her teeth.

'Something like that,' I said, rolling a bandage around her arm. Saltanat gave me one of her speciality suspicious scowls.

'So, do you want to tell me about it?' I asked.

'About what?'

'About Albina and you, what there was between the two of you,' I said.

Saltanat sighed in exasperation, stretched out on the bed, staring at the ceiling. We'd already taken the room next to ours, with a connecting door between the two suites. Saltanat had bathed Otabek and held his hand while he curled up under the covers and escaped into sleep. I dry-swallowed a handful of the extra-strong painkillers I'd managed to cajole out of the pharmacist, waited for the pain in my shoulder and foot to also take a nap.

'I told you I was adopted,' she began. I nodded.

'Well, Albina didn't choose you to be her pet. I wasn't so lucky.'

'She adopted you?'

'That's right.'

'But why? She was young, she could have had children of her own.'

'I don't think Albina had the slightest interest in sex,' Saltanat said. 'Oh, she knew how to use the promise of it as a weapon, sometimes it was all she needed to get what she wanted. But actually carrying out the deed, that would have made her vulnerable, and she couldn't abide that.'

Saltanat stopped, turned away from me.

'You don't have any cigarettes, do you?'

'No, I only smoke yours,' I said, hoping to make her smile. 'And besides, they're bad for your health.'

A grunt was Saltanat's only answer.

'So Albina adopted you?'

'Yes, but not in the way you think. She didn't want a child to love, but one she could train.'

I looked puzzled, and Saltanat began to explain.

'In my country, the authorities are very cautious, and they value loyalty very highly. What they don't believe in is trust. Some families have always supplied the elite in the security services, because it's a lot easier to guarantee loyalty if you have a hold over someone's children, parents, grandparents. She'd been trained by her father to fight, spy, kill, just as he'd been trained by his father. That's how it's done.

'Albina married very young, a marriage of convenience to the son of one of the other families. He was killed during "an anti-Uzbek rising of disloyal citizens", leaving Albina a childless widow.'

'Is that why she came to my orphanage?' I asked.

Saltanat shook her head.

'I don't think so. For a start, you're Kyrgyz, not Uzbek, so you would never have been accepted, never trusted. Maybe then, she was looking for a son. But later, once the family put pressure on her, she toed the party line.'

'Then why pick you, why pick a girl?' I asked.

Saltanat stared at me for a moment, her black eyes impenetrable.

'Because my mother had been in the security services, trained by her father. She died in a car accident outside Samarkand, which is how I ended up in the orphanage.'

'Why didn't her family look after you?' I asked, guessing the answer even as I asked the question.

'Because she wasn't married to my father. She was their shame, and I was hers. So, off to the orphanage with Saltanat, and forget there was ever a little girl of that name.'

Now I understood the depth of bitterness within her, realised why she was so reticent about her past life. I knew no words could comfort her. Instead, I stared at our joint reflection in the ornate gilt mirror.

'How old were you when you left the orphanage?'

'Nine.'

'And Albina trained you?' I said.

'In her own image,' Saltanat said, a wry smile breaking through the mask of composure, 'until the pupil outdid the master. To start, it was about getting me physically fit; you know what orphanage food is like.'

For me, the food in my orphanage had been better than the food I'd been given at home, but it didn't seem tactful to mention that.

'Then it was about learning skills; swimming, running, climbing. All the things kids want to do anyway, but with Albina it was an obsession. Stopwatches, records, and punishment if you didn't do better than the time before.'

'She was cruel to you?'

'Not cruel,' Saltanat said, 'more that her interest in me was entirely practical, the way you might train a guard dog, or teach someone how to cook. I think she only became cruel later.'

I saw her face tighten with memories, wondered about holding her hand, sat still.

'After that, it was learning to shoot, rifles, pistols, arrows. Stationary targets at first, then moving ones. How to fight with a knife, unarmed, with anything that came to hand. How to defend yourself, how to track someone, disguise yourself, live off the land. All the skills that might one day come in handy.

'The only time we stopped was when Albina had to go away on a mission. I never knew in advance, just one day I'd wake up and she wouldn't be there. But I'd practise anyway, in case she came back and caught me lazing around.'

'It sounds terrible,' I said.

'Not really,' she said. 'We lived better than most people, good food, good housing, the best teachers. When it comes to defending the status quo, nothing's too good for the top guys. And remember, it was what my family did. I'd have had the same training if my mother had lived.'

I wasn't sure exactly how I felt about her role as a trained killer, but it wasn't as if I'd ever been under any illusions about Saltanat as a placid housewife.

'Every few months, Albina would go on road trips, not

just Uzbekistan but Kazakhstan, Kyrgyzstan, looking for potential recruits, children she could train up to be foot soldiers to the elite. It must have been on one of those trips that she visited your orphanage.'

I was silent, wondering how different my life would have been if I'd taken Albina's hand, been led into a new way of living, perhaps of dying. And how I would have felt about Saltanat if we'd grown up together.

'So what made it go wrong?' I asked.

'I was fifteen when Albina went away, didn't come back for five months. I never found out the details, but she'd been hurt working undercover, shot twice, thigh and shoulder. She healed, but she was never quite as supple, maybe a pace behind her best. I was better than she was, and she resented that.'

'What happened then?'

'We'd always pulled back in practice before then, held the knife a centimetre away, got the neck hold but didn't snap the spine. No point in training an agent if you lose them before they go out into the field.

'One day, we were practising with knives, close quarters. We used blunted knives so we might get the odd scratch or two, but nothing serious. But when we started, I saw Albina was using a real blade, razor-edged on both sides. And that's how I got this.'

Saltanat ran her fingernail down the length of her scar.

'You know how much head wounds bleed,' she said. 'It looked like I'd been slaughtered. I thought she was going to cut my throat.'

I remembered the sheep we'd sacrificed for Chinara's forty-day *toi*, the ceremony commemorating her life, how the sheep had bleated as we dragged it towards the waiting knife.

'What stopped her?'

'One of the other trainers saw what had happened, stopped the fight. Of course, Albina swore she didn't know the knife was for real. But I knew. And we never fought like that again. But that's when she really started to hate me. For being stronger than her, for having seen her weakness.'

'She was shot here?' I asked. 'In Kyrgyzstan?'

Saltanat gave me the 'are-you-stupid?' look I'd grown to know so well.

'I don't know,' she said. 'And even if I did, you don't expect me to tell you?'

I shrugged.

'It was a long time ago. And besides, she's dead,' I said.

'Secrets stay secrets. In my country, anyway.'

I rolled over to look at her, at the raven's wing of hair splayed out on the pillow, at the dark eyes whose depths I could never fathom.

'My country's not as good at keeping secrets,' I said. 'That's why we have revolutions. And the news a foreign agent's corpse has been found in the centre of Bishkek, that's going to be a secret for maybe twenty seconds.'

'So?'

'That means I have to go and see Tynaliev, explain the situation, before he wonders if I've gone rogue, and puts a TOS out on me.'

Saltanat nodded; she knew what TOS meant.

Terminate On Sight.

Chapter 58

I finally managed to persuade Saltanat it would be better if I went to see Tynaliev on my own.

'It's going to be hard enough to get to see him myself,' I argued. 'You think he's going to allow a trained foreign assassin to get within two hundred metres? We'll both get shot, no questions asked.'

'He'll want to know where I am, what I know,' she said.

'I'll tell him I haven't seen you for the last two days, you crossed the border yesterday, you had nothing to do with Albina's death.'

'He's going to believe that?' she said.

'It doesn't matter what he believes,' I replied, 'as long as whatever happens is to his benefit. He'll call his counterpart in Tashkent, offer his deepest condolences on the Uzbek ex-member of his staff who fell foul of a group of pornographers, and was murdered. Then he'll assure him everything possible is being done to catch the authors of this terrible crime. Honour satisfied, crisis averted, case closed.'

'So what am I supposed to do?' Saltanat said.

'Wait here until I call you. If you don't hear from me in a couple of hours, go somewhere, but don't tell me where, and take the battery out of your phone. Call me from a throwaway in twenty-four hours, and if I don't answer, head across the border.'

'And from there?'

'If I'm not answering, you'll know I'm dead or locked up. That means Tynaliev is tied in with Graves and the porn. If he is, contact Usupov, get him to send the material I gave him to the papers. Better still, you send it to the Uzbek papers, and the BBC and CNN. There's no way Tynaliev could survive a media strike like that.'

'Why not do that anyway?' she asked.

'I need to know if Tynaliev's involved or not. Bring him down and he's innocent, the stability of my country is threatened. It's not as if we're Switzerland to begin with.'

'Twenty-four hours, right?'

'Unless I call you first.'

'And if you don't?'

I stumbled for the right movie cliché, pulled her close to me, hugged her. I pushed the image of Chinara on the Ferris wheel out of my mind, thought only of the here and now, the woman in my arms.

'Then we'll always have Bishkek.'

I felt a lot less confident when I arrived at Minister of State Security Tynaliev's town house. The one time I'd been there was when I came to tell Tynaliev that his daughter, Yekaterina, had been found butchered above Ibraimova, near the Blonder Pub. In daylight, the place still looked like a mafia *pakhan*'s armed compound, with more guards than the White House. Two men with Uzis tracked my progress as I parked the Lexus at a suitable distance to prove I was suicide-bomb-free. The armed guard at the gatehouse inspected my police pass as if looking for a reason to shoot me, handed it back to me, thumbed towards the scanner. Trust no one was the motto of the day.

I handed over my gun, walked through the scanner, and a guard led me to the front door.

'Wait here,' he ordered, with all the politeness you'd expect from a man with a machine pistol in his hand.

'I called the minister earlier, said I was on the way,' I said.

The information didn't send the guard into a fit of grovelling; I couldn't have said I was entirely surprised. I didn't add I'd given a list of conditions for coming in, the most pressing of which was not being gunned down on sight.

'Wait here,' he repeated, letting his hand rest on the Makarov on his hip just to make sure I'd fully understood. I was finally escorted into the hallway, and from there into the same small, overheated study where I'd first met Tynaliev. The minister stood there, cracking his knuckles in a way I didn't find reassuring.

'You've sorted this business out, I hope, to everyone's benefit?' he barked.

'In a manner of speaking, Minister,' I said. 'I can tell you where the porn films were made, point you at the main suspect. I'm sure you'll be able to spin the case so you come out of it with the maximum credit, without embarrassing us or your Uzbek counterparts.'

'Sit,' the minister said, and it wasn't a request. He poured himself a small vodka, picked up a second glass, looked at me.

'You don't, if I remember,' he said. 'I was always told never trust a man who doesn't drink.'

'My mother always said never trust a man who does,' I said.

He tossed back the vodka, poured another, and smiled, the same wolfish grin I'd seen before.

'Perhaps you should have listened to your mother,' he said, and sat down behind his desk.

'If I could remind you—' I began, before he interrupted me with an impatient gesture.

'Yes, yes, the order's already gone out, the Circle of Brothers was trying to discredit you by planting kiddie porn in your apartment, you're reinstated with no loss of pension, pay or seniority.'

'I'm grateful, Minister,' I said, and for once when talking to a government official, I meant it.

'There is a problem, though,' I went on, 'with the making of the film, the bodies we found and, of course, the murder of Gurminj Shokhumorov.'

'What sort of a problem?'

'There had to be a considerable investment in making those films, the equipment.' I shuddered, thinking of the belts and knives in Graves's cellar. 'Finding the victims, ensuring they weren't missed, not to mention the distribution, the bribes that had to be paid all along the line. So obviously, this wasn't the work of a poor man.'

'You've found links to the Circle of Brothers? Something we can use to smash them?' Tynaliev asked.

'I've no doubt they helped with the distribution, at least some of it,' I said, choosing my words with care, 'but this isn't the sort of thing they would get involved with. Too unpopular.'

'Explain,' Tynaliev said.

'The Circle makes its money through what most people consider facts of life. Bootleg vodka, gambling, trafficking drugs to Russia and the West, prostitution. Men pay money to fuck, women fuck for money, the way of the world, oldest profession and so on. People say, well, if not them, someone else. And everybody likes to take a drink now and then. But something like this isn't acceptable to most people. And that weakens the Circle in all their other activities. The money starts to dry up. And the foot soldiers in the Circle, they start to wonder if it's the turn of their daughters, their sons to become film stars, meat for the mincing machine. So everyone's unhappy. Bad for business.'

I stood up and took one of the bottles of sparkling mineral water. I held it up to the minister, asking his permission. He nodded, I unscrewed the top, drank. Now came the time when my mouth would be dry, and I'd have to fight to keep the fear out of my voice.

'So you need someone powerful and rich to do all this. Someone with *som* in his pocket to make people look the other way, to buy his way out of any trouble. And if people won't be bought, then get rid of them with no consequences.'

'That sounds like half the people I know.' Tynaliev smiled.

Now came the hard part, and I took another drink before speaking.

'The problem is, Minister,' I said, 'I know who is responsible. People you know as well.'

'Are you fucking with me, Inspector?' Tynaliev said, and his voice conjured up images of tiled interrogation rooms, blood spatter on the walls, broken teeth on the floor crunching underfoot.

'No, Minister,' I said, pleased I sounded unafraid, confident even. 'There wouldn't be any point in me doing that. We both want whoever did these awful crimes to be punished, don't we?'

'Who?' he said, his voice the sound of prison doors slamming shut.

'Obviously, I've got documentary evidence to back up my case,' I said.

'You mean you've taken out insurance? Left the files with someone you can trust?'

'I'm dealing with a powerful man, Minister. I wouldn't want the case to fizzle out if an "accident" happened to me, I'm sure you agree.'

I didn't need to spell out that my 'insurance' would pour a world of shit on Tynaliev if he was involved and had me put in the ground.

'I ask again. Who?'

'Morton Graves. And a woman. Albina Kurmanalieva.'

The names hung in the air like distant smoke. Tynaliev looked at his vodka, then pushed the glass away.

'I have met Ms Kurmanalieva, just once. A striking woman, very single-minded. If my tastes were to run to more mature women, I have no doubt that ours would be a friendship on many levels. I trust you can back your claims with evidence?'

I nodded.

'And also against Morton Graves? He's one of this country's major foreign investors. He's brought trade here, exports what little we have, brings foreign currency in, provides jobs, even medical care and housing. And you know how good we are at doing all that for ourselves.'

'I know, Minister. But that's not all he does.'

'You don't like rich people, do you, Inspector? Or foreigners? Or me?'

I stood up, and I saw Tynaliev's hand move under his desk. Panic button, or maybe a gun. But I didn't care.

'This isn't about what I do or don't like, Minister. And I can't imagine someone as important as you cares what I think. It's about justice. For seven dead babies dumped in a field to rot. For an honest orphanage director who was shot for protecting children. For the boys and girls whose final hours were nothing but pain, shame and humiliation. That's what it's about. Minister.'

Tynaliev sat back, and I heard the expensive leather of his chair creak.

'You're either a very brave man, Inspector, or a remarkably stupid one. It hasn't occurred to you that you might have been sent on a wrong track by your Uzbek lady friend? Maybe shift any blame from them to us?'

I shook my head, my legs suddenly feeling weak. I saw my hand shake as I raised the bottle to my mouth. I sat down and finished the water.

'I think you'd better explain, Inspector, don't you?'

It wasn't a question, more like a death sentence. I just didn't know for whom.

Chapter 59

Over the next hour, I outlined the points in the case I had against Morton Graves, reducing Saltanat's involvement to that of an occasional helper, omitting her role in Albina's death entirely. If I was going to sink without trace, I wasn't going to drag her down with me. He listened in silence, only interrupting occasionally to clarify individual points or the sequence of events.

I finished and looked at Tynaliev. He didn't look convinced.

'You obviously are aware that I know Morton Graves?' he said. 'That we share certain business interests? So I suppose you're wondering if I'm involved in his other activities? If I enjoy watching rape and murder porn? Maybe even join in with the fun and games? That's why you've taken out insurance?'

I shrugged, noncommittal.

'I don't think you knew anything about the porn, Minister, or the illegal adoptions, or the rapes and murders,' I said.

I've interrogated enough suspects to know when they're lying to me, and I watched Tynaliev for his reaction.

'But you're not sure?' he said.

'I'm a policeman,' I said. 'Murder Squad. You once said I was the best. That's because I suspect everyone. Including you.'

Tynaliev stood up and walked towards the window, his back to me as he spoke.

'You did me a great service once, Inspector, in the tragedy of my daughter's murder. You brought me the man behind her death, in such a way as to minimise scandal and political upheaval. I owe you for that.'

He turned and walked to the door.

'More to the point, Yekaterina owes you that, for giving her justice,' he added, and a hint of sorrow crossed his face, quickly replaced by the mask of a politician.

'Wait here,' he said, and left the room.

I looked over at the vodka bottle, felt more tempted than I had been for months. I might have insurance in the form of documents with Usupov and Saltanat, but that wouldn't help me if I was found floating face down in the Chui.

Tynaliev came back, this time with a gun in his hand. My gun. If you're going to die from a bullet in the head, I decided, there was a sort of poetic justice in it being the one you'd used to kill other people.

Tynaliev sat behind his desk, my gun pointed loosely in my direction, not loosely enough for my liking.

'This could be the story. You somehow got your gun past my security people, maybe a temporary failure in the scanner, or you bribed someone to smuggle it in beforehand. You came to my study, waved the gun about, and then confessed to taking part in filming the rape and murder of young Kyrgyz citizens. You told me you couldn't stand the guilt and shame any longer, then you put the barrel of your gun in your mouth and blew your brains out all over my very expensive Parisian wallpaper.'

He paused, raised an eyebrow, moved the gun to aim directly at me.

'I don't think there would be a problem with anyone

believing that story, do you? And your "insurance"? Lies spread about by an unnamed foreign power, out to discredit me and cause political unrest. Not much of a legacy you'd leave behind you, Inspector.'

'If you're going to do it, then do it,' I said. 'Otherwise, with all due respect, Minister, I don't think you've got the balls.'

Tynaliev nodded, considering his options, pushed the gun towards me.

'Put it away. We're going to visit my friend, Mr Graves.'

Chapter 60

We left the minister's house in a convoy of three, topped and tailed by SUVs filled with Tynaliev's security team. The lead car had some sort of radio device, because every red light changed to green as we approached Graves's villa. The metal gates swung open and we drove in. I could see the scorch marks on the gravel from the grenade I'd thrown over the wall, but there was no sign of the car. A handful of Graves's thugs stood at strategic points around the drive, and the tension and reek of violence hit me like a hammer on the head. One sudden move, a scowl that became a challenge, and guns would start blasting at everything that moved

Tynaliev took a call on his mobile, listened, spoke a few words in English, then opened the car door.

'Out,' he said. 'And come with me.'

I wondered if this was a set-up; there seemed no alternative but to obey. Flanked like a warlord by his warriors, Tynaliev walked to the front door of the villa, still marked with shrapnel scars. As we arrived, Graves opened the door, put out his hand. The two men shook, both too confident to indulge in anything as obvious as showing off their power.

'Mikhail.'

'Morton. Can we speak in Russian, so the inspector can understand you?'

'*Da.*'

Morton Graves seemed even more intimidating than when

I'd seen him before. Then he was violent, insane, obsessed. Now, a calm business persona gave him respectability. But there were still the same hard muscles under his shirt, his shaven head massive, his eyes calculating, unreadable.

'You're here to investigate the attack on my compound?'

Graves pointed to the scarred door, the scorched gravel, shrugged his shoulders, as if genuinely surprised such a thing could have happened to a respectable businessman.

'Please, I'm forgetting my manners. Do come in. *Chai?* Something stronger?'

His Russian was precise, if oddly inflected, slightly old-fashioned. I found the courtesy with which he spoke more menacing than when he'd announced he was going to kill me. We followed him into a room that obviously served as an office. The bodyguards remained outside, sizing each other up, working out who was the hardest.

'I was surprised to get your call, Mikhail,' Graves said. 'Not least when you said serious charges had been laid against me.'

He smiled, and I sensed the confidence of the man, his ruthlessness. Tynaliev sat down and gestured at us to do likewise.

'This is the officer accusing me of something?' Graves said, staring at me as if I were prey and he was one of our mountain eagles waiting to swoop, then strike.

'Inspector Borubaev—' Tynaliev began, before Graves interrupted him.

'Forgive me, but I was under the impression the inspector had been suspended, for possessing and distributing hard-core pornography. And he has some sort of involvement with the Uzbek security forces. Not really very wise, or patriotic, wouldn't you say, Inspector?'

'Don't piss me about, Graves, you'll regret it if you do,' I said. 'I know what you've done, what you like to do. I've been there, and I've got the burn marks to prove it.'

Graves smiled, lit a cigarette. The smoke wreathed around his head and for a moment he looked truly demonic.

'I don't have the slightest idea what you're talking about, Inspector,' he said, the amusement and contempt in his voice obvious.

'You'll know about Albina Kurmanalieva?' I said.

Graves was instantly alert, his eyes moving between Tynaliev and myself.

'A potential business partner,' he said. 'I have various interests in Tashkent, and we've been discussing ways to maximise our investment and profit there. You've met her, I think, Mikhail, as a guest at my house?'

Tynaliev nodded, but said nothing.

'I'm afraid you're going to have to revise your plans, Mr Graves,' I said. 'Ms Kurmanalieva was found dead in Panfilov Park earlier.'

Graves's face gave nothing away. For all the emotion he showed, I might have been discussing the price of horse meat.

'This is terrible news, Inspector,' Graves said. 'Was it her heart? I always thought she was very fit.'

'In a manner of speaking,' I said. 'Her heart didn't have any blood to pump around her body. She'd been stabbed and bled out on the spot.'

'Murder? Do you have any suspects?' Graves asked.

I hesitated before replying. I didn't know how much Tynaliev knew, and I certainly didn't want to draw his attention to Saltanat as a possible suspect.

'My colleagues will be investigating her death, and I'm sure they'll keep the minister fully informed. But I'm here about a number of other deaths.'

'However I can help, Inspector. But I have no idea what you're talking about.'

'I'm talking about the rape and murder of young boys and girls, here in the cellar of this villa. About filming them for rich sick perverts like yourself. For illegal trafficking of young children. About murdering and dumping the ones you had no use for.'

Graves laughed, the sound of a cut-throat razor scraped across brick. He stubbed out his cigarette and a smile crossed his face, to be quickly replaced by anger.

'This is absurd,' he said, turned to Tynaliev. 'Are you going to allow this nobody prick to talk to me like this?'

'I'm sure there is no basis for his claims, Morton,' Tynaliev said, 'but I'm sure you'd prefer to have his allegations thoroughly crushed.'

Graves spread his hands in a gesture of resignation.

'Very well, Inspector, what do you suggest?'

'We should take a look in your cellar, Mr Graves. The torture chamber where you filmed all those rapes and deaths. Where your friend Albina Kurmanalieva tortured me.'

'My cellar? How do you even know I have a cellar?'

Graves feigned puzzlement for a moment, then nodded.

'We had a break-in here the other evening. Nothing was taken apart from a few unimportant papers; we surprised the intruders but they managed to escape. You wouldn't know anything about that, Inspector?'

Now it was Tynaliev's turn to stare at me. I shook my head, not wanting to take that path.

'How would a villa this size not have a cellar?' I said. 'So I suggest we go and inspect it.'

'Morton?' Tynaliev asked.

Graves shrugged, led the way to the cellar door. On the threshold he paused, his hand on the latch.

'This really is unnecessary, Inspector, I don't know where you got your information, but your sources are obviously either complete fantasists or business rivals of mine. I have nothing to hide.'

He opened the cellar door and switched on the light.

I felt sick as I limped down the stairs, the raw taste of bile and vomit suddenly sour in my mouth. I felt the pain in my foot, the tug of the stitches in my shoulder, the tightness of the burn scars on my hand. This was where my life could have come to an end, where my career might still collapse in a cover-up and money changing hands.

The bare bulb spat light out onto the walls, and lit up the shelves. They were still there, but the whips, chains, belts? All gone. The floor was scrubbed clean, the walls newly painted, the smell of disinfectant heavy in the air.

Graves looked around, innocence hanging like a cloth over his face.

'Just a cellar, Inspector. Nothing sinister here, I'm sure you'll agree?'

I didn't know what to say. Of course Graves was intelligent, he wouldn't have been such a successful businessman otherwise, but he'd second-guessed me. I could have sworn he wouldn't be able to part with his trophies, his church, his acts of worship, but I was wrong. And I knew that in some other cellar, in some other quiet and secluded villa, the torture chamber was ready to start work again.

Tynaliev turned to me, raised an eyebrow.

'Inspector?' he said, the anger in his voice evident. He turned to Graves, offered his hand.

'Morton, I am most grateful for the complete cooperation you've shown us,' Tynaliev said. 'I'm sure the Inspector will wish to apologise.'

Both men turned to look at me. I remembered the fear I'd felt strapped down and helpless. Of the smell of sweat and vomit that seeped out of the walls. Of the wide-open eyes of children who looked for help and were given only death.

'Gentlemen,' I said, and started to make my way back up the stairs, 'you can both go fuck yourselves.'

Chapter 61

I waited by the car while Tynaliev said his goodbyes, a hand-shake, a brief hug, then he was with me. He pointed to the rear seat of the car.

'In,' he ordered, and I obeyed.

'I think you've just about used up the last of my favours, Inspector,' he said. 'I've persuaded Mr Graves not to insist on your badge. I've also told him he no longer plays a part in our investigation. And nor do you.'

I said nothing as we drove off in the centre of the convoy.

'I told him I had every confidence in his integrity and honesty,' Tynaliev continued. 'I also said we intend to stamp down very heavily on such antisocial activities as the manu-facture and distribution of pornography.'

'So you believe me, then?' I said. 'About the cellar, about Graves's involvement.'

Tynaliev gave me a world-weary look, settled back in his seat.

'It doesn't matter whether I believe you or not,' he said. 'You have no evidence, no witnesses, nothing. And even if you did, think of who Graves is. A businessman who's brought a lot of wealth to this country. Who employs hun-dreds of people, if not thousands. Who puts *plov* and *kleb* on a lot of tables. Weigh that up against, what? A few dead orphans no one knew, cared for, wanted?'

'Rather cynical, Minister,' I said.

'No, Inspector, it's practical. Without evidence, you can't put him on trial. Continue to make allegations, and he'll leave Kyrgyzstan, and take his wealth, his jobs, with him. What good will that do? Do I think he did all the things you say? I don't know. But he's not stupid. He'll see this as a warning, a hint not to stray from the path.'

'That's not enough, not for those dead children.'

Tynaliev's voice was soft, almost paternal, explaining the realities of the world.

'Perhaps not. But it's as good as they'll get, you know that.'

He turned, opened the window, lit a cigarette, watched the smoke spin out into the air, snatched into nothingness.

'This is an end to it, do you understand? Finished. And one more thing. I'd advise your friend to head over the border in the next twenty-four hours, before anyone connects her to the Panfilov Park murder.'

I stared out of the window, the breeze stinging my eyes, turning everything blurred, indistinct.

'What do you mean, that's it?' Saltanat said, her face harsh with disbelief.

'Tynaliev wants the matter closed. Nothing's going to happen to Graves, not with the connections he's got.'

'And you're just going to roll over?'

'He wants you out of the country and me back behind a desk.'

Saltanat stared at me, and I sensed something new in her eyes. Contempt.

'It's all political,' I said. 'Graves invests here, everyone makes money, we don't have to rely totally on the roubles

305

sent home from Moscow. The state survives, the government stays strong. That's the way it is.'

Saltanat said nothing, moved around the hotel room, pulling clothes out of drawers, off hangers, stuffing them into a large kit bag.

'What are you doing?' I asked, realising the stupidity of the question even as I asked it.

'Taking your minister's advice. I've had enough of being shot at, hunted, stabbed. Enough of knife fights, guns, the taste in my mouth when I saw those filthy films. And it's all been pointless.'

'Graves won't dare start up again. He'll close down his adoption business, he'll be watched from now on.'

'Great,' Saltanat said, zipping up her bag. 'Maybe he'll come and move to my country and start making his home movies again. You know he thinks he can get away with anything. And what does the famous Murder Squad inspector do? Shrugs, nods, walks away. So that's what I'm going to do.'

Saltanat slung her bag over her shoulder, and headed for the door.

'You know, Akyl, I really admired your honesty, even your anger. You chose to do the right thing, even when it could have got you killed. You waded through the shit, but you didn't let it corrupt you. But now?'

She shook her head.

'Either you're no longer the man I thought you were, or you never were. You've got blood on your hands, Akyl, and it's not just from the bad guys.'

'I love you,' I said. It was all I could think to say, and perhaps it was even true.

'No, Akyl,' Saltanat said, her hand on the door handle, a look of compassion crossing her face for a few seconds. 'You might wish you did. But you're in love with Chinara. So. End of story.'

She stared at me, revealing nothing.

'I'm taking Otabek with me. Someone has to care.'

And then she was gone.

Chapter 62

I turned the computer screen away from the internet café desk, but no one was paying me any attention. I finished typing my letter of resignation, read it through, sent it to the chief of police at Sverdlovsky station, adding a blind copy to Tynaliev for good measure.

Outside, the summer heat was baking Chui Prospekt, dust hanging in the air and coating the pavements. Inside the café, a weary air conditioning unit gave an occasional cough and splutter, doing nothing to cool the air.

I lit a cigarette, ignoring the notices about not smoking, looked at the memory stick in my hand. I plugged it into the computer, opened the video it contained. A couple of days earlier, I'd gone to my lock-up to collect a few important items, and also sent money to Karakol to ensure the seven dead unknown babies were given a respectful funeral. They were laid to rest in a communal grave, in the same cemetery where I buried Chinara, a peaceful place overlooking a valley with the mountains in the distance.

And then I turned film-maker.

The picture was grainy, amateur, shot on a handheld phone. But it showed Graves's villa, late at night, the walls lit by floodlights, making blurred puddles on the road. The side door opened, and a man emerged, walking towards the car parked outside. The camera zoomed in, and it was Zhenbekov, checking the coast was clear. He was followed by Graves, his height and shaven head unmistakable. Zhenbekov unlocked the car, climbed behind the wheel, while Graves took the passenger seat. The headlights flicked on, and the car started to move.

Then the image turned pure white, dazzling, before slowly coming back into focus. The car was a heap of fragments, twisted metal, splinters. The passenger door hung open, crooked on one hinge. A figure staggered out of the wreckage, twisting and whirling around. Graves, but most changed. His clothes were on fire, and burns scarred his head like patches of red and black paint. He had lost a hand, or rather was holding it with the one still attached. The film was silent, but it was easy to imagine the scream coming out of his mouth, shocked by the impossibility of what was happening to him.

He fell to the ground, rolling in an ecstasy of pain, blood splashing from his severed wrist onto the pavement, the way blood flows from a sacrificial sheep at a forty-day *toi*. Perhaps he remembered the screams and cries in his cellar, relived the pleasures of the knife and whip. Possibly he thought of the wealth and power he was leaving behind. Or maybe he just died, in pain and alone.

I attached the file to another email, a one-off address in another country, and pressed send.

I remembered Saltanat walking away, never hesitating, never looking back.

We create rules to live by, to tell us how to act, to help us sleep at night. And when life shreds them into fragments thrown to the wind, all we can do is carry on.

But there's always a price, because betrayal comes in many disguises.

First we betray our friends. Then we betray those who love us.

And finally, inevitably, we betray ourselves

Maybe it's love that redeems us. Or when we do what we know is right, whatever the consequences.

After a few moments, a reply to my email arrived in my inbox. I opened it, my palms sweaty with anticipation, hope, fear. It was from the foreign address where I'd sent the film.

There were no words, only a short video clip.

A young boy, maybe eight years old, stood in front of the Sher-Dor Madrasah in Samarkand, dwarfed by the towering minarets and the ornate tiger mosaics. Otabek stared into the camera, his hair still cut in that odd lopsided fashion, clothes slightly too big, those of an older boy, but he looked healthy, well-fed. He clutched a woman's hand, as if for protection, or reassurance. The woman was visible only from the waist down, slim long legs in black jeans tucked into shin-high lace-up combat boots.

He wasn't smiling, looked guarded, but I could sense some of the fear had left his eyes, that he was no longer consumed by a terror that could pounce at any moment. He raised his free hand to give a tentative wave to the camera, then the screen went dark.

I watched the clip, over and over, until the café attendant tapped my shoulder and told me I'd run out of time.

Acknowledgements

As with my previous Akyl Borubaev novel, *A Killing Winter*, I owe a great deal to many people, whose continued help and encouragement is already acknowledged there.

To that list must be added:

In Germany: Sebastian Fitzek.

In Kyrgyzstan: Oksana Itikeeva, Umai Sultanova.

In the UAE: Isobel Abulhoul, Annabelle Corton, Baron Elliot, Michael Judd, Yvette Judge, Maryann Miranda, Meerim Morrison, Nyugen Ngoc, Martin Tyler.

In the UK: Stefanie Bierwerth and her team at Quercus, especially Kathryn Taussig and Matthew Cowdery; Jakob Tanner at Waterstones; Marcus Wilson-Smith, whose Kyrgyz photos are the redeeming feature of my Facebook page (www.facebook.com/tomcallaghanwriter).

As before, I owe huge thanks to Tanja Howarth, friend and agent extraordinaire, and my old pal Simon Peters, for criticism, encouragement and a killing eye for typos.

My biggest debt, of course, is to everyone who read *A Killing Winter*, and who I hope will enjoy *A Spring Betrayal* as well.

All the characters and events in this book are entirely fictitious, and any errors, misinterpretations or distortions of actual events are mine. Kyrgyzstan is a beautiful country with friendly people, and I hope no one will be put off visiting it by reading what is, after all, a crime novel.

Read on for an exclusive extract from the third title in the Inspector Akyl Borubaev series, *A Summer Revenge*.

I can't tell any more
Who's an animal, who's a person,
Or when the execution's due.

Anna Akhmatova

Chapter 1

I'd smelled violent death before, that sour mix of blood, urine and fear bubbling away like some vile soup. Having been an inspector in the Bishkek Murder Squad, there was no way I could avoid it. Stabbings, shootings, murder by bottle, boot or bullet, I'd smelled them all. The stink settles into your clothes, your skin, your soul; nothing ever fully washes it out. And no matter how many times you smell death, you never become used to it.

I pushed the door open a little further, hoping the only other person in the room was the one no longer breathing. The man's body was huddled in the far corner, the other side of a double bed, as if he'd tried to take shelter from his death. I turned on the light, wished I hadn't. The large abstract painting on the wall had been created by long scarlet smears and splashes someone had turned into letters. It looked like a child's first attempt at writing, as if the finger dipped in blood was unused to the Cyrillic alphabet we Kyrgyz use.

SVINYA. Pig. Short, sweet, and from what I'd learned earlier, accurate.

I walked over towards the body, crouched beside the corpse. It wasn't hard to tell where the red ink had come from. The man's ears, eyes and tongue were missing. Well, not missing, just not attached to him any more, but scattered across the tiled floor like abandoned rubber toys. The wounds gaped like ugly open mouths, the sort that yell and swear and sneer.

A punishment killing? This will teach you not to hear, see or talk about our business? Perhaps, but that didn't explain why someone had scrawled *SVINYA* above the body. That seemed personal, an epitaph or a proclamation.

There's something depressingly familiar about most murders, the unmistakable way the body sprawls as if all its muscles had snapped at once. A lifetime's energy and ambition, dreams and anger, gone without trace. No wonder it's hard to believe life is anything more than a series of random collisions, with one final inevitable crash.

I touched the man's cheek. Cooling but still warm. Hard to tell how long he'd been dead with the stifling summer heat in the room. Back in Bishkek I would have waited for the crime scene people, for the ambulance. Not here. I couldn't tell whether the mutilations were post-mortem; I hoped for his sake they were.

I wondered why none of the man's neighbours had heard anything; there must have been some sort of scuffle. No one noticed someone arriving at the apartment, no one heard screams?

I gave the room a swift search, hoping to discover what I'd come for. I pulled open drawers, hunted through the wardrobe. Finally I found it, taped to the underside of the bedside table. The blueing looked worn, and the metal had scratches down one side. But it was a Makarov, loaded, just as I'd requested. I didn't open my wallet to pay. I couldn't imagine he'd need the money.

I took a final look at the body, to see if there were any

indications of what had killed him. That was when I spotted it – a small puncture mark on his neck, bruised as if someone untrained had jabbed him with a syringe. If he'd been drugged, that would explain why there'd been no noise. Toxicology reports would confirm that, I guessed, although I wouldn't be around to read them.

I dropped the gun into my pocket. I wasn't going to call the police, leave an anonymous tip. The hot weather would make the body's presence known soon enough.

I took the stairs rather than the lift, a rule I do my best to always keep. Stairs give you a couple of options, lifts give you none. And if there's somebody with a gun or a knife, they're ready and waiting for you when the lift doors open. I used my shoulder to push open the bar on the fire escape door, strolled out into the night, hands in my pockets. Another rule: people notice you if you're furtive, so pretend you haven't a care in the world.

I walked on for about half an hour, turning left or right at random until I came to the creek, where I sat down and watched the wooden boats moored up four deep. The sluggish black seawater lapped and spat against the stonework. The air smelled of curry and salt and petrol fumes. In the distance on the other side of the water, the towers of the city sparkled and shone. My shirt was soaked with sweat, my hair plastered to my forehead. Even a Bishkek summer was never this hot, and I felt blistered, worn, as well as jet-lagged after the cramped four-hour flight.

I wondered whether I should simply return home, knew it wasn't an option. If I failed the man who'd sent me here, he would pour never-ending shit on my head. Since I'd left the police force, I was now officially 'little people', which meant

I was powerless against state bureaucracy, let alone a vendetta from a government minister. For only the four-hundredth time I debated whether resigning had been the right move, whether I should have stayed where I was, doing what I did best. Solving murders, catching killers.

I lit a cigarette, stubbed it out; adding to the hot air already filling my lungs wasn't a great idea. The thought of a cold beer was appealing, but I'd given up alcohol completely after my wife Chinara's death the previous year.

From somewhere behind me, the midnight call to prayer sang out from the minaret of a nearby mosque. All my life I've heard the *adhan*; though I'm not a Muslim, I've always found it a haunting sound, especially at night. So I listened as the muezzin's voice spilt like honey out over the water and merged with the whisper of tides, the creak of wooden boats. I waited until the final notes faded away, turned to walk back to my hotel.

I needed to think about the mess I was in up to my neck. And what I was going to do about it, alone, uncertain, in a city so alien I might as well have been on another planet. I was in Dubai.

Chapter 2

A week earlier, late one evening, I'd been summoned to meet my old nemesis, the Kyrgyz Minister for State Security, Mikhail Tynaliev. We had a curious relationship, considering most people who challenge Tynaliev end up regretting it, often from inside a shroud.

Initially, I'd done him a service, finding the man who'd organised the butchering of Tynaliev's daughter, Yekaterina. The minister had taken on the role of judge and jury, and no one ever uncovered the body. Then I did him a disservice by ignoring his orders and killing Morton Graves, a connected foreign businessman, paedophile and murderer. So I wasn't at all certain I wasn't going to end up in Bishkek Penitentiary One, sharing an overcrowded cell full of people I'd helped put there.

There's a story Stalin would summon his ministers in the middle of the night, sending a car to fetch them. Turn left and into the Kremlin, and you were escorted into Uncle Joe's presence. Turn right, and an execution basement in the Lubyanka was your final destination, your trousers stinking of your fear. I knew the feeling.

The driver of the car sent to pick me up had told me to bring my passport, refused to say another word on the drive to Tynaliev's town house. Motion-controlled lights turned the air blue-white, and the armed guard at the sentry gate-house kept a keen eye on us as we parked.

I held my passport up to the glass, said I was expected. Perhaps I should have said summoned.

'Armed?'

I shook my head. The guard beckoned me through the security scanners, jerked a thumb towards the house. I nodded thanks, began the trudge down the path. Just as I reached the door, it opened, and Mikhail Tynaliev stood outlined against the light.

'Thank you for coming, Mr Borubaev,' he said, the emphasis on Mr, but there was no welcome in his voice. 'Please come in.'

I entered the hall the way an apprentice lion-tamer might enter the cage. I had no idea why Tynaliev wanted to see me or why I'd had to bring my passport, but I didn't imagine it would be anything I'd enjoy. He led me through into his study, sat down on one of the leather sofas. I'd been in the over-decorated room before and I hadn't enjoyed the experience then.

'Drink?'

'*Chai?*'

Tynaliev shrugged, reached for the decanter by his elbow.

'Still not drinking? Probably a good idea, where you're going.'

He poured himself an industrial-sized vodka, took a sip, nodded appreciation. He gestured towards a chair beside his desk, one of those fussy faux-antiques with spindly gold-painted legs.

'Missing your old job?'

It was my turn to shrug. Tynaliev looked as formidable as ever, broad shoulders, a head slotted between them with no sign of a neck, hands that could stun a suspect with a single punch. People said he was more than willing to take over an interrogation if answers and teeth weren't being spat out fast enough.

'I'm able to get you your old job back. If you want it. Unless the bits and pieces of private investigation you've picked up are making you rich?'

Tynaliev obviously knew I had enough *som* in my bank account to buy a couple of cheese *samsi* for breakfast. What he didn't know was I missed the chase, the challenge. Being Murder Squad is as addictive as being hooked on *krokodil*, Russia's new home-made wonder drug, and probably just as life-threatening. But it goes deeper for me. Someone has to speak for the dead, for the old man killed for his pension, the schoolgirl raped and strangled, the wife who refused sex when her husband came home drunk. Solving a case is like closing the victim's eyes, so they can finally sleep.

'That's very generous of you, Minister,' I said, '*Spasibo*. If there's ever anything I can do for you . . .'

Tynaliev almost smiled. It wasn't pleasant. 'Before you start work again, perhaps you'd like to take a little holiday? Somewhere warm, with beaches? Just for a week or so.'

I looked regretful. 'If I could afford it, nothing would be better, but . . .'

Tynaliev poured himself another, equally large vodka. If he'd had a smile on his face, it had melted like ice under a sunlamp.

'Don't fuck around with me, Mr Not-Yet-Inspector. Just sit there and listen to what I want you to do.'

I did as I was told. It looked like I wasn't going to get my cup of tea after all.

Chapter 3

'I'm going to tell you a story, Borubaev. A hypothetical story, you understand?'

I nodded. Tynaliev could recite the entire Manas epic – all half a million lines of the long Kyrgyz poem – if it meant I got my job back.

'A senior colleague of mine – no need for names – has fallen in love with a woman much younger than him.'

I nodded, making sure I kept a straight face. I had a pretty good idea of the colleague's name. Every doctor in the world has heard the 'It's not me, it's about a friend with a problem' story. And everyone knew Tynaliev's wife spent most of her time at their *dacha*, a luxurious country cottage on the outskirts of Talas, while Tynaliev spent most of his spare time working his way through a long line of ambitious and attractive young women.

'This young woman,' I asked, deliberately keeping my voice neutral and professional, 'does she reciprocate his feelings?'

'She said so –' Tynaliev shrugged '– and there were the usual presents, trips, restaurants. The problem was, my colleague was – is – married.'

'Always difficult, Minister, even if the wife is understanding.'

Our hypocrisy hung in the air like cigar smoke. Tynaliev took a sip of vodka, looked away, unwilling to catch my eye.

'That's not the problem, Inspector.'

I was pleased to see I'd regained my rank, wondered if my salary would be backdated. You get tired of *samsi* for breakfast.

'The young lady in question announced she wanted to go on holiday. Naturally, my colleague was more than happy to help with the expenses, flight, visa.'

'Naturally,' I agreed. 'Where was she planning to go?'

'Dubai. For the shopping.'

'And she went?'

Tynaliev nodded.

'And didn't come back?'

He nodded again, sipped his vodka. He suddenly looked older, less certain of himself. Discovering you've grown old will do that to you. Or learning it's your money and power that lures the girls to your bed, not your looks or charm or the size of your *yelda*.

'And you want me to go to Dubai to find her? What did she take that's so important, Minister? Money? You've got more than you know how to spend. Documents? Secrets? Something that could harm you politically?'

I watched as anger and pride flickered across his face like summer lightning.

'Inspector, as I said, my colleague—'

'Minister, I can't help if I don't know the facts,' I said, one reasonable man talking to another. 'If she was your lover, then tell me; I'm not a judgemental man.' I paused, folded my arms. 'And if you won't tell me, then I don't stand much chance of finding her or doing the right thing when I do.'

'I rely on your complete discretion, Inspector,' Tynaliev said, looking at me as if he'd prefer to rip my throat out.